For a time in history, the man who erected a saw mill was considered the pillar of his community. The logger who faced death moment to moment, in the pinnacles topping a red-wood or on the trembling ground and churning rivers, was a fearless pioneer, the spearhead of empire and manifest destiny.

This is the saga—not of Paul Bunyan and the mythical loggers—but of the real heroes, whose perilous river passage through a town would empty a schoolhouse and crowd the bridges with cheering children. It is a story of hard living and swift death, the slim form of cat-like Pete Hurd loosening the solid jam, and thrown and buried beneath two million rushing feet of logs. It is the tale of massive John Turnow, the Wild Man of the Olympics, who haunted the forests and his fellow man with the extra strength of his madness. It is the roistering account of pent-up energies, released in the logging towns—of Swede Annie's, where anything goes, and Fan Jones' Sky Blue House, and the birling competitions on the Fourth of July, when a slippery log rolled in the river for two days and neither Jim Oliver nor Tom Stewart lost his footing for a second.

That breed died with Jigger Jones in the machinery of civilization, but the exploits of Jigger, Silver Jack, Fred Maynard and the others are the living substance of a legend.

HOLY OLD MACKINAW

A Natural History of the American Lumberjack

Stewart H. Holbrook

A COMSTOCK EDITION

SAUSALITO • CALIFORNIA

Library of Congress Catalogue Card Number: 56-7306

ISBN 0-89174-039-2

Second Printing: July 1980

Cover design by Bill Yenne

Printed in the United States of America

COMSTOCK EDITIONS, INC.
3030 Bridgeway, Sausalito, CA 94965

Contents

Foreword

THERE HAS BEEN a plenty of books about pioneers in the United States. Explorers have been the subject of much fact and fiction; so have trappers, traders, and missionaries to the Red Men. Enough to fill a large library has been written about cowboys, Indian fighters, railroad builders, and the men and women of the covered wagon. If there has been a serious book about the American logger it has escaped my notice, and I have been looking for a long time.

The logger I mean is the lad who ranged three thousand miles through the forest from Maine to Oregon, steel calks in his boots, an ax in his fist, and a plug of chewing handy. The lad who at intervals emerged from the dark savage woods for the purposes of calling on soft ladies and drinking hard liquor.

This logger was as much a pioneer as any of them, more than most. Before houses could be built and farms plowed there had to be a clearing and there had to be logs and boards. The loggers took care of the business, hewing down one forest after another. It was hard and dangerous work, but loggers were a tough race, a species early set apart from farmers and townsmen of all sorts, and they retained their primitive purity until civilization caught up with the timber line and laid them low.

The pure logger strain came into being on the grim wooded shores of Maine three hundred years ago. The strain probably rose to fullest stature in the Lake States of the late nineteenth century, and it is now passing out of existence on the West Coast and in the Pacific Northwest.

It isn't a matter of timber. There is plenty of timber left. It isn't likely that Americans will ever know a timber famine. But the timber is being harvested, mostly, by a new and different breed of men—men who smoke many cigarettes but chew little plug; men with families, who wear conventional clothing, vote in elections, and play tennis and golf. Few of them need to know how to handle ax or peavey, and few of them are given to kicking plate glass out of barroom windows. They roar no louder than their city brothers whom they so greatly resemble. In short, they are good, solid, commonplace American citizens.

A mere corporal's guard remains of the boys who knew logging in its great and red-eyed heyday—when streams and rivers from Maine to Minnesota were filled with long logs, and bellowing bull teams lurched down the skidroads of the Far Western timber. Boy and man, for more than thirty years, I have known these rugged lads at first hand and for them I have an affection that is very deep.

Because they have been so scurvily ignored by academic historians and because we shall probably never see their like again, I have tried to set down an honest picture of the American lumberjack, at work and at play, as he has performed for the past three centuries. Only the lumberjack of the timbered North is considered. Logging in Southern pine and cypress is a story in itself and it deserves to be written by someone who knows the subject.

Portland, Oregon.   S. H. H.

HOLY OLD MACKINAW

1

Saga of The Jigger

IT WAS TOLD of Jigger Jones that when he was a young head-chopper in the Maine woods some fifty years ago he would walk a felled spruce, barefoot, and kick off every knot from butt to top. That was before my time in the timber, and I never saw him do it, yet all who knew The Jigger, even in his old age, doubted the report not at all. He was what loggers meant when they said "a rugged man," and he was almost but not quite indestructible.

Jigger Jones also was almost the last of his race—that race of men who cut a swath of timber from eastern Maine to western Oregon and yelled like crazed devils every spring, when the drive was in and they were released from the savage woods for a few days, as they pounded the bars in Bangor, Saginaw, St. Paul and Seattle.

Jigger didn't know it, of course, but his life and especially his death had the dignity and tragedy of a classic pattern. Into them were packed all the three hundred years of experience it required to produce and destroy a unique and mighty race of men. Some of that tribe, as in Jigger's case, were killed physically by civilization; as for the others, civilization has mowed them down spiritually—removing the high, wild color from their lives, ironing flat their personalities, and reducing them to the status of proletarians. The professors would term Jigger's brief story an epitome, and so it was.

I didn't catch up with Jigger Jones until early in 1910. It was at a logging camp in northern New

England, and the weather was around thirty-five below, accounted fair coolish even in those parts. Jigger was standing in the camp yard when I, a young punk of a new camp clerk, hove in on the tote team.

Jigger wore neither toque nor mittens, which was unusual in that clime, but I looked first of all at his feet, to know by witness if the legends I had heard about him were true. They were. The Jigger was barefoot. He walked up and down on the packed, creaking snow, passing the time of day with the teamster, and occasionally he would stop and stand on one leg like a stork, rubbing one foot against his pants leg. It was a fact that he never wore socks, summer or winter, except on rare and state occasions such as funerals, when he felt that he should put on all the style possible. Around camp he commonly went barefoot, although he would pull on a pair of shoepacks or rubbers when he went into the woods to take charge of the crew. A red woolen undershirt and drawers and a pair of heavy pants completed his outfit.

Jigger was an excellent foreman in the old tradition. Like all those old camp bosses, he was no mere cog in an industrial machine, a number on a payroll. Jigger was an individual who stood upon his two hind legs and asked no quarter from Man, Capital, or even God, in the form God usually showed Himself to Jigger, which was high water, deep snow, or a thaw in January.

None other than Jigger Jones is credited with the famous lumberjack slogan that would put any chamber of commerce to shame. If on arrival in a new camp he happened to be well oiled, as was usually the case, he was given to letting the boys know about it by roaring "I can run faster, jump higher, squat lower, move sideways quicker, and spit further than any son-of-a-bitch in camp." This genial announcement was always made in good humor, but in good faith as well. If he couldn't live up to quite all of it, he could come near enough to cause grave consideration in the minds of those who thought otherwise.

As a camp push, or foreman, he had few equals. He knew, for instance, when it was going to rain, snow, or freeze at least twenty-four hours before it happened, no small feat in New England and Quebec. When asked what signs he used, he said all he knew about the weather was what he read in the forecasts in *Ayer's Almanac*. He knew to a day, almost, when the ice would go out of any of the streams tributary to the Kennebec, the Androscoggin and the Connecticut; and he knew men and timber. A notable slave driver, nevertheless he would walk into saloons in Berlin, New Hampshire, or Sherbrooke, Quebec, and impress a sizable crew of drunk and fighting *habitants* to go with him to drive the Nulhegan, one of the most dangerous streams for cant-dog men in the North Country. Without pencil or paper he would cruise casually through forty acres of mixed fir and spruce and come out with an accurate estimate of the eventual log scale of both species.

With an ax handle or sawed-off peavey he often faced a rebellious crew and offered to kill, not to lick, them all; but he knew he had only to break a few skulls to quell the mutiny. He never cut wages until he was forced to by higher-ups; and on at least one occasion he purposely misunderstood orders from the head office to make a ten per cent slice on a certain November 1, and did not put the pay reduction into effect. Men got scarce later that season, and many camps went shorthanded, but Jigger's crew was complete and happy. His only explanation of his foresight was that he had read in *Ayer's Almanac* "where it says we was goin' to have a shortage of choppers this-a year." All his references to the almanac, of course, were satirical. He never looked inside one and was sure that anyone who did was haywire.

Jigger Jones was christened Albert at the time of his birth in Maine in the early 1870s, but few knew him as anything but The Jigger, a name whose origin has been lost in the imperfect history of woodsmen. And it seemed to all young loggers that there had never been a time, no matter how remote, when one hadn't heard of Jigger Jones and his doings. His life and works had been so mighty that he existed part real, part myth, from the eighties until violent death did him in near a White Mountain village in 1935.

He was a small man, standing not more than five feet six, and he weighed around one hundred and forty pounds. He was strong. In his middle years he would pick up a drum of gasoline from the ground and slap it into the back of a tote-team body. He was actually as quick as a cat. These two gifts contributed considerably to his life span, but they were useless in the face of the machine age.

After one term in a district school, Jigger went directly to work in a logging camp, as cookee or cook's helper, at the tender age of twelve. But Jigger wasn't tender at twelve; he was rugged.

Conversation among the crew at mealtime was strictly forbidden. One night some new men, carrying noble hangovers, heaved into camp just in time for supper. One of them insisted on talking loudly at table. Jigger, dutiful, told him to shut up. The fellow, twice young Jigger's size, swung off the seat, struck the boy, and floored him. Then he jumped on Jigger and began pounding him. Jigger hugged the big drunk close, set his keen young teeth into an ear, and hung on. When some of the crew pried the pair apart, a good hunk of the ear remained in Jigger's mouth. Between two men of equal age and size this incident would have created no more than polite interest; but the youth and grit of the young cookee made it something special. So in honor of the occasion the crew passed the hat and bought Jigger a fine new red woolen shirt to replace the one torn in the scrap, and a full pound of B. & L. Black, a favorite chewing tobacco of the time.

Jigger soon graduated from the cookhouse. Having used an ax since he could walk, he did not require the usual preparatory courses of swamping out roads, knotting felled trees, but hired out as a chopper. In those days saws were not used for felling timber and axmen took great pride in the smoothness of the scarf of their undercut. Jigger's was like a planed board. He learned to fell a spruce or pine so that, in falling, it would drive a stake previously set in the ground. In no time at all he was a head-chopper.

Jigger had no thought, probably, of learning the business and of working upward and onward, but due rather to his restlessness he next became what was known as a hair-pounder, or teamster. He liked the excitement of sliding down ice-hard roads, standing upright on the long logs, and yelling bloody hell at his four horses. But he didn't like the bother of putting on the bridle chains which were placed around the sled runners to act as a brake on the steep hills. On one frosty morning on Swift Diamond Stream, he took a hill with a big load and no bridle chains. The load was too great for the team. With sparks of fire flashing from their hoofs and the devilish yelling of Jigger in their ears, the frightened animals tried to keep ahead of the sled, but could not. The weight and momentum of the monstrous load rushed them off the glaring road and into the timber, where the logs piled on top of them, and on top of Jigger, like great jackstraws. Three of the horses were dead, a fourth had a broken leg and so had Jigger. Jigger killed the injured animal with a pole ax. In the language of the woods he had sluiced his team.

Sluicing a team is likely to hang over a logger for a long time. Its shadow, indeed, is something akin to that cast in other circles by the failure to touch second base in a World's Series. But Jigger lived it down. By the time he was twenty years old he was put in charge of a camp on the Androscoggin River.

Old-timers have told that Jigger's first season as a camp push was something to go down in the annals. He was the smallest man in camp, and of course, in those days, he had to fight and lick half a dozen "able" men before he got his feet on solid ground. He did this with neatness and a fine show of imagination. Although he denied its truth in later years, tradition has it that he hit one of the tough lads over the head with a peavey and then rolled the body into the river as though it had been a log. "That story is a goddamn 'zaggeration," Jigger protested.

In any case, he had been in a heap of fights. On the rare occasions when he made any pretense at bathing, I was impressed by the deep marks of "loggers' small-pox" all over his chest, shoulders, and stomach—the work of many steel-calked boots stamped there by opponents. That his face was entirely free from such marks was attributed to the fear in which men held Jigger's teeth. "When I got holt on a feller's ankle," he recounted with relish, "I chawed clean through boot, hide, an' all."

Yet there wasn't an ounce of venom in his soul. In a tribe of traditionally generous men, he was outstanding. Literally, he would give the red woolen shirt off his back to the first friend or the first no-good bum who came along. He considered it ethically indefensible for any man to leave for camp, from town, until he had spent his last dollar, lost his hat, and awakened with his coat pleated from sleeping against a radiator in some river-front hotel. And when Jigger wanted to go to town, he never used the standard excuse of loggers—"I want to get my teeth fixed." Jigger said: "I'm going down to get fixed up."

One of Jigger's greatest contributions to the logging industry was the virile and amusing profanity he always had on tap. He could and did damn a person or a thing in a manner that made the Pope's excommunication sound like a recommendation of character. But he never used—at least in his more mature years —vulgar and shopworn phrases like "blue-eyed, bandy-legged, jumped-up ol' whistlin' Jesus H. Mackinaw Christ." Such ejaculations, he held, were sacrilegious. Unfortunately, because of its phallic and other anatomical references, little of his bluest and best billingsgate can be reproduced. Much of it was interesting in that it connected various biblical characters, of whose history he knew little, with references to things known to all woodsmen.

One of the worst things he could call a man embodied an allusion to the *pediculis pubis,* with which he claimed the patient Job had been afflicted. Of a logger who was notably unkempt, Jigger said that he was "dirtier than the combined britches of Matthew, Mark, Lute (sic), and John." Of another logger he would say, with just a trace of envy, that he was a "bigger picaroon man than ol' King Solomon hisself."

He might term a very lazy man "a reg'lar Joel's jilpoke." If he wished to indicate that something or other was very broad he would say that it was broader than a certain part of the anatomy of Amos. Diligent search of the Bible leaves these connections obscure, and it was probably Jigger's love of alliteration that brought them into being.

In the realm of alcohol Jigger stood alone. His drinking abilities passed all belief, unless one had seen them displayed over a period of years. He actually drank everything from clear grain alcohol to canned heat, and from horse liniment to painkiller; that is, everything except champagne and cocktails, both of which he held to be injurious to the stomach and kidneys.

Speaking of Jigger's stomach, I shall never forget the March morning in 1920 when I left Jigger's camp. The thermometer was down "two feet below zero" that morning. Jigger, sleeping in a bunk across from mine, sat up on the edge of the bed in his bright vermilion underwear. He reached under his bunk and came up with a crock of Graves' Pure Grain Alcohol. He poured a draught into a tin dipper and drank it neat. Then, barefoot and in his underwear, he strolled down to the brook through the deep snow, cut the ice in the pond, and brought a pail of water back to the shack. He remarked that it was middling coolish. While pulling on his pants and shoepacks he worked on half a cut of B. & L., squirting the juice onto the sizzling stove—to kill the germs in the air, he always said. In a few minutes he took another shot of the grog. Then, just before the gut-hammer's *clong clong* broke through the cold silent darkness outside, he pawed again under the bunk and this time brought forth a bottle of milk of magnesia.

"I guess I better take a dose of this," he said. "You know, I got to be powerful careful of my stomach. . . . It ain't very strong."

Jigger Jones would have lived to be a hundred years old, probably much older, had he been allowed to remain deep in the logging woods where he belonged. Whole trees had crashed upon him; he had fallen forty-five feet off a dam at First Connecticut Lake; a team of logs had run him down; large men had jumped on his chest with calked boots; and for more than half a century he had lived in snow all winter, in icy water all spring, on the drive—but neither exposure nor accident seemed to have the least effect on him. It was only when circumstances forced him out of the logging camps, and into the ways of civilization, that he took the first step toward the grave.

When the New England pulpwood industry went bad

in the 1920s, the aging Jigger found camp foremen's
jobs scarce, and he went to work for the United States
Forest Service. They put him atop Mount Chocorua,
in New Hampshire, as a fire lookout, and later moved
him to the summit of Carter Dome, highest fire tower
in northeastern United States. Jigger could spot fires.
He made a dandy lookout—alert, competent, and con-
scientious—just as long as there was actual fire hazard
in the woods. But when rains had soaked the forest
and even a city slicker would have known there could
be no forest fires, Jigger took to seeing bats, winged
eels, and other phenomena familiar to able drinking
men, even in high altitudes. Much as the Forest Service
liked The Jigger, they had to let him go.

Presently, and after a brief toot in town, Jigger
became a sort of watchdog for a bloated capitalist who
had a summer home and large shooting preserve in
northern New England. During the dangerous dry
months it was again Jigger's duty to sit in a lookout
shack, this time atop a bald peak whose sides were so
sheer as to discourage most mountain climbers. How,
in the name of God, he ever managed to tote material to the very top of this dome and there set up a
small but practical still must be left to the imagination.
But he did exactly that, and for weeks, until it blew
up in a blaze of glory and fired the lookout cabin
itself, the only smoke visible for miles around was that
from what Jigger was pleased to call Jones' Tin-Plated,
Triple-Worm, Little Giant Still. The product of this still,
which Jigger boasted was the highest in all America,
was said to have made men breathe easily at four-
thousand-feet altitude. Jigger called it Eagle Sweat.

Following detection of this contrivance and his subsequent discharge from the capitalist's menage, Jigger
took a job as foreman at a CCC camp. This was undoubtedly the beginning of the end. He took to riding
about, on occasion, in an automobile; and there was
also the effect that life in a CCC camp must have had

on his morale. City guys had ever been anathema to Jigger, and in his eyes all CCC boys were such; yet he set out manfully to make real woodsmen of them. But he couldn't fire anybody, as of yore. He couldn't even curse anybody, much less whale some sense into them with a peavey handle. And "professors" came to camp to lecture the boys about the evils of gonococci, which Jigger held could be laid low and harmless by immediate applications of strong tobacco juice, as witness his own excellent health and pure reproductive ability at close to seventy years. . . .

And there were rules about shaving and bathing and clothing and the hell and all. Not that Jigger paid any attention to any such rules, but it bothered him to know they existed, even in theory. Perhaps the study periods bothered him most, although he never attended them. What did it profit a man, he would ask, to know that a fir was an *Abies balsamea,* if he didn't know on which side of a tree the moss grew? "And a skunk ain't no bottle of Floridy water, even if you calls him by one of them fancy Polark names," he said. (By "Polark," i.e., *Polish,* Jigger designated any foreign language, either dead or living.)

It was all pretty discouraging to one who had spit Spearhead into the eyes of mean French Canadians and had bitten ears off gigantic Blue Nosers from New Brunswick. Although the CCC boys, and their officers, too, learned to like The Jigger immensely and to have deep respect for his lore of the woods, Jigger's mind often turned back to the great days when, as boss of a hundred wild riverhogs, he had chased the logs from headwaters at Connecticut Lake down to Holyoke, Massachusetts, and on at least two occasions, when the log booms had broken, right down to salt water at Saybrook, on Long Island Sound.

When this melancholia fastened upon him, Jigger would, in spite of all the CCC officers could do, get off the reservation and go to town, any town, where he could "get something for" his stomach, an organ that must have been made of nothing less than boiler plate.

It was then that the pseudo-sophisticated younger generation of the White Mountain area were struck dumb and startled before the vastness of a he-man's binge. When he rolled out the strophes to "The Redlight Saloon," the Great Stone Face in Franconia Notch was seen to tremble slightly, it was reported, and the few moose left in New Hampshire charged, bellowing in fear, over the state line into Maine.

It was a sort of swan song, one of Jigger's last great efforts to howl down the civilization that was catching up, hemming him in. Men who heard The Jigger on these latter benders said his cry was like that of a trapped animal—fierce, wild, and defiant, yet with a ring of fear at the bottom. So, when the CCC regretfully let Jigger go, the end was not far off; but the end was not as it should have been. Folk had long said of Jigger that he would surely go to his death by being trampled under the claws of purple pachyderms, while a six-legged boa constrictor caressed his neck—fauna he had often met with in his years of serious drinking. Others had predicted, for years on end, that he would finally tumble off some mountain cliff high enough to bust him up proper. None could have guessed that death would call for The Jigger in a conveyance he wholeheartedly loathed—an automobile.

Released by the CCC, Jigger had taken to trapping, an art he had practiced off and on since boyhood. He did very well with wildcat and lynx, that last winter of his life, bringing several of the clawing devils alive into town. He could get more for them alive from zoos than their fur would bring. Then came that cold day in February of 1935.

Starting out over his line Jigger found a lynx in the first trap. He killed it. And then a mighty thirst struck him. Instead of continuing on over the trap line, as he knew he should have done, he hurried back to the village where he could claim the lynx bounty. Immediately he got the money he bought a quart of drinking liquor, then another, treating everybody in town who would drink.

After two days of this Jigger suddenly awoke to the fact that he had not visited his traps in forty-eight hours, a gross violation of a law that had been getting considerable attention from game wardens. This wouldn't do, for Jigger had often felt the heavy hands of the wardens in times past.

So, in what he must have known to be a weak moment, he engaged a driver and what he contemptuously referred to as a "horseless carriage" to carry him to a point where he could take off on snowshoes near his trap line. Hitting along on all four, the car slithered off the icy road and crashed into a telephone pole.

The country doc to whom they brought the dying Jigger could hardly believe that a mere automobile accident could lay low such an indestructible fellow as he had known The Jigger to be. True enough, his skull was broken in two places; he had concussion; and his arms, legs, shoulders, and ribs were smashed. Still, in the past, Jigger had taken such things in his stride.

But it wasn't a mere accident. It was something much larger than that. It was the last round in a one-sided battle between all civilization and one unadulterated savage of the species lumberjack. And it was a churlish fate that removed him in such manner, even though he had his boots on, the old timber beast who could run faster, spit farther, jump higher, and belch louder than any ory-eyed so-and-so north of Boston. All the old-time loggers at the funeral, during which Jigger wore socks, remarked that it was one hell of a way for The Jigger to get sluiced.

2

The Flowering of a Lumber Town

THE ROCK-MAPLE FLOORS of Bangor's two hotels showed the impress of a thousand and more calked boots, and the proud plank sidewalks of the young city were deeply holed by rivermen's shoes, too, and splintered as well. For Bangor in Maine was to be the very first of the great lumber towns and in some respects the greatest of them all.

Conditions were perfect to turn the trick. Unwatered rum cost three cents a glass, a glass was a dipper-full, and a thirsty logger helped himself with the tin dipper that was chained to the open barrel. And down Exchange Street, a piece, two rather pretty ladies had rented a house and put up a small sign announcing "Gentlemen's Washing Taken In"—a genteel and harmless euphemism. No chamber of commerce was needed to make Bangor; the lodestones were there already and talk in a hundred bunkhouses, back in the deep timber, would take care of the advertising.

Coordinating conditions also were magnificent. North from Bangor, and drained by the river that turned her sawmills, there stretched two and one-half million acres of black and wonderful timber. Once he saw it, the scene gripped the fancy of young Henry Thoreau, a-visiting here from Concord, down in Massachusetts.

There stands the city of Bangor [he wrote in 1846] like a star on the edge of night, still hewing at the forest of which it is built, already overflowing with the luxuries

13

and refinements of Europe and sending its vessels to
Spain, to England, and to the West Indies for its
groceries—and yet only a few ax-men have gone upriver into the howling wilderness that feeds it.

A howling wilderness it was. The tall black spruce
was dwarfed by the towering white pines that rose up,
straight as masts and light as cork, close to two hundred feet above the ground. How far north of Bangor
ran this forest, no man knew. Some said it reached
to the Pole itself; everybody said it would last forever.
It would take a small war and two pretty stirring
orations by Dan'l Webster to learn where the Yankee
pine left off and the Canuck pine began.

Through this vast forest ran the Penobscot, with all
its lakes and tributaries, in season a swift-moving highway down which with no power other than brawn and
a peavey the forest could be brought to mills and tidewater at Bangor. It was a temperamental highway,
difficult to manage in spite of dams; but manage it
they did and for a full century sharp-shod men walked
fair down the middle of it on bobbing logs.

Fifty miles south of town, down the deep Penobscot,
was the open sea. The tides in the river were remark-
ably high, and the deep-sea skippers liked the port of
Bangor, for here they could, at low water slack, fill
their casks easily from over ship's side and find the
Penobscot water fresh and saltless, though in time it
came to have the flavor of pine in it.

A numerous fleet, Bangor-built and Bangor-owned,
carried lumber from here to the world and brought
back rum, and molasses and sugar to be made into
more rum to get more logs to make more lumber to
trade for more rum. It was all a perfect cycle from the
lumbermen's viewpoint, while from that of the practicing logger—the man who used the ax and saw—
Bangor was nothing less than Paradise. Booze, bawds,
and battle with roistering loggers—there was really

nothing else in life, except timber, and that was handy by. Bangor set the classic pattern that would follow the timber line West to the Pacific shore, distant by three thousand miles, one hundred years, and two trillion board feet of lumber.

God indeed smiled on the rising lumber capital of the world, and He caused one of His apostles to name it. The citizens of the humming town on the Penobscot wanted a town charter, in 1791, so they drew up a highly official and legal application. The name of their new home in the forest, they decided, should be Sunbury, which handsome name was inscribed in the application and the document turned over to the Reverend Seth Noble to carry to Boston, where the Great Seal and governor's signature might be put upon it.

The Reverend Seth Noble was a local divine whose voice was such that it could be, and often was, heard above the drone of four hundred and ten saws and the combined howls of wolves and loggers on carouse. But the Reverend Seth cared little for the chosen name, which smelled of paganism. He erased it and inserted in a neat round hand the name by which his favorite hymn was known in the old hymnals, "Bangor."

The name fitted Bangor, Maine, and so did the hymn itself, although the loggers probably did not realize how well:

> Hark from the tombs a doleful sound;
> Mine ears attend the cry—
> Ye living men, come view the ground
> Where ye must shortly die.

And die they did, up there in the gloom of the two million acres of tall black stuff—when a sudden waft blew a tall pine the wrong way; when there was the sickening slump in a mile-long landing of logs before they rolled Death over a man; or, the whiskered Old Fellow with the Scythe might hold off, jokingly, until the logs were fair in the stream, then strike you down into the white boiling water of the Ripogenus, on the west branch. Death always stood just behind the logger and very close to the riverman.

That's why loggers lived the way they did. Death might come out of the trees above, with the merest *whisss* of warning, or it might wait in the form of a watered rock, just around the next bend in the river. . . . Little wonder they pounded on the white pine bars of Bangor's groceries and yelled for another drink all around.

The early years of Bangor saw only moderate progress. The first settler hewed out his home there in 1769, and within a year the first of a long line of sawmills was going. But Bangor didn't get its town charter for two decades, and the first ship with a Bangor house flag didn't go down the ways until 1811. Shortly thereafter, and suddenly, there came a brief era of speculation.

Indians, white hunters, and even a few land-lookers had long told of the mighty trees in the vast forest of the Penobscot. These tales finally permeated to the populous cities of Portland and Portsmouth and even to metropolitan Boston and Philadelphia, where lived men of vision and substance. Good pines that were handy to streams, they knew, were already becoming scarce along the Connecticut, the Saco, and the lower Androscoggin and the Kennebec. Late in the eighteenth century men of means began buying Penobscot timber.

The District of Maine—there was no State of Maine until 1820—was happy to be shut of its timberland. It disposed of much of this by grants to colleges and academies and to soldiers of the Revolution; and it sold even more through lotteries. Money was hard to come by, for the provincial governments. Timberland not only was worthless; it was in the way.

You had, as they said, to let daylight into the swamp before corn and potatoes would grow.

So the buying and granting went on. William Bingham, a wealthy Philadelphian, sent a timber cruiser on a voyage through the woods of central and eastern Maine, and then Mr. Bingham bought, for twelve and a half cents an acre, a goodly slice of Maine for himself. In one hunk Mr. Bingham purchased 2,107,396 acres of white pine and spruce in which no ax, save it be an Indian's stone tomahawk, had been heard.

It is beyond the minds of men today to conceive of two million acres of virgin timber in one solid block, owned by one man. For more than a century afterward a horde of loggers hacked away at the Bingham Purchase, driving part down the Kennebec, part down the Penobscot; and of a winter's work one logger would say to another that he had been working on the Kennebec Million, or the Penobscot Million.

There were many lesser but still large purchases, too, and Bangor soon became the scene of a land speculation that would be matched only in the Far West of later years. This was only proper, for the Penobscot country was really New England's last frontier, the only frontier in America where men moved from West to East to reach it.

In 1835 land brokers' offices crowded the saloons and "gentlemen's washing" houses all along Exchange Street, and they ran like the water-front sawmills—all day and all night. Timberland that had brought six and twelve cents an acre a few years before was now changing hands at six dollars, eight dollars, and even ten dollars. Fast courier lines, a sort of Pony Express, were set up between Bangor and Boston. Smooth gents formed the somewhat diaphanous Bangor Lower Stillwater Mill Company, obviously more interested in lots than in mills, and staged a combination auction-banquet, the latter presided over by a caterer from New York. Champagne was poured from original bottles into washtubs, and all invited to belly-around and drink hearty. Fortunately, for the amazed loggers, this affair was held in June, when the drive was in and a man was handy—and thirsty.

The wildcatters turned over $127,000 in timberlands that day, and the loggers who would later cut the timber got ory-eyed on free champagne.

The speculation boom, of course, soon burst, but actual logging along the Penobscot was just getting a good start, for men of action had come along with the men of vision. Railroad construction had been pushed twelve miles upriver as early as 1836, to reach Oldtown and Orono. Its rails were wood, with scrap iron spiked along the top, and its locomotive had been made in England by Stephenson himself. The redoubtable General Sam Veazie bought this road and started out to make it go.

General Veazie, while perhaps the most aggressive[1] of the early Bangor lumbermen, was quite typical. He soon built or bought control in nineteen mills at Oldtown, thirteen more at Basin Mills, and still twenty more in his own town of Veazie, which town he got a friendly legislature to set aside for him. The general thought it would be nice, and efficient, to elect men from his own company payroll to fill the rather important offices of tax assessors.

As early as 1825 the legislature had granted a charter to a company[2] formed to collect the great mass of logs of mixed ownership that floated down from the woods and to segregate them for the various mills at and between Oldtown and Bangor. General Veazie bought this franchise and ran things in his own way, possibly to his own advantage, for there was hell a-popping and much fighting about logs until the other

---

[1] On occasion even boss lumbermen engaged in fisticuffs over logs.

[2] The Penobscot [log] Boom Company.

lumbermen got the State to appoint a three-man commission to handle affairs at the Penobscot log boom.

But Veazie was not alone in his aggressiveness. There was Jefferson Sinclair, a great figure to whom many gave the credit for starting the boom idea in the first place. There was Moses Giddings and old Arad Thompson, individualists from 'way back, and the Pearsons, the Lumberts, the Bruces, and a score of others, all of them up on their hind legs and r'aring to go. Among them, and aided by just such aggressive and prehensile logging operators in New Brunswick, they brought about what to this day in Maine is referred to as the Aroostook War.

The "war" took its name from the then vaguely bounded country known as The Aroostook. The international boundary was as yet undetermined, but not so were the intentions of the Bangor logging operators and timber owners. They wanted *all* that great straight pine, come hell and high water, and they charged that the New Brunswickers were jumping the claim and cutting in Maine woods.

The State of Maine sent its land agents up to investigate. They discovered many rafts of logs, allegedly cut in Maine timber, being floated down the Aroostook River and into New Brunswick. They seized some of the rafts, only to have the Blue Nosers[3] cut them loose under cover of darkness. There was considerable hullabaloo, during which oxen were seized and stocks of wild hay burned. Among the actual loggers on both sides a heap of assault and battery took place, some of it naturally running to mayhem, through the loss of ears in combat.

Now the logging operators and timber owners set up a howl that was articulated through the Maine legislature loud enough to reach Washington, D. C. But Washington moved too slowly to suit long-mem-

[3]Citizens of the Maritime Provinces of Canada.

oried folk whose towns and cities—aye, and whose
camps and sawmills—had been burned by the British
a few years before. In 1839 Maine loaded some old
brass cannon onto oxcarts and scows and sent militia
north to man Forts Kent and Fairfield.

Some excellent sniping was done back and forth with
ball and cap rifles, but the artillery did not go into action. Sir John Harvey and Lord Ashburton had come
forward as peacemakers for Great Britain, and General
Winfield Scott and Dan'l Webster acted for the embattled Bangor lumbermen. The Webster-Ashburton
Treaty (1842) setting the present boundary, was the
outcome, and the Maine troops returned to their homes.

With the Aroostook Question officially settled, both
Penobscot and New Brunswick lumbermen continued
to poach upon each other's preserves, but the only
actual fighting done was carried on by the loggers
themselves, who enjoyed it hugely, never allowing it
again to become an International Incident but keeping
it alive for local amusement and practice.

With comparative quiet restored along the border,
Bangor went into the years of its glory. Williamsport,
Pennsylvania, would later cut more lumber than Bangor. Saginaw and Muskegon in Michigan would cut
more boards in a month than Bangor did in a year;
and, in time, a *single* sawdust plant would rise on the
Columbia River in the Pacific Northwest that could
cut twice as much lumber as *all* of Bangor's four hundred and ten saws. Yet the fame of the Penobscot city
became so great that no less than ten other Bangors
were founded, hopefully, on the loggers' and lumbermen's trek South and West. A number of things contributed to this lustrous shining of Thoreau's star on
the edge of night.

Bangor was the first city of size whose entire energies were given to the making and shipping of lumber and to the entertainment of the loggers who cut
the trees. Then, too, it is from Bangor's canny and

inventive men that stems so much that has been found sound and practicable throughout the years. And lastly, there were the surefooted lads of Bangor who, spring after spring, walked two hundred and more miles on heaving logs straight down the middle of the Penobscot. These men made such a name for themselves, by their agility on a moving log and by their foolhardy courage anywhere, that west of Bangor a Penobscot man came to be known as a Bangor Tiger—quick of foot and ready for battle.

Good as they were, the Bangor Tigers, like loggers elsewhere, lacked a forthright tool for driving the timber down rivers. For a century past, rivermen had got along the best they could with a tool as primitive as a stone ax. It was a swing dog, in its then most modern form, and a pretty poor rig it was. Around a short pole, some four feet long, hung an iron collar to which was attached a hook, or dog, for the rolling of logs. It was awkward, and dangerous, for the dog would move up and down and sidewise. Thus the dog was not always "there" when wanted, and a man giving a good quick heave on the staff might find himself flopping headlong over the log and into the stream. Rivermen cursed it, and it sent many of them into the water, not to rise until a million feet of logs had passed over them. Then they ceased to worry about swing dogs. But Bangor inventors didn't.

One afternoon in the spring of 1858, Joseph Peavey, a blacksmith of Stillwater Village, near Bangor, lay on his stomach in the old covered bridge that crossed the Stillwater branch of the Penobscot. Through a crack in the floor he was watching the efforts of a crew of rivermen below him to break a big jam of logs.

Old Peavey watched a while, and listened while the rivermen passed blistering remarks about the goddamn so-and-so swing dogs. Then, as he afterward told, the Big Idea came, like a shaft of sudden sunlight through a hole in a covered bridge. Peavey jumped up, shouting a blacksmith's equivalent of "Eureka!" and ran as fast as he could to the Peavey blacksmith shop. Here he directed his son Daniel how to make a *rigid* clasp to encircle a cant-dog staff, with lips on one side. These lips were drilled to take a bolt that would hold the hook, or dog, in place, allowing it to move up and down but not sidewise. Below the bulge in the cant-dog handle Daniel placed graduated collars of iron which added greatly to the strength of the handle. Then, as a piece of crowning genius, old Joe had his son drive a sharp iron spike into the end of the rig. . . . Thus the tool was born that would in the years to come roll untold billions of feet of logs into the many rivers that run between the Penobscot and the Pacific, and from Hudson's Bay to the Gulf of Mexico.

Old Joe Peavey's last name would soon be known wherever logs were rolled, though the greatest single invention in the technology of logging would bring him no fortune.

Peavey got William Hale, noted Penobscot river boss, to try out the new tool. Hale pronounced it the soundest rig ever put in the hands of a calk-booted man. So Joe Peavey made a drawing of it and set out on foot for Bangor and the post office, with the intention of getting it patented. On the way he stopped to see a blacksmith friend in Orono.

Joe Peavey liked a glass of Medford rum, sometimes two glasses. His Orono friend poured liberally and old Joe, his stomach warm, displayed the plans he was sending to the patent office. This called for another round of rum, and so on. When Joe awoke next morning and shook the fog out of his old gray head, drawings and application for a "Patent Cantdog," *not* a peavey, were on their way to Washington, submitted by the Orono blacksmith.

But regardless of first patents, the Peavey family went into the business of making the tool Joe had invented, and the fourth generation of them are at it today, in Brewer, just across the Penobscot from Bangor. The name had long been admitted to dictionaries and is a generic term applied by woodsmen to all cant dogs. Not one logger in a thousand today knows whence and how came its name.

Joseph Peavey didn't stop with the rivermen's tool. He is credited with the Peavey hoist, for pulling stumps and raising the gates of dams, and with the hay press, by which loose hay could be baled into small tight wads for transportation into the logging camps.

The idea of a large sorting boom to handle logs for many mills has already been mentioned. It was devised at Bangor in 1825, and was copied later on the Hudson, the Saginaw, the Mississippi, and other streams in the West.

Bangor men invented the Bangor Snubber, a machine for regulating the speed of sledloads of logs on steep hills. And the log-branding ax, or hammer, was a product of Bangor, and it is the logger's one concession to Art.

A log with no owner's mark on it and floating down the public highway of a river is anybody's log, so the practice of branding logs came early in the industry. Before the Bangor invention of a branding ax, men who had to be marvels with an ax cut the owner's mark in the ends of logs. These marks, by necessity of the tool used, had to be a grouping of straight lines. They ran to what were called, Dart, Double-dart, Diamond, Crowsfoot, Anchor, Short Forty, Long Forty, and such.

With the branding ax, its face a steel pattern of the brand's design, lumbermen could allow their imaginations free rein. Log brands have run to wondrous patterns since then, and include Derby Hats, Wine Glasses, Beerkegbungs, Aeolian Harps, and Hearts and Flowers. Thus did inventive Bangor devise an outlet

for the long-suppressed artistic urges of logging operators.

During the period 1830-1860, sawmills grew and
multiplied along the Penobscot. Bangor doubled, then
redoubled its population to seventeen thousand. Ships
for lumber came so thick that on many days small
boys could walk across the harbor from Bangor to
Brewer on their decks. The channel to the sea once got
so full of heavy pine slabs that Army dredges had to
come to clear it, making it even deeper; and monstrous
great ships, like the graceful *Belle of Bath* and the
staunch *Phineas Pendleton,* could dock at Bangor with
room to spare underneath the keel.

Below or above Bangor, the river was never empty.
From the mills clustered at Oldtown and Orono came
long rafts made of sawed lumber floating down to the
docks, to be taken apart, board by board, and stowed
in the holds. Log rafts, too, some of them half a mile
long, came into Bangor for sawing in the city mills.
As for men in calked boots—they simply swarmed
over everything and everywhere.

Out on a Bangor street one sniffed the air and found
the perfume of pine in it. In the shops one smelled
rum and molasses. It was pure affinity. Lumbermen
sweetened the loggers' beans and tea with molasses;
they made it into rum for the loggers' entertainment.
And the logger, he put the pine dust in the air.

The big lumbermen built mansions all along State
Street in Bangor, where some of the houses still survive. These first lumbermen were lusty fellows and
they, too, set a pattern. It was a pattern that has been
dimmed by the passage of time and dimmed again
by the efforts of their scandalized descendants, but it is
tolerably clear—and fascinating.

Most of these big lumbermen would drink Madeira,
to be polite, when they entertained at home, but they
liked Medford and West Indies rum, which they drank

in vast quantities. They were kind to dumb animals, their favorite being the fast and tireless Morgan horse. These they imported from Vermont for themselves and their mistresses, whom they kept in semiregal style, if compared with the Spartan life enjoined on the young men and women of the Bangor Theological Seminary.[4]

Nor was the calk-booted proletariat without its entertainment. Quite early in Bangor's life the Devil himself took possession of much of the property centering around Haymarket Square, on the west side of town, and held his own securely until the timber line had moved west to Michigan. It was here, on Harlow Street, that the noble Fan Jones built and operated her justly famous Skyblue House.

Fan Jones was a woman of wide vision, looking both landward and seaward. There was a huge chimney on the outside of her place and this she caused to be painted sky blue, the blue of the brightest sky ever seen. It was never allowed to fade, but was repainted twice a year, brighter and more lovely each time. And this chimney was so placed that its heavenly color served as landmark for womenhungry loggers coming downriver from the woods, and as a promise of snug harbor to the sailors coming upriver. If a man got lost in Bangor, whether by land or by sea, it was no fault of Fan's; and she did very well by this public-spirited service.

Haymarket Square came to harbor a score of hell-holes where grog and other vice abounded. It was a fitting subject, close to hand, on which the young divines of the theological seminary could practice calling down God's curse. Yet Satan had so well fortified it that in 1911, when Bangor suffered the worst fire in its history, the flames ate up five churches, a school, a bank and dozens of homes of the pious, but left the

[4]The Seminary derived much of its early support from lumbermen.

Haymarket with not so much as a blister of paint on its scarlet lights.

Bangor and the Penobscot did not reach the peak of lumber making and shipping until 1872, yet their importance in the lumber industry had faded a full decade before. By the time of the First Battle of Bull Run the bulk of Maine's white pine forests had gone through the saws, and Michigan, the next white pine stronghold, was the lumber colossus. A heap of spruce would go down the Penobscot just as some of it does in 1938 —in tiny, four-foot sticks—but most of that spruce has gone into the chippers and digesters of pulpmills, to be regurgitated as long rolls of paper on which to print comic strips.[5]

[5]In a small neat park, near Bangor's fine library, is a group of statuary, "The Last Drive," depicting three calk-booted figures, two of them with peavey in hand. It is the work of Sculptor Charles E. Tefft and is the only mark left to indicate that Bangor was once the greatest lumber city on earth.

3

The Beginnings of Sawdust

BANGOR WAS TO BE THE FAIR and fullest flower of the Eastern lumber industry, and nigh two hundred years of preparation went into its making. That preparation began in 1631 when colonists made the rude harness of a dam and set the Salmon Falls River to swishing an up-and-down saw in South Berwick Township, Maine, on the New Hampshire border. It was the first sawmill in America. The Dutch had earlier erected on distant Manhattan Island a sawmill to be run by wind power, but records indicate it to have been a failure. It wasn't for nothing that Maine put a white pine tree on its flag.

There was an all-covering forest to be cut in New England before the colonists could practice agriculture. This forest was friend and enemy. As a friend it was the source of houses, ships, and fuel. As enemy, it made dark and damp the ground that must have sunlight to grow grain; and it was a sinister protection for savages. For two centuries to come, a man who would erect a sawmill and thus encourage the cutting of trees was held not only a leading citizen but a beneficent and patriotic fellow as well. What was most needed, in short, was some daylight in the swamp.

The early sawmill men were loggers, too. They went into the woods, which were always near by, cut a few logs, then ran them through the saws. When the pond water got too low to turn the wheel, they would shut down the gates and turn logger again. Not until the beginning of the nineteenth century did loggers grow

27

a race apart, yet by the time Bangor led the lumber industry, environment and what might be called natural selection had a new breed of men in the making, a species quite distinct from the more sober and home-loving fellows who handled the forest's products once they had arrived at the sawmill.

New England colonists had scarcely got their first wind when they started two industries that were to dominate their lives for a long time to come. On July 4, 1631, they launched at Medford, Massachusetts, the *Blessing of the Bay,* first New England-built ship; and in the same year the *Pied Cowe* arrived from England with machinery for the sawmill that was presently set up at South Berwick. Henceforth, the building of ships and sawmills was an everyday occurrence.

Shipbuilding appears to have been a well-organized business from the first, especially at Portland and Portsmouth; but most of the early sawmills were erected by community effort, raising bees, at which settlers congregated to drink rum and help lift the mill timbers into place. One may read in yellowing records of the prodigious amount of potable alcohol required to put even the smallest mill together.[1]

Although the general trend of the lumber industry was from Massachusetts north into the New Hampshire Grants, thence east into Maine, the Saco River in the latter State was the very rialto of the early mills. One of the Saco mill operators was John Alden, son of the Pilgrim who spoke out of turn and was married by Priscilla Mullens. Another early timber baron was Sir William Pepperell. Sir William commanded the colonist forces in the expedition against Louisburg, Cape Breton Island, in 1745, and was the only baronet of New

---

[1] The account books of Major John Pynchon show that in erecting a sawmill in Suffield, Connecticut, in August of 1672, and in "setting down ye dam," the major had occasion to purchase the following goods: 1 bottle brandy, 1½ Gals. liquor, 1 bbl. cider, 2 bottles liquor, 3 Gals. rum.

England birth during colonial times. He appeared at his log landings along the Saco attired in a coat of scarlet cloth. It is the earliest record of brilliant garb, worn in connection with logs, and one wonders if it were not from Sir William that stemmed the loggers' liking for bright red, whether of sash, shirt, mackinaw, or a good pair of woolen drawers.

These colonists were he-loggers from the very beginning of things. They spat on their hands, gave another snap to their galluses, and dived ax first into the King's timber to such effect that the Crown became alarmed. In 1691 when a charter consolidated most of the New England colonies into the Province of Massachusetts, England put a ban on all the largest and best pines and "okes." All pines of twenty-four inches and more at the butt, standing within three miles of water, were reserved for the Royal Navy; and upon these trees England ordered its officers to cut the mark of the Broad Arrow. The penalties for cutting marked trees were very severe, approximating those against swearing, heresy, fornication, and murder. The law, of course, was flouted and small mills continued to eat into the timber, caring little whether a tree had a Broad Arrow in its bark, or merely the flint head of an Indian's arrow. (The reds often took pot shots at the loggers.)

Anne, by the Grace of God, Queen and so forth, was the first British monarch to attempt seriously to enforce the Broad Arrow policy. For the sum of two hundred pounds yearly Anne commissioned John Bridger as her Surveyor General. That was in 1706. Among Bridger's duties were to set aside, mark with the Broad Arrow, and to *protect* such "trees as be fitt and proper."

It was an appalling job that Bridger set out to do. Officials two hundred years later found it difficult if not impossible to prevent loggers from cutting whole *sections* (six hundred and forty acres) of timber that loggers thought were in the way of "Progress," to say nothing of a stray pine here and there. So Bridger and his unhappy successors found themselves marked and alien men in a time and place where nearly every colonist was a logger of parts.

Bridger apparently realized the hopelessness of his task, for he was very lenient with poachers; but his successor, Dunbar, set out with a high hand to enforce a law as unenforceable as that against the drinking of hard cider. Dunbar, says Belknap, the New Hampshire historian, seized and marked large quantities of lumber already sawed; and he raided sawmills and clapped offenders into gaol. Apparently he did not realize the kind of men with whom he was dealing. They outwitted the Surveyor General much of the time, and when one of them was caught, the others rioted and put up forcible resistance. No such flouting of law was seen until prohibition came to Maine, thus making loggers wilder than ever and sending them into the ginger-liniment-peruna era, years ahead of the rest of the country.

The Surveyors General of timber not only failed to maintain the Broad Arrow policy, but this policy created a widespread resentment that played a much greater part than most histories indicate in bringing on the Boston Tea Party and sending Paul Revere, potted as any logger, if legend be correct, a-riding through the Middlesex night.

With the War of the Revolution over, Maine, politically still a part of Massachusetts, went into the business of logging with an ax in each hand—one for cutting down trees, the other for building ships. It was a great and gaudy era that was to last close to a hundred years. First, they would cut the white pine only, leaving the vast quantities of spruce as unfit for any use; then they would log the State all over again. The spruce topped the pine cut for the first time in 1861.

The early loggers found the long Connecticut and the short Merrimac and Saco pretty highways over which to ride their produce to market, and they made fine meadows out of timberland in no time at all. That is, except for the upper reaches of the Connecticut, which were more than three hundred miles away and would have to wait a bit.

They advanced early on to the Presumpscott, taking that timber in their stride, and, still marching eastward, they tackled the Androscoggin, and also the Kennebec, the great central river system of Maine. Meanwhile, tidewater mills had begun to dot the Maine coast line all the way from the Piscataqua to the St. Croix. Both Maine and New Brunswick men began logging on the St. Croix, part of Maine's Eastern boundary, at about the same time. Calais was the big lumber port here, and as early as 1805 a marvelous sluice had been constructed to bring lumber in a hurry from the mills above Calais to tidewater and ships at the city's docks. Incidentally, this sluice, reckoned the last word in its day, was built for and owned by two maiden ladies of Scotland, the Misses Margaret and Susanna Campbell, possibly the first of their sex to be connected with America's red-eyed and hell-roaring lumber industry.

Portland was the center of the mast trade that flourished in the first half of the eighteenth century. Bath soon followed Portsmouth as the place where ships were actually built, and it was at Dresden, near Bath, where one of the boldest attempts in all lumber history was made. It came in a flash of near-genius in the fertile mind of Dr. James Tupper, who is described in Charles E. Allen's *History of Dresden* as "a man most eccentric, hospitable and generous to a fault; was a warm and true disciple of Baron Swedenborg. . . . He was a man of strong and vigorous intellect, a deep thinker."

At this period, 1791-1792, England was still feeling huffy about the recent war and loss of her colonies. She would allow entry to no sawed boards, although there was not even a duty on squared timbers. Doctor Tupper looked at the Atlantic, found it nothing more than a large lake, and swore, by the Suffering Old Deity—so often called upon by loggers—that if the English would have none of his lumber, then they should have some of the fine tall pines of Maine in the form of hewed timber. With a crew working under him he constructed at Bath what was probably the strangest craft ever launched in Maine or elsewhere. He christened it *The Experiment,* and it was well named.

The thing was basically a raft, nothing more. It was made by treenailing ax-hewed timbers together in the form of a ship's hull. It was then full-ship-rigged, the plan being to send her out across the Atlantic under her own sail, like any ship. As a concession to the crew, the good doctor placed a small vessel on the craft's deck—just in case. Then, his sailing crew changed their minds.

This monstrous "ship," made of about one thousand tons of timbers, lay for weeks in the harbor at Bath, while the doctor stomped around the grogshops trying to drum up sailors to man her. Finally he succeeded. The thing sailed out of Bath under her own canvas, and headed up the coast. But here, off the Grand Banks, a storm blew up. The crew, so the record indicates, deserted very readily, putting ashore in the vessel carried on the craft's deck. Aged Blue Nosers of New Foundland recall hearing their grandpappies tell of seeing the remains of Dr. Tupper's great idea, full of salt and marine borers, being pounded slippery smooth along the rocky coast.

Two other such attempts to raft timbers across the sea were made from Bath, but met with failure. The doctor had started something, though, and again, in the 1880s, log rafts started from Halifax for Boston. They never got there.[2]

Inland, too, Maine men were showing considerable imagination. There was the Moosehead Lake business, and the "Telos War."

At Moosehead Lake in Maine the waters of the Penobscot and the waters of the Kennebec were not more than two miles apart. As early as the 1830s this fact got a good deal of thought in the minds of the Kennebeckers. Up there at the far and remote end of the Penobscot's West Branch, they knew, was great white pine such as couldn't be cut any more between Moosehead Lake and the ocean.

Finally, in 1839, William Boyd and William Moulton, two large operators on the Kennebec, came out boldly with a plan to divert Penobscot waters into Moosehead Lake. Thus they could drive logs cut on Penobscot waters into the lake, tow them across with headworks,[3] and sluice them into the Kennebec.

In spite of the fact that an Erie Canal was working well in the Far West of the day, the Moosehead Lake proposal was a plan bold enough to stagger the imagination of backwoods men of the time. But it was Bangor lumbermen who were staggered most. What? Turn God's own water from the Penobscot and into the Kennebec! The very thought stank of tinkering with the Lord's plans. And from Bangor, which is a Penobscot town, such a howl went up that it was heard in Augusta, the State capital. Penobscot preachers pounded their pulpits and shouted that it was against

[2]Not until 1906, and from the Columbia River on the other coast of America, would a log raft be made that could withstand the pounding of the sea.

[3]Headworks consisted of a capstan and much rope. The capstan might be set on shore at the end of a lake, or on a raft anchored in the middle of a lake. Horses or men turned the capstan, pulling in the rope and a boomful of logs. It was slow work.

God, which helped a good deal in those days. Penobscot lumbermen marshaled "menaces" by the score into the press, and they also "took care of the boys," down at Augusta. The legislature frowned and the matter was dropped.

Canals and canal building, however, permeated the air of Maine, and twenty-five charters to canal companies had been granted before 1840. The most famous of them was built by quite rugged individualists. It was the Telos Canal and it worked well and without benefit of charter until it grew into a *cause célèbre* that resulted in the "Telos War," still talked about around the bunkhouse stoves of Maine pulpwood camps.

At about the same time the impious Kennebeckers were seeking to divert God's (Bangor's) own Penobscot waters for driving purposes, the men of Bangor also had been studying geography. They saw on their maps, and their land-lookers fortified the maps by witness, that a dam on Lake Telos and a sluice from Telos to Webster Lake would cause waters of the Allagash River to flow into those of the Penobscot.

This, it seemed in Bangor, was not at all against God's plan; for the Allagash flowed into the St. John River and the St. John flowed into New Brunswick— foreign parts where lived nothing but a pack of Tories who might howl, if they would, and be damned to them. In March of 1841 the dam was built on Lake Telos, and in the spring a freshet of Allagash water took logs a-fluking down a natural ravine and into Penobscot waters and so to Bangor.

This was slick enough, but now the Bangor lumbermen had a falling out. Without going into details, which are complicated by other dams and sluices in the same neighborhood, Rufus Dwinel got control of Telos Canal and announced that it would cost other lumbermen exactly fifty cents a thousand feet to sluice their logs through it. However, Dwinel, a Bangor man, was dealing with Bangor men, and they leaped at once to attack this undermining of the Flag, the Home, and individual effort, or whatever euphemisms were used in those days.

David Pingree, one of Maine's biggest timber owners of all time, led the charge of the embattled individualists. They "saw the boys" at Augusta and they threatened to sluice their logs through Dwinel's canal by force. Dwinel replied by moving seventy-five rugged and resolute loggers to the canal head and arming them to the teeth. "Come on, you barstards," they howled, giving to the noun the full flavor of the broad Penobscot "a."

The affair was settled in the legislature and without bloodshed, and Allagash waters aided the Penobscot until all the pine had gone downriver.

In time, too, the Kennebeckers would get some of that Penobscot water they had attempted to divert early in the century. Mention has been made of Boyd and Moulton who in 1839 had planned to build a canal and sluice at Moosehead Lake. In 1893, the Bradstreets of South Gardiner, a Kennebec town, started in to do what Boyd and Moulton had been prevented from doing. This became the famous Bradstreet Conveyor, which was really quite an engineering feat and Maine's final great effort.

Ira D. Peavey, of the Bangor Peavey family, was in charge. The works consisted of two conveyors, of six hundred feet each, a sluiceway, and a dam on Carry Brook. The first conveyor, operated by steam, took logs from Carry Pond, on *Penobscot* waters, by means of an endless chain with iron dogs at intervals, and dumped them into a second conveyor, operated by a second engine, and delivered them to a sluiceway that was two miles long. The sluice was filled with water from Carry Brook and landed the logs in *Kennebec* waters.

The rig, one of the most stupendous in logging history, worked well and long. It was used until 1901 and brought out an estimated total of one hundred million feet of logs. Kennebeckers always got their water —and their logs.

In respect to the two regions, there was always great rivalry between Penobscot and Kennebec loggers. When Bangor was a rough backwoods village, the loggers who went there to work from the comparatively civilized Kennebec brought their dunnage with them in highly flowered carpet bags. Penobscot loggers, who, if they carried any dunnage at all were likely to have it in an old meal sack, jeered at such sissy doings as the carrying of carpet bags. And to this day, in Maine and New Hampshire, a knapsack is referred to as a "Kennebecker."

The first speed-up in lumber-production technique did not reach Maine until 1821, and then it came from the sawmill end of the industry, just as more and greater speed-ups would come in time. Loggers changed their methods very slowly, looking askance at every new element, changing to power equipment only when driven to it by the hungry maws of the mills, holding fast to oxen and then horses until long after those animals were extinct in most industries. . . . Yet the loggers knew what they were about, for during three centuries they managed to keep the millponds full of round-stuff.

The shadow of the coming speed-up fell across Maine in 1821 when the Bath Steam Mill Company began burning slabs instead of using water for its power. The word "steam" had magic in it. It was a proud word in those days, and so it remained until late in the century. Mills from Calais, Maine, to Portland, Oregon, used the word in their corporate titles to display their up-to-dateness.

The Bath Steam Mill was an immediate success.

Hampden had one by 1835; Hallowell, in 1837. By 1850 there were thirty-six steam-powered sawmills in the State. The saws were still the old up-and-down affairs.

Out in Bentonville, New York, a blacksmith named Benjamin Cummings had in 1814 made and patented a circular saw. Quickly tried out in Bangor, it was pronounced worthless. But in 1820 Eastman and Jaquith of Brunswick, Maine, took out a new patent on the same idea, and circular saws came into use shortly thereafter. They could not be said to be in general use in Maine until around 1850.

By now the saw filer, the man who sharpened the cutting edge of the saw, had come into his own. They were a most secretive order of men, these early saw filers, but hardly Masonic, for they did their best to keep any secrets they had from their own colleagues. Indeed, they did everything they could to make their art as esoteric as though they had been dealing in lodestones and the transmutation of base metals into gold.

A saw filer in those days performed behind closed and locked doors. Anyone wishing to talk to him, even the big boss, had to ring a bell put up for that purpose outside the filing-room door, so that the filer might conceal his technique by getting his devilish apparatus out of sight. With modifications, and lacking the locked door, this secrecy of sawmill filers continued until automatic filing machinery pretty much did away with "secrets."

An edging table came into use in 1825. "Yankee" gangsaws came soon after, running twenty, even thirty, saws to a single rig. And with steam in the boiler, the sawmill men cared nothing about freshets or droughts, just as long as the logs kept coming down from the woods.

But by the time sawmill filers had come to be personages, the loggers, the men who worked back in the timber, had ceased to know much about sawmills and less about the sawmill speed-up. Nor did they give, as they said in their quaint way, a good goddamn. The process of creating a new race of men had been slowly and surely going on since colonial times. It was a cruel process, as most natural processes are; yet, like them, too, it was most efficient, and out of it had emerged a species of men the like of which had not been seen before—and certainly not since, for civilization of the first third of the twentieth century killed them off, actually or spiritually, just as surely as it sent old Jigger Jones to his preposterous death, Anno Domini, Nineteen Hundred and Thirty-Five.

4

Daylight in the Swamp

No MAN CAN SAY just when the species *logger* appeared. The early American hewers and sawers of wood were called "lumberers," whether they worked in the forest or in the sawmill. Most of them did both, cutting the forest into logs during winter, and in summer sawing the logs into boards. Yet the professional logger, the man who would work in the woods or at nothing at all, was sighted as early as 1801 by E. A. Kendall, a visiting Englishman, who wrote of this new species of man:

> But, his habits in the forest, and his voyage [the river drive] for the sale of his lumber, all break up the system of persevering industry, and substitute one of alternate toil and indolence, hardship and debauch; and in the alternation, indolence and debauch will inevitably be indulged in the greatest possible proportion. . . . The lumberer is usually too poor to possess land. If he possesses land, it soon must leave him to pay for rum. . . . But along with vice, where there is misery, we divide ourselves between anger and compassion. If his toil is unsteady, it is also unprofitable; and he suffers at least as much from the scantiness of his wages as from any deficiency in his work. The strength and execution of his arm almost exceed belief; and he fells the forest with at least as much activity as others plough the soil. Meanwhile, it is often amid cold and wet that all his labour is performed. . . . To ward off damps and chills he drinks spirituous liquors; the liquors weaken his system. . . . Intermittents attack him. . . .

Yes, the "intermittents" would attack him. They would appear in various forms, such as pink and whiskered little men crawling straight up the sides of buildings all around Haymarket Square in Bangor; as a gigantic anaconda, far from its native jungle, writhing horribly across the Sawdust Flats at Muskegon, Michigan; or as a great, green grizzly bear, complete with wings and calked boots, walking on its hind legs down Burnside Street in Portland, Oregon. The fauna of the bottle would keep up with the receding timber line.

But dismal picture though it be, and one-sided, Mr. Kendall's description of the logger was accurate enough, in 1801 or in 1901. What the Englishman did not see was that the life of the logger would in a single generation or so produce a race of men who in the large didn't give a tinker's damn for property; and who were as hardy a race of men as ever walked. Natural selection by forthright elimination would do it.

Of, say, a crew of fifty green loggers, going into the woods in October, about half would find the life too rigorous. They would soon quit and leave. Of those remaining, the less alert and sure-footed would be struck by falling timber or crushed flat on a log landing. The spring drive downriver, most dangerous of all woods work, would surely remove a few more. Once the drive was in, two or three others would die of acute alcoholism or in saloon brawls. . . . As for the survivors, they were immune to disease and you couldn't kill them with a pole ax.

It was a cruel yet perfectly natural selective process, and it produced in the survivors a crew of veritable hellions—rough, tough, lusty, and thirsty; men fit to follow hard on the tracks of the explorers and trappers and to cut the forest and drive it down rivers. Although they never thought of it that way, and although historians and other writers have largely ignored them, the loggers were the real American pioneers. When they had cut one forest, they would drink hearty and howl long and loud while "blowin' her in." Then they would pack their turkeys on their backs and hit out over the Hump. Hell, man, there was plenty of timber, timber without end, just over the Hump, and by the Holy Old Mackinaw, they'd cut her, cut her close, wide, and handsome!

The authentic species, even to their garb, had appeared in solid and characteristic form long before 1856. In that year a Mr. C. Lanman observed of Maine loggers, in his *Adventures in the Wilds of the United States,* that

> "they are a young and powerfully built race of men, mostly New Englanders, generally unmarried, and though rude in their manner, and intemperate, are quite intelligent. They seem to have a passion for their wild and toilsome life, and judging from their dresses, I should think possess a fine eye for the comic and fantastic. The entire apparel of an individual consists of a pair of gray pantaloons and *two* red flannel shirts, a pair of long boots, and a woolen covering for the head, and *all* these things are worn at one and the same time."

Thoreau, no sissy himself, looked at the logger and found him a formidable fellow. Timothy Dwight, a noted observer of the 1820s, recognized the true species emerging when he wrote that the loggers "are almost necessarily poor. Their course of life seduces them to prodigality, irreligion, immoderate drinking, and other ruinous habits." Dwight was too delicate to indicate what those "other ruinous habits" were, but he must have known that loggers already had sworn they would leave not one virgin along the Kennebec.

It was said of loggers that they lived in trees, hanging by their tails, and that they would eat, and digest, hay, if you but sprinkled whisky on it. The former statement is an exaggeration, but not much. The early

camps were more primitive abodes than those of the
cave dwellers; the cave men cut pictures on their walls,
a civilized gesture. The logger at home peered through
a haze of smoke to see nothing but more logs piled up,
one upon the other, to make the sides of his camp.
That is, if he could see through and around the mass
of steaming and stinking clothing that hung all over
the place.

The camps were staunch enough; some of their remains could be seen a hundred years after, furnishing
food for untold generations of hedgehogs. The chinks
in the logs were stuffed with moss. The first roofs
were bark; later came cedar shakes and poles covered
with tar paper. The bunks, when there were any,
might be double- or triple-deckers; mere poles onto
which were tossed some hay or hemlock boughs. The
bunks had no rated capacity; as many men got into
them as could. No foolishness about housing regulations.
Along the lower tier of bunks ran the deacon seat.
This classic piece of camp furniture was the split half
of a log, a foot or so in diameter, supported by legs,
its flat side up. It ran from end to end of the camp,
along two sides.

In the center of the room—there was only one
room—was an open fire, set in sand and stones, and
placed hopefully, in respect to smoke, directly under a
large hole in the roof. On this fire the cook performed,
with swinging cranes, and around it, sitting and kneel-
ing, the loggers guzzled tea and dipped into the bean-
pot. The only other piece of furniture in the place was
a grindstone.

Such was the early pattern, a savage and excellent
cradle in which to nurture the timber beast. It was said
of these camps that the oxen lived better than the men,
for the oxen, in a camp as well built as the men's,
were bedded down on clean straw, while loggers slept
on boughs. Ox teamsters often slept in the hovel, as
logger barns are called, by choice.

In a short time, however, a separate room was made for the cook's premises and dining room. The tables were of rived pine or spruce, and later covered with oilcloth. For many years, though, the cook baked his bread against the open fire; and even after stoves came in, he continued to bake the beans in a beanhole dug in the ground, held by loggers to be the only fit way to treat a bean.

The fare was pretty much salt pork, beans, bread and molasses, and tea, black tea strong enough to float an ax on; and this fare improved but slowly until late in the nineteenth century. There was no talking at meals. The foreman, or bull of the woods, ruled the camp outside the cookhouse but in the cookhouse the cook—and the cook might be a boiler, a sizzler, or a stew builder—was Godamighty. Cooks were violent fellows, when aroused, and it was their right and custom to slap a man down off the table seat if he raised his voice.

The origin of this custom of mealtime silence is lost in history. Some lay it to the cook's desire to have the men fill their gut and get out as quickly as possible. Disciples of Marx lay it to the ogre of Capital, lurking in the background and gnashing its teeth at every moment lost to actual log production.[1]

The logger's needs in camp were few and those few were supplied him from out of the company *wangan* box, a word that has half a dozen spellings and means two entirely different things. The wangan in camp is the camp store—usually a large and padlocked box in the old days—from which the logger may have tobacco, clothing, and such. The charges for these goods are called "wangan," too. But on the river drive, the wangan is where camp is made for the night.

[1] The custom largely prevails in 1938, from coast to coast, and it would have been a great thing for doctors and patent-medicine makers were it not for the fact that a logger's stomach, as everyone knows, is of pure cast iron.

What light the early camps had came from flaming pine knots. Later came whale oil, kerosene, and finally, but not generally, electricity.

The logger's day began, so the loggers said, any old time after midnight, with the cookee's long wail of reveille. "Daaay-light in the swamp!" was a favorite getting-up cry, and it was heard, even in dark December and January, anywhere from half-past four to five o'clock of a morning. The ox teamsters were already up to feed and water the animals.

This morning call was the cookee's one opportunity to show originality, and he made the most of it. Some cookees had quite elaborate calls. One La Flamme liked to shout: "Oh, my! Oh, my! Dere ain't nobody h'up, an' de daylight, she's all aroun' in de swamp!" That was pretty fair for a *canayen,* who wasn't very used to the language. Another lovely call, whose author's name is regrettably lost, was chanted to a military rhythm: "Get up, get up, get up—dyin' old Christ, ain't you goin' to get up?" One cookee known as English John Thomas was a yodeler of parts and it was his custom to rout the boys by giving voice to J. K. Emmett's "Cuckoo Song," with, it is said, all the variations.

Instead of the human voice some camps used a conch shell, a tin horn,[2] or the gut-hammer. This instrument is a piece of iron, usually triangular in shape, hung just outside the cookhouse door. Upon it, with another piece of metal, the waker-up beats his tune. Here, too, the cookee could show his personality, and to the true artists among them, sounding reveille was as much a ceremony as to a sergeant-bugler. One Elizar Therrien, who had waked strong men from Calais, Maine, to Hoquiam, Washington, was one of the masters of gut-hammer. He began his tune with a leisurely movement—three sustained bell-like notes, pealing like the crack of doom into the ears of sleepy loggers. When

[2]Often known as the "gaberel."

the last note was just dying, he would go into a roulade, beating the iron faster and faster and louder and louder until the very hills seemed to tremble. This was big medicine, and one knew it from the swelling chest of Elizar. By God! when he rang the gong, the boys had to get up.

When the last echoes of the quick roulade had died away, he would strike the iron five times, slowly and deliberately, letting each solemn note die away in the forest before he struck again, just as though saying "roll . . . out . . . or . . . roll . . . up" (i.e., "roll *out* of bed and get to work, or roll *up* your stuff and hit the road").

With their bellies full of beans and the lye that passed for tea, the loggers would grope their way through the winter darkness. Often, even by the time they had walked a mile or so to the landings or unfelled timber, the light would still be too poor to do any work. They'd sit around in forty-below weather, talking and smoking until they might tell a pine from a hemlock.

Midday lunch might be eaten in camp, or it might be brought to the woods on a sled and eaten there, the tea steaming but the biscuits frozen nigh stiff and the pork little more than slabs of cold lard. Then they'd work until it was dark again and stumble their way back to camp. It never occurred to them that things could, or even should, be otherwise.

Twelve, even fourteen, hours out on the big white blanket, snow to their ears, against a background of blackgreen forest. The forest was black but not silent, for it snapped and crackled and boomed from a savage cold, and was quiet only when the falling-wedge went home and the great tall pines, protesting volubly about the weather, went swishing down to deep silence in the snow.

Poets said the trees shuddered and quaked when a

man with an ax walked among them. The loggers
saw nothing, heard nothing of this quaking. They saw,
close to hand, five months of timber that would have
to be cut before they might have a woman and a bottle
of drinking liquor in Bangor or East Machias or Calais
or Lewiston or Berlin or Woodsville.

So they cut the trees. They cut them with axes up
into the 1880s, then with saws. They put the logs on
rude go-devils[3] to yard to the main roads.

At the main road the logs were loaded onto sleds,
pulled by oxen, later by horses, still later by steam
log-haulers, and away they went down to the icy river.
The road was icy, too, for all night long a lonely
man, entertained by owls and wolves, sat on a sprinkler
sled and drove over the road, spraying water that
froze the instant it struck the sled tracks. Come daylight, here was a sheer highway, smooth as glass and
glittering, over which two small horses could pull a big
mountain of white pine logs.

The road wasn't ice on the hills. Here it was kept
bare of snow and ice, or hay and dirt were thrown on
top of the snow to act as a brake upon the sled runners. If the hill was very steep, a snubber was used
—a thick rope around a stump, to be paid out slowly
as the sled went down. Or, if the logs were long
ones, one end of them was dragged on the road at all
times, and on the hills a bridle chain of big links was
placed around the runner, to dig into the ground and
hold back the load.

Once down to the river the logs were piled in
long landings. When the ice went out in the spring,
in went the logs, with the drivers after them, chasing
them down to the mills. . . .

Until the advent of crosscut saws, loggers performed
wonders with an ax. They could fell a tree wherever

[3]A go-devil was nature's own sled, made from a forked birch
with a crosspiece nailed midway of the V, and hauled by a pair
of horses.

they wanted, even into the teeth of a head wind; and the scarf they made was so smooth that it showed scarcely the mark of the blade. Commonly, in the very ancient days, a logger took his pet ax to bed with him, tucking it under the sack or coat that was his pillow. Most loggers wore beards all winter, but those who preferred a mustache only, kept the other growth down with an ax.

On a Sunday, as honest men still living will tell, such a logger would sit, ax in hand, on the deacon seat and with a whetstone bring the blade to a near-razor fineness. He would then slap some soapy water into his beard and thereupon shave handsomely in the manner of men time out of mind.

No logging camp could operate without axes, and in time it came to be that no camp could operate without haywire. This wire was the stuff with which hay for the oxen and horses was bound into bales, for compact toting into the distant camps. Teamsters shaking out a bale to feed the animals took to saving the wire strands, throwing them over an oxbow nailed to the side of the hovel. They would do to mend a busted hame strap, or to put a link in a broken chain. And loggers used the strands to strengthen an ax helve or to wind the split handle of a peavey. Cooks strung haywire above the stove over which to dry clothes and to hang ladles; and often to bind the very stove together. In the zither era, so old-timers have vowed, a length of haywire came in handy to replace a broken string, and they say never was a more resonant G sounded, clear and deep as any harp.

It was told, too, but is offered here only as apocrypha, that a dentist of Greenville, Maine, once constructed a neat bridge of haywire and the molars of a fawn, which worked very well and lasted eleven years.

What is more positive, though, is that logging camps gave a new and useful slang phrase to the American

language. For in time a camp that was notoriously
poor in its equipment came to be known as a "haywire camp"; and from this usage it spread to mean
broken, busted, sick, crazy, no-good, and a score of
other things, none of them praiseworthy. It is possibly
the only authentic logger word the lay public has accepted.

Of social life in the woods there was almost none.
When that fourteen-hour day in cold and snow was
done, a man was ready for the bunk—hemlock needles,
hay chaff, lice, bugs, and all. He went to bed as
soon as he had smoked his pipe, and there he slept.
One who has never heard a room filled with one hundred and more sleeping loggers has no idea of a
nocturne. They worked hard and they slept the same
way.

Of a Sunday in camp many writers have painted
an idyl of sylvan charm—with loggers reading, writing,
making ax handles, searching for spruce gum, or visiting other camps. The picture is nice, yet more often it
was otherwise. A Sunday in camp was a day to lie
prone in a bunk, or to play poker or high-low-jack
with tobacco for stakes. If a gallon of liquor could be
smuggled in, so much the better, but in any case, cards.
There was usually a fiddler and several light-footed
fellows who could dance. When the French Canadians
came, late in the century, there was considerable mass
singing, whole crews of them sitting along the deacon
seats, stamping their feet and shouting the endless
verses to "Alouette" and "En Roulant Ma Boule."

For reading, there was long one and only one piece
of it in camp and it wasn't the Bible. The literature
was a copy or two of Richard K. Fox's *Police Gazette.*
All a logger knew of the Tweed Ring he read in the
Gazette, and likewise of Jim Fisk, Josie Mansfield,
Jesse James, "The Black Crook," and Madame Bern-
hardt. It was through the pretty, yet startling pink

columns that he was informed of such folks as Maggie Cline, John L. Sullivan, Steve Brodie, and Dr. Mary Walker. He probably never read "The Ballad of Reading Gaol," yet the *Gazette* told him how Mr. Wilde happened to be in jail. It gave him bad news, too, telling him he had *not* held a winning ticket in the current drawing of the Louisiana Lottery.

Now and again well-meaning preachers came to camp to "do good," something the pure logger strain has loathed since the earliest times. The preachers usually found the loggers indifferent rather than hostile, which speaks well for the loggers' tolerance. Unlike the sailor, the logger had few superstitions. His concessions to theology, if they could be termed such, began and ended when he had rolled a fellow—killed on the drive—into some bark, as a coffin to bury him in; then he took off the dead man's calked shoes and hung them from a handy branch, possibly cutting the unfortunate's name into the bole of a tree. It was likely done more as a warning of a dangerous spot than as a rite.

Sad as it was, neither the arts and sciences nor religion played a very big part in the life of the logger. He painted no pictures, wrote no books, and the few songs he composed are pretty awful. The mass of him couldn't even carry a tune; they simply bellowed. He took little interest in the vast natural laboratory in which he lived. And a tree was something that contained so many thousand feet of boards, or, he might figure it to contain fully one quart of hard liquor. In any case, the tree was to be cut as quickly as possible. "Let daylight into the swamp."

As for God, He was something to be called upon, along with His Son, to aid in bringing down suitable curses upon the unseasonable elements that bedeviled him—high water, low water, deep snow, thaws, rains, and all manner of hurricanes.

When the logs were piled high along the river banks,

it is just possible that the logger sent up a veritable prayer; a prayer for thaw and rain that would melt ice and make a good driving pitch in the stream. Then he would throw away his ax, pick up his peavey, and ride those white pine sticks down to an authentic Eden, where lived many pretty women and where violently strong liquor ran without end—or at least would run for two or three weeks.

5

The White-Water Men

RAILROADS PLAYED LITTLE PART in getting New England's timber to the mills. It took white-water men to do that, and a white-water man was simply a logger who was "good on the river." He cut logs all winter, then drove them, riding bareback with spurs in the soles of his shoes, down to the saws that ate them up and whined for more.

It was said of an especially good riverman that you could throw a bar of yellow soap into the water and he would ride the bubbles to shore. This is doubtless an exaggeration, yet those men who survived even half a dozen drives were nothing less than cats on the logs. The job itself took care of that. If you went into that pitch of boiling white water, alive with thousands of churning logs, swimming was of the exact value of a prayer.

It was accounted a mild disgrace to lose one's peavey on the drive, and the old-time river bosses deducted its cost from a man's wages. Thus when a driver tumbled into a stream, his cynical fellows would shout "Never mind the men, but be careful of the peaveys—*they* cost three dollars."

Breaking a jam was the most dangerous part of the business, but the whole affair was superb as a spectacle and the jam-breaking itself one of the most breathtaking shows ever staged anywhere.

There is no such thing as a history of river driving and rivermen. All the chapters for such a history have been locked in the minds of men now graying into

middle life and more. One brief chapter has haunted
the mind of one who was a small boy when William
McKinley was President and when one of the last
great drives of long logs went down the Connecticut.

We lived in North Stratford—he who was a lad at
the century's turn recalls—and none of the boys in
our town wanted to be cowboys or soldiers or police-
men. To be a riverman and go down with the drive
was the ambition of all of us. To "card" logs through
white water, to steer a bateau down Fifteen Mile
Falls, to break the log jams—these were the greatest
things any man could hope to achieve. Even to pilot a
locomotive on the Grand Trunk was as nothing. We
wanted a peavey, a pair of calked boots, and a fast-
moving stream full of logs.

The coming of the drive to Stratford was heralded
by various signs, all of them sure and invariable. First
were the drums of the logs themselves, upriver, the
booming that made your heart beat faster. Then the
advance guard—slim, easy-riding logs that somehow
had managed to break away and get miles ahead.
These were graceful sticks, moving swiftly in the broad
river, seemingly anxious to meet their fate at some sawmill town downriver—fastidious logs, running away
from the jams their more laggard fellows would surely
encounter.

Another sign was when the boss of the drive, a most
important man in the spring, drove down Main Street
with a team of the Company's fastest horses. The
horses were black as midnight, black as the bushy
eyebrows of the boss, but they were no blacker than
the long cigar the boss chewed. The boss was important enough to have a man drive for him and wherever
they went they drove very fast. . . .

Soon the logs began coming thicker until you scarcely could see the water between them. The river became
a mass of sluggish bodies, rolling this way and that,

grumbling all day and all night. No door could shut
out this noise. And who wanted to shut out such
pleasant thunder?

Down at the bend of the river a few men were
stationed, "tending out," they called it, poling the logs
from the "off" bank lest they be halted in the eddy
and make a jam. . . . And on and on came the miles
of logs.

Rumors traveled fast among young boys, and we
never failed to know when the *wangan* train was due.
These were huge wagons hauled by six, eight, and ten
horses each. The *Mary Anne* was the name of this
circus caravan. The wagons had long blue bodies with
the Company's initials painted on their sides. The
harnesses were trimmed with bright brass and be-
decked with tassels more gaudy than the rivermen's
shirts. When they rolled down Main Street they made
a mighty clanking, and the sun on the brass sent bright
spots racing across the buildings on the shady side of
the street. All in all, it was a bigger time by far than
when Sig Sautelle's Great Renowned Two-Ring Circus & Menagerie came to town.

We were on hand at the wangan grounds, on the
edge of town, when the tents came out of the wagons
and were set up. We lugged water and wood and were
allowed by the teamsters to unbuckle the hames on the
gallant big horses. Soon there was the aroma of cooking in the air.

The cooks on the drive were generous with the Company's food. It might be Pat Ryan, or Watson Blod-
gett, or Old Dan Kelliher; but whoever he was, he fed
us on beans and he loaded us down with gigantic
cookies that were marvels of size and goodness. The
like of these cookies has never been seen elsewhere
but on the drive; they were as large around as small
plates and thick as three ordinary cookies.

On the night when the drive hit town there was a
great to-do after supper. The quiet village suddenly

surged with life as two hundred or more rivermen
milled up and down Main Street. Many of them wore
brightly colored shirts, and all carried canary-yellow
greasers with red flannel collars. They wore their calked
boots, too, and played havoc with the floors of the three
saloons.

The "nice people" stayed at home this night; or, at
least the women did, although they were as safe on
the street when the drive hit town as at any other time.
Rivermen were rough fellows but they minded their
own business and had rather a decent code.

We couldn't go into the barrooms, but there was
plenty for a boy to see on the street. We watched Big
Arthur O'Leary as he carefully and methodically threw
four or five brawny rivermen, one after the other, into
the street, telling them they might come back when
they had decided to be gents.

By the bridge that crossed the river into Vermont
we would see half a dozen fights, a sort of battles royal
with eight or ten men engaged. There was no particular reason for it; they were fighting because of the
joy of being alive and going down with the drive.

It was the one night of the year when Stratford
throbbed with noise—alcoholic shouts and laughter,
the stomping of hard boots, the plunking of slot machines, and the new Edison phonograph in O'Leary's
bleating high-pitched about "A Bird in a Gilded Cage."
Underneath all was the steady bass of the muttering,
grumbling logs, going by in the night.

Next morning as we went to school we saw that
the logs were moving more slowly. We fidgeted at our
desks because we couldn't see the river from the
schoolhouse. Yet we knew what was happening, for
the rumble of logs had almost died away.

At noon we wouldn't stop for dinner. We rushed
down to the bridge. There we saw it with our own
eyes—the river piled high with logs. Yes, sir, a jam!
Stretching for half a mile downriver was the huge bulk

of logs, crossed like so many jackstraws; long spruces up-ended, their dripping bodies standing straight out of the mass. We could hear creaking and a mild groaning as the water ground the logs more firmly together.

The river was backing up fast, and 'way down below we could see small figures on the logs and the banks, working feverishly. Now and again, it seemed to us watching, the great mass of logs would give a long, deep sigh.

There was no keeping us in school; all on the river knew that, even the teacher. We ran as fast as we could down to the bend.

Below the jam the Connecticut was a mere trickle. They'd have to work fast, we knew, or soon the water would be backing up into the village. And they *were* working. We watched breathlessly as they danced like puppets to and fro across the barrier, looking for the key log, the king log, the single log that must be moved before the jam could be broken. There was a clanking of peaveys, a cursing to high heaven, and many shouted orders, as the men tore first at this log, then at that. Over all was the ominous feeling of impending danger. You couldn't shake it off, so you talked in whispers.

There came a cry of warning. Slim Pete Hurd, one of our rivermen heroes, had "got holt on" the king log. We could see him twist it from its grudging fellows and roll it down. Then there came a quaking and a shifting of the huge mass as the drivers ran for shore, balancing themselves with their peaveys on the struggling logs. Not all of them made the shore, for the water and the pent-up logs would not wait, even for rivermen. The jam "hauled" with a rush of tossing logs, and some of the men had to ride her out, Death riding everywhere among them.

Through the thunder of the mad logs we heard a cry: "Pete's gone!" And, looking downstream where the crest of the floor was rolling, we saw a slim body

thrown high in the air, to fall again—into the white
water and among those grinding logs. . . .

On the way back to the village we did not talk
much, for there was a lump in every boy's throat.
When we got to the bridge the logs were moving fast
and freely, but we didn't stop to watch them.

Over on the wangan lot that night there were no
cheery campfires, no brave white tents. Near the bend
of the river, where the jam had been, a few logs
floated idly. The river grumbled no more. The village
was still as death. The drive had gone down.

That was how the drive looked to a small boy in
1901. Romantic and colorful, but a small boy couldn't
see the other side, which was chiefly work. It began
in that misty half-light peculiar to rivers before the
sun comes up. It ended when a driver couldn't tell a
log from a shadow. There were four meals a day—
breakfast, first lunch, second lunch, and supper. The
lunches, like as not, were brought to the men where
they poled at the logs, for there was no time to fool
away with a lunch hour.

That made a middling-long day, for driving was
done in April, May, and June. It was just as well that
it was long. Then a man could tumble down in his
tent after supper and sleep like a drunken god, on the
wet ground and in his clothes. If there was wind, it
howled through the tents and often brought snow with
it, but no tired riverman ever knew it. His feet would
freeze first.

During the day he worked like a demon most of
the time. The boss, a very dragoon or he was no boss,
saw to that. And there were other forces, such as the
driving pitch, to hound the driver on. A man had to get
his logs downriver to the booms while the freshet ran
wild and high, or he'd have to wait until fall, and perhaps until another spring. To leave a drive dry on

the meadows and in the shallows was a disgrace not only to the boss but to every man of the crew.

Those old-time drivers took pride in their work. They checked off the days and took stock of their progress. They'd tell each other we was only to Wells River a year ago, and here we are at Bellows. Bet she's a record. . . .

Yes sir, mister, those red-shirted fellows would ride 'em, ride 'em through white water and green, ride 'em right through the milltail of hell. Sometimes the milltail was running so fast that the boys just kept riding and never came back at all. At Perry Falls, on the Connecticut, just below First Lake Dam, hell's milltail ran too fast for many of them. You could read there, cut in the bark of trees, the names of Charles Seymour and Dan Sullivan and Jake Regan, and simply "Haley & Quinn," two lads who rode the milltail on the same day and to the same destination. . . . Old men tell that even today, a clear-eyed person on a fair night of moon can see Haley & Quinn a-riding logs that seem whiter than any white pine down Perry Falls. It is probably only a trick of the moonlight.

The river took an awful toll. The work was only for resolute men, and life on the drive was grim as a new bluesteel ax. Yet there was nothing grim about the drivers. They told each other that she was a long *route*, if you didn't weaken; and the more lewd among them howled warning and promise that when the drive was in no honest harlot should go to bed with an empty stomach.

Once in a long age the drivers would contribute something to life other than more logs. There was that classic moment on the west branch of the Penobscot.

The actors were Jim, eldest of the six brothers Gallagher, all of them rivermen, and Dave Crain, boss of the drive that year. Crain's twenty million feet of logs were piling up back of Dead Man's Point. Something

radical would have to be done, and quickly. Dave sent
Jim out to break the jam, meanwhile ordering the rest
of the crew to stand back out of the way. Then, when
they were all in the clear, Crain gave voice to the undy-
ing command:

> They're all back pretty fur;
> Let her go, Gallagher.

That was the way it happened. Dave Crain wasn't
given to verse. It was simple and entirely without plan,
like all such magnificent moments, and it resulted in a
four-word command as famous as "Don't give up the
ship."

Once in a while a woods or river boss reached the
stature of a legend. John Ross did. He was a Penobscot man who had charge of many drives on the west
branch between 1864 and 1887. In those days the
drive here was conducted by the Penobscot Log Driving Company, a mutual concern representing many
operators, and it was bid off each year. If no bid met
with approval of the company's directors, a master
driver was appointed and he was often John Ross.

It was a titanic job, on either the Penobscot or the
Kennebec. There might be two hundred million feet
of logs, or a mere one hundred million feet—anyway, a lot of logs. The master driver had to inspire
or at least to rule a horde of wild men. These wild
men had to be placed at the right points along the river.
The "right" points changed from day to day, from
hour to hour, and men must be moved accordingly.
The master had to understand the habits of a score of
tributary streams, the capacities of many dams, and to
know, even as God, what the weather was to be.

And John Ross *was* God, on the west branch, for

much of three decades. A steamboat on Chesuncook Lake was named for him. Small boys would yell, "Say I'm John Ross or I'll kill you!" This was fame indeed. Even in his lifetime Ross achieved the immortality of having a song written about him. One John Golden, logger and riverman, claimed authorship of the ballad. The lyrics are interesting for the light they shed on Ross's reputation as a hard-hearted master so hungry for more logs that he wouldn't wait for one of his slaves to consummate a possibly legal wedding. The doggerel began:

> O the night that I was married O,
> I laid on marriage bed,
> Up rose John Ross and Cyrus Hewes
> And stood by my bed head
> Saying: "Arise, arise, young married man,
> And go along with me;
> To the lonesome hills of 'Suncook
> And swamp them logs for me."

The Cyrus Hewes mentioned was a well-known Bangor lumberman, apparently as anxious for logs as was John Ross. It might just as well have been one of the Babbs, the Stricklands, or the Morrisons, all famous names in that time and place.

A more widely traveled master driver than Ross was James L. Smart. Smart ranged the whole New England forest like a moose. It was said of him that he knew every rock, rapids, and eddy on the St. Croix, the Penobscot, the Kennebec, the Androscoggin, and the Connecticut. He grew into a legend, too, but no song was written about him and his name is fading.

For many years logging and driving on the Connecticut were dominated by the Van Dyke brothers, high-handed men who paid their bills when they were forced to it. If a logger quit a Van Dyke camp during the winter, he had to wait until spring for his pay. There seemed to be little recourse in those days, so men waited and cursed, praying for an organization— they seldom talked of a "union"—that would scare decency into those timber barons who thought always of logs and never of men.

On one occasion, when the drive got to Bellows Falls, a sheriff appeared and slapped a plaster on a wagonload of grub for the Van Dyke drivers. By the time the crew of one hundred and fifty men had missed breakfast and first lunch, they started raising ned and continued until one of the Van Dykes paid the sheriff and released the food.

Often, on the Connecticut, the cookhouse and wangan floated downriver on a raft, tying up for night. It, too, was called the *Mary Anne,* just as when it traveled in wagons; but when it floated it carried the famous Company stove—"Biggest stove ever used on the drive"—that weighed thirty-five hundred pounds and was something to see. One spring this floating Mary Anne crashed plumb into Colebrook bridge across the Connecticut, and the cookhouse, stores and all, went to the bottom, and for weeks afterward boys did a good business fishing new calked boots and boxes of plug chewing out of the river.

Bill Schoppe was long a noted boss on the Connecticut. So was Frank Smart, and later came Alphonse Roby. It was the longest drive in New England and possibly the longest in the country.[1]

Many good drivers of New England streams had learned their logs on the St. John and the Miramichi rivers of New Brunswick. So many of them were Scotch and Irish that often they all were lumped together as the "Rorys and Anguses." A favorite cry of the Rorys

---

[1]Most logs on the Mississippi were moved in big rafts, not as loose sticks.

and Anguses was "I was born on the Miramichi. The farther up you go, the tougher they get, and I was raised on the headwaters."

Every river in northern New England, it would seem, had a character, real or legendary, known as Sebat. He might be Big Sebat or Little Sebat, or Black Sebat. These various Sebats appear to have stemmed, in tradition if not by blood, from an authentic Black Sebat who drove logs on the Penobscot and Kennebec in the sixties and seventies. He was part if not wholly Indian and tales of his prodigious strength and endurance have lasted three quarters of a century.

And every river, every stream almost had its legends about some light-footed riverman who could ride a log anywhere a log could go. In his half century on the Connecticut, Alphonse Roby recalls that Dan Bossy was a "catty" man without peer. Jack Haley, for many years in charge of the Androscoggin drive, says the same, and Bossy's fame is known to drivers along the Kennebec and up in the Allagash country. These men who knew Dan Bossy in his prime put no faith in the story that, wearing roller skates, Dan rode a log across the river at Berlin, New Hampshire, but they vow that Dan was the cattiest man they ever saw, and that should be enough.

Nor is there much doubt about who was the dirtiest cook, on the drive or in the woods. This distinction belonged to Joe Bullie, a Frenchman from around Trois-Rivières, Quebec. Joe "sizzled and boiled" food in Quebec and New England for sixty, some say seventy years. All agree that his "stuff tasted all right, if you didn't have to look at the dirty cuss."

Once on Hall Stream, as Afton (Rube) Hall, old-time woods scaler recalls, the crew discovered that Joe had been using the molasses barrel for a sort of patent rat trap. This trap Joe arranged by placing a teeter board, baited with meat, over the open barrel. When a rat ran up this board it would tilt and the animal would fall into the thick molasses. In the morning Joe would fish out his catch.

On discovery of this arrangement Dick Sweat, a direct actionist, jumped onto the table, walked down it with his calked shoes, and kicked Joe's cooking all over the place.

Once, by mistake, a woman cook was sent to a camp run by the redoubtable Jigger Jones. She had long hair and the hair was not well planted; much of it got into the cooking. Jigger got through the baked beans without trouble, but he left a piece of pie untouched on his plate. "What's the matter, Jigger?" asked one of the crew. "Don't you like her pie?" "Sure," replied The Jigger. "It's elegant pie, and you tell that dame if she'll take it out and give it a shave, I'll eat it."

Most of the woods cooks, however, were clean and worked wonders with the small variety of supplies furnished. And cookhouse supplies grew better and of greater variety until, around 1900, a man sat down to better fare in the woods than he likely would get in town.

Of female followers of the drive regrettably little is known. They had them, on all of the longer drives, but only one seems to have left her fame secure. She was known only as Old Colorado, and she followed the boys down the Connecticut from near its headwaters at First Lake to the mills at Mount Tom, not far from Holyoke, Massachusetts.

Where she got her name is not known. Some ancient men seem to recall that she hailed originally from Colorado. Others think she was a native of New England who had been to Colorado during the silver excitement there, and had returned to her own heath to talk of Leadville and Cripple Creek ever after.

In any case, Old Colorado was a fixture on the Connecticut River drive for more years than man can tell. She was very old. In experience, they say, she dated

back to Eve herself. She joined the drive, every spring,
soon as it left First Lake. Along the route she lived
in a tent, in barns, in rooming houses of the river
towns, and sometimes her bagnio was a clearing in the
bushes.

The quality of her wares, it is said, was only pass-
able, but the cost was reasonable enough, being never
more than a dollar and more often fifty cents. Indeed,
during the hard times of Cleveland's second administration, when wages on the river were very low, this
kindly woman dropped her tariff to twenty-five cents.

What might well have been called her fine delivery
service made Old Colorado successful. From First Lake
to Holyoke, a distance of some three hundred miles,
she was ever close to hand. In the larger towns along
the river she had to meet competition; but on the
stretches in between, it was Colorado or nothing. She
had wholesale as well as retail prices. Once, just above
Bellows Falls, a crew of forty men were tending out,
keeping the logs from jamming. It was monotonous
work. Colorado happened along, just to see how the
boys were doing, and one of the bored drivers asked
her for "an estimate on the whole crew." Colorado
was thoughtful a moment, looking the gang over.
"Eighteen dollars," she said. It was a bargain, even
in tough times, and it was consummated on the spot.

For the most part, however, men in the woods and
on the drive were not given to spending much money
in camp or along the way. They preferred to keep it
(many times they couldn't get it) until the logs were
cut and piled on the banks, or the drive was in at the
mills.

All winter long loggers would patch their clothes,
face their mittens, mend their rubbers, and be nig-
gardly in their dealings, that they might have a big
stake for the blow-in. They would watch their wangan
charges closely and moan about the great cost of

smoking and chewing tobacco. Some of them would keep their "time & wangan" accounts in little books, but more simply cut notches in a stick they hid in their bunks. One series of notches meant so many days' work, another represented Spearhead and B. & L. tobacco, while a great big notch might mean a pair of rubbers, an undershirt, or some such stupendous purchase at the camp store.

But when loggers came to town in the spring they were different men. None ever spent money more quickly or riotously. In river towns the old simile was "Spending money like a drunken logger."

For the spring blow-in each logger had his favorite sport. Bangor, of course, was the first and greatest of New England spree towns. But many a logger has waked in small East Machias and wondered where he was and how he got there. The same was true of towns like Calais, Fort Kent, Greenville, Waterville, Skowhegan, Ellsworth, Rumford, and Augusta, all in Maine; and of West Stewartstown, North Stratford, Berlin, Woodsville, and North Walpole in New Hampshire.

It was in small Woodsville where one Ed Smith, a common and obscure logger, leaped into lasting fame among lumberjacks. Ed was in town on a drunk, and as he wandered a bit unsteadily along the main street his eye was caught by what looked to be a beautiful woman in the show window of a local store. She was blonde of hair, pink and white of skin, and she was dressed in silk hose and a pair of corsets. Ed sized her up a moment. Then he whooped once, with the true rutting whoop of the logger, and leaped feet first through the window. The heavy plate shattered and it fell in a rain of jagged glass all around Ed, but left him unscratched. It was undoubtedly the height of Ed Smith's life, for the next spring he was caught by a log at Perry Falls and friends hung his calked boots from a limb.

Occasionally the more ambitious of loggers went to

a really big city like Portland to blow her in; and there is record of a few of them getting as far as Boston, chiefly to view the wonders in Austin & Stone's Museum and to gaze on fat girls in tights at the Old Howard Atheneum, probably the favorite showhouse of loggers and Harvard undergraduates.

Generally, though, loggers liked to spend their money in towns along rivers, and often a jack blew her in, every cent, without so much as seeing a gaslight. Greenville, at the foot of Moosehead Lake in Maine, was said to be "two hundred miles from nowhere," yet things were so arranged there that a man might have everything he could think he needed without the trouble and expense of going to Bangor. Another such place was The Forks, for many years a blowing-in spot for Kennebec loggers who simply couldn't wait until they got to Waterville or Augusta.

At remote Errol, New Hampshire, twenty miles from any railroad, was the somewhat noted Umbagog House. It stood not far from where the Magalloway loses its identity in the broader waters of the Androscoggin, a strategic spot. The thousand and more loggers going into the woods for the Berlin Mills Company[2] had to pass the Umbagog House. It wasn't important when they were going in. But when they came out, there she was, the Umbagog House, the first thing they saw looming up amid the stumps. Many a man never got past it.

Nat Leach was proprietor of this tavern and he knew his trade. The bar was of white pine, unvarnished save by spruce pitch on the sleeves of mackinaws. There were forty-two rooms in the house, and Nat commonly put ninety men to bed, in season. The rest slept on the floors of the lobby, barroom, and halls.

Getting those lads up in the morning, after a heavy night, required some doing; but in time Nat evolved a

[2]Now the Brown Company, Berlin, N. H.

process that worked very well and made him famous. With an open bottle of hard liquor in his hand, a glass in the other, Nat would go from drunk to drunk. He would hold the bottle under a nose. "Have a snort?" he would ask. In no time at all, and at little cost, Nat had them on their feet and navigating.

Dry towns and sometimes state-wide prohibition were an inordinate bother to lumberjacks. In such circumstances they did the best they could with whatever liquid best came to hand. If liquor was not available, they would drink anything in the line of liniment and extract. At times they bought the entire stocks of patent medicines from the shelves of small-town druggists or general stores. One veteran authority on patent medicines whose stomach is still functioning recalls of buying Peruna by the case, and of once getting by mistake a case of what he terms "Mrs. Pinkham's Peruna." Either sort made a fairish drink, but neither was so good as Beef, Wine & Iron, or straight Jamaica ginger, he recalls.

French Canadians were able white-water men, and most of them were likely with an ax, although not so good with horses. The first great influx of them into New England came in the seventies and eighties. There was an ebb tide in the nineties, then another flow that continued well into the present century, when there were many pulpwood camps in which scarcely a man spoke English. The given names of about half of them were "Jean Baptiste" or "Napoleon."

The Irish had arrived in New England a bare twenty years ahead of the first Canuck invasion. The Irish made good rivermen and even better loggers. Both ax and peavey came handy to them. They were tough, fearless, and hard workers. And, as come-latelys so often do, the Irish resented the later migration from Canada. One of these wild Irishers, and typical of many of the best of them, was Roaring Jim Boyle who for two decades conducted a one-man war against the French Canadian "furriners."

When Rollin W. Holbrook was engaged in logging some of the last white pine that grew in northeastern Vermont, he once hired a crew of fifty Frenchmen and put them to work at a camp on Mount Monadnock. Presently, Roaring Jim Boyle and his two sons came to the Holbrook place and asked for a job cutting timber. They were strapping big fellows. Mr. Holbrook gave them tools and sent the three men up to the camp. That was in the morning. That night, and all night long, Frenchmen continued dribbling in to the Holbrook home. They came in twos, in fours, and in larger batches. Some of them showed signs of rough usage. They couldn't speak much English, yet they made it clear that they wanted their time; and they made it doubly clear that they were returning to Canada at once, never to return.

Come daylight, Mr. Holbrook jumped into a sleigh and went to camp. There he found Roaring Jim and his two sons whaling into the pines like a hurricane. Not a Frenchman was left on the mountainside. "What's the meaning of all this?" the logging operator asked. "Where are all those Canucks?"

"I tell you, Mister Holbrook," Roaring Jim said. "Me and the two boys here can cut all the logs you want. . . . You don't need none of them furrin bastids around." It turned out that Jim and his sons had threatened to kill all the Frenchmen if they didn't leave and had even started to work on some who didn't move fast enough. "But we give 'em time to pack their pokes," Jim added tolerantly.

In time this Jim Boyle grew into a mighty woods boss and as notable a character as one could find in ten townships. Once, in the Willard House at North Stratford, a French Canadian called him a bad name and asked him outside to fight. "Come on, everybody," boomed the voice of Roaring Jim. "Come on out and see the battle between the lamb and the lion."

Jim was a natural subject for lumberjack tales. It was said that when Jim finally became boss of a camp on the Nulhegan River he immediately celebrated by going to town and getting drunk. He returned to camp late that night and went to bed in an upper bunk. When he awoke it was barely light enough to see the camp window. His body heated by the booze that was now "dyin' out" and his mind telling him that he had made a serious mistake by getting drunk just when he had been promoted to boss, he resolved, apparently, to do something to make up for lost time. Roaring Jim sat up on the edge of his bunk. "Two-dollar-a-day men foller me," he howled. "Dollar-and-a-half men go out the door!" And Jim Boyle dived through the window at the head of his upper bunk, taking glass, sash and all, with him.

Jim Boyle and his kind were the sort of camp and river bosses they liked in those days, but Jim Boyle and his kind have long since gone over the Hump to the place where white pine grows exactly one mile high without a limb to the three-quarter mark, and where the sap of rock maple trees is one-hundred-proof alcohol.

6

First Migration

WHEN WHITE PINE TREES had been reduced to stumps and daylight struck fair in all parts of the swamp, the New England loggers knew that their work there was done. . . . They'd be getting on, mister.

The place was now free of wolves and tall timber, a land safe for farmers and traders, for bankers and such city slickers. But it was no place for loggers. Once the swamp was clear, there was only one thing to do, so the boys packed their turkeys on their backs, took a double snort of whisky, and were away over the Hump to the next forest. Always be plenty of timber, they said.

Their first great migration was not so sudden or so dramatic as their next two moves would be. It began as early as 1836, when Charles Merrill of Lincoln, Maine, bought a vast block of timber on the St. Clair River in Michigan. It was the first sign of things to come.

A year later the brand-new sawmill town of Augusta, Michigan, was founded by men of the old sawmill town of Augusta on the Kennebec.

Three years later, John McKusick, traveling with an ax and a pair of snowshoes, built a shack and named the future logging metropolis of Stillwater, Minnesota, after his old home town on the Penobscot, where Joe Peavey was blacksmith.

And in 1845 Isaac Stephenson, soon to be one of the Titans, came from New Brunswick, by way of Bangor, to start an immense lumber business in north-eastern Wisconsin.

Such was the pattern the first migration would follow—from New England direct to the Lake States. Before midcentury Maine lumbermen had laid their claims in the mighty timber domains of Michigan, Wisconsin, and Minnesota. They'd have all of fifty years' logging, before they would have to move on again.

This first major migration lasted well into the Civil War period, reaching its peak in the fifties. The boss lumbermen and their land-lookers went first. They didn't have to look long to find white pine in the Lake States, and it could be had cheap enough. The government had little ready cash and too much timber. "In July of 1848," wrote Isaac Stephenson, in his memoirs, "I went to Sault St. Marie [Mich.] where in the barracks of Fort Brady I, with Daniel Wells, bought areas of timber on the Escanaba, the Ford and the Sturgeon rivers. We paid $1.25 an acre."

A dollar and a quarter an acre was pretty much the standard price of government timber for years. And when the tired and thirsty veterans of the Mexican War found they could turn their timber scrip—the "bonus" of the day—into perfectly good drinking liquor, why, some real bargains appeared on the market.

It was cheap enough, *"even at a dollar and a quarter"* an acre—as one of the buyers admitted in a gross understatement. Once the advancing timber barons got a good look at the vast night of forest that ran from the western tip of Lake Erie to the western tip of Lake Superior, and beyond, they bought a few thousand acres each and returned to Maine, hotfoot, to get cash and loggers.

They had little trouble getting the cash, and even less in getting the loggers. Small armies of them came to Michigan by the Erie Canal to settle Bay City and Saginaw, and to spread North and West. Although it was an era of heavy drinking in all walks of life, boatsmen and innkeepers along the Big Ditch were astounded at the amount of rum required to move the red-shirted men of the Maine backwoods into the backwoods of Michigan. On occasion the loggers got completely out of hand and wrecked barges and taverns, but on the whole they were content to guzzle, and to bellow:

> I've got a mule, her name is Sal;
> Fifteen miles on the Erie Canal;
> She's a good old worker and a good old pal,
> Fifteen miles on the Erie Canal.

As soon as they got to the other end of the Canal —and the "other end" might be Saginaw, or Green Bay, or Ashland, or Duluth—they set immediately to work cutting the product that would keep the Canal busy for five decades.

It is slight exaggeration to say that only the restless loggers of New England pioneered settlement in the Lake States. Early among the "great names" along the saw-dusty Saginaw were the Eddys, the Murphys, the Dorrs, the Gubtils, and the Leadbetters, all from Maine. Thomas Merrill of Lincoln, Maine, founded a tough old Michigan firm that followed hard on the receding fringe of the timber line through Wisconsin, Minnesota, Washington, and British Columbia. Horace Butters of Maine went to Michigan to log and to invent a skidding machine.

Cadwallader C. Washburn[1] of Maine became governor of Wisconsin and owned a heap of timber there. The Sinclairs, the Wellses, and the two Stephensons went direct from Maine to Wisconsin, sending back time and again for more Penobscot boys and New Bruns-

[1]He dropped the final "e" of the family name.

wickers and P. I.'s (Prince Edward Island men) to harvest logs along the Oconto, the Peshtigo, and the Menominee. William H. Bradley and the Randalls of Maine logged virgin timber near Eau Claire. The Withee brothers and N. B. Holway, all Kennebec men, pioneered at La Crosse.

In Minnesota the Coburns of New Hampshire and Dorilus Morrison[2] were early loggers along the Bear River; and in the St. Croix Valley, both sides of the river, was a host of Down Easters, many of them potent—Stanchfield, Washburn (Cadwallader's brother, who also made flour), De Laitre, Bovey, Eastman, Tozier, Hersey, and Staples.

By the 1850s few if any of the Lake States lumber districts were without evidence of the migration from Maine. These Maine lumbermen knew and liked the quality of Maine woodsmen and sawmill workers. As early as October 9, 1838, they were advertising as follows in the *Bangor Whig & Courier:*

> WANTED to go West, one first rate head Sawyer, two of the second class, one who understands Circular Saws, and one Teamster. The above to start immediately. Also, in 3 or 4 weeks, a gang of 10 or 12 Wood Choppers, to cut Pine for steam Boats. The best reference will be required. Inquire of CHANDLER & PAINE.

Thus quiet farmers along the Erie Canal were to be wakened in the dead of night by howls of Bangor Tigers on the way to fresh jungles of white pine.

Some of the Eastern loggers, both big and small, tarried a while in New York and Pennsylvania, but the greater part of the horde moved straight to Michigan, or even a little father west, before they unpacked their sleighs and unyoked their oxen to browse a bit,

[2]Born at Livermore, Maine. He became mayor of Minneapolis.

before snow-fly, in the wild grass along the Saginaw, the Menominee, and a newer St. Croix.

There was good reason why so few of the nomadic loggers tarried in the Middle Atlantic States. There was little to stop a logger—long. New York and Pennsylvania had been steadily cutting their own timber while the Maine and New Hampshire loggers had been busy at home.

As early as 1813 large drives of logs were coming down the upper Hudson, for cutting at Glens Falls, largest lumber-making center of the Empire State. By 1849 Hudson River loggers had a mutual boom association, patterned after that on the Penobscot at Bangor; and in 1850 New York led all states in lumber production.

Yet there is not in New York State, other than locally by counties and towns, any great tradition of lumber. A number of conditions contributed to this lack of sawdust atmosphere. New York, as related, began cutting boards at about the same time as did Maine. By 1840 there were 6356 sawmills in the state, far more than Maine ever had. But these were small mills, for the most part—operated by men who were part-time farmers, part-time lumbermen. Nowhere did mills appear in such concentration as at Bangor. They cut for the local trade and the lot of them together could not make enough lumber to supply the needs of the fastest-growing state in the Union.

Maine and New England shipped most of their lumber elsewhere; so did the Lake States. Timber was their prime crop, their one great dominant and often domineering industry. In New York, and also in Pennsylvania, industries of all kinds flourished—coal, iron, petroleum, to cite a few. Timber was merely one, not all.

The Erie Canal brought billions of feet of Lake States lumber to New York, both for use and export,

and fame came to Albany[8] as the greatest lumber mart
in the world. But those endless piles of boards in Albany
were cut by New England loggers who had gone to
Michigan.

In York State, though, an important change occurred
in the terminology of loggers, one that has often been
discussed around the barrel stoves of bunkhouses.
Heretofore, to the east, the device on which a logger
hauled his product was known as a "sled." Somewhere
in York State the sled became a "sleigh," and sleigh
it would remain until it reached its farthest west, in
the white pines of Idaho and the yellow-pine country of
Oregon and Washington.

The situation in Pennsylvania was similar to that in
New York. Logging began early in Penn's Woods. It
started in the eighteenth century, and somewhere in the
1860-1870 period (the statistics are a bit fuzzy), lumber making reached its peak. For a year or two Pennsylvania led the nation in production.

So, when the New England lads had finished the
bulk of their white pine and wanted more, there wasn't
much use stopping long in New York and Pennsylvania. All of the Middle Atlantic pine had long been in
private hands, and much of it was already cut. There
was no stuff here at three cents an acre, or even three
dollars an acre. . . . No sir, mister, better not stop this
side of Saginaw where they say the white pine grows
bigger than ever it did along the Penobscot.

One should remember that it wasn't a dearth of
timber that drove the Maine men West. It was a dearth
of *white-pine* timber, something vastly different in those
days. When they talked about timber, by the Holy
Old Mackinaw, they meant white pine, the veritable
pinus strobus of the college professors, and that only.
They took the cedar—for shingles—where it grew
with the pine; and on occasion they took the hemlock,

[8]Later, fame as a lumber market came to Tonawanda.

chiefly for its bark to sell to tanners. Spruce they left as
wholly worthless. That's why New England was logged
all over again and why its lumber peak came in 1907,
ages after the pine soldiers had gone.

No, it was white pine the loggers wanted. By the
time Maine's pine had come to an end, so had the best
pine of the Middle Atlantic. The Bangor Tigers would
have to go to the Saginaw, or farther West, to get their
claws into some bark they liked.

For a brief period Pennsylvania cut more boards
than any other state. At and around Williamsport centered the sawmills, bigger, better, faster than anything Bangor had known before the Civil War. Some of
the Maine men stopped there a short time, chiefly to
work in the woods, but much of the sawmilling and
logging was done by Pennsylvania "Dutch," a large
number of Irish and Germans, and a few French
Canadians. And Williamsport was notable for the first
strike of consequence involving loggers and sawmill
workers.

In 1872 the order files of mills in and around Williamsport were spiked high with demands for lumber;
it was the big flurry of business just before the Panic
of '73. More than three hundred million feet of logs
were in the Susquehanna Boom, ready for milling, and
drivers were at work bringing down more.

Operators sat up nights devising means to increase
production. Mill bosses were ordered to "rawhide,"
which meant to drive the men and machines for all
that was in them; and the workday was lengthened
to fourteen hours.

In previous years such a speed-up would probably
have resulted in nothing more than bunkhouse belly-
aching about the Big Bosses. However, the spirit of
labor organization was very much in the air and
Pennsylvania was the breeding ground of "new and
dangerous ideas." Already the Molly Maguires, secret

order of Irish Catholic workers, had brought terror to the coal fields of the state; and in Philadelphia the Noble Order of the Knights of Labor had been founded. Although neither the Knights nor the Mollies seem to have played any direct part in the ruckus at Williamsport, the very fact of their being unquestionably put ungodly ideas into the heads of the sweated Susquehanna mill workers and loggers.

On June 29 a strike was declared by the almost wholly unorganized mill workers and boom men of Pennsylvania's lumber-making metropolis. All mills were shut down and so they remained for three weeks, while concessions were made and rejected by both sides. Then the operators decided to open, come hell and high water. They brought in a crowd of strike breakers and to these were added deserters from the ranks of the strikers.

Several of the mills reopened, but not for long. The strikers attacked the plants in force, sending raiding parties armed with clubs through the mill yards and in some instances into the mill buildings. Loggers and rivermen came down from the woods to help and got in more excellent fighting than they had seen in a decade of barroom assaults. There was considerable violence and bloodshed. Soapboxers preached on every corner, and the hotheaded called on the "slaves" to burn the mills. Williamsport preachers declared that a strike was an act against God.

The boss lumbermen responded in characteristic Pennsylvania fashion. They appealed, not to God, but called for troops, and Governor Geary sent them. The strike was quickly broken, but far from settled. It would break out again a decade later, along the Saginaw and on Lake Muskegon, to better effect for the "slaves."

One other thing of historical importance to the lumber industry happened in 1872: Michigan cut more logs and made more lumber than did the states of

Maine and Pennsylvania *combined*. If there were any ethnologists practicing in those days, the news from Michigan told them positively where the nomads of Maine had settled—for a while, anyway.

The First Migration had been completed.

7

Big Doings Along the Saginaw

IN 1859 JAMES BUCHANAN was in the White House, the Dred Scott Case had been decided, but hardly settled, and old John Brown made a raid on the arsenal at Harper's Ferry. In September of that year the young city of Saginaw in Michigan came of age by building a swell new hotel.

Saginaw,[1] the coming lumber colossus, needed a swell new hotel. The ground was ready, and characteristic. It was forty feet deep of sawdust, piled and packed hard as rock atop the marshes along the river. For thirty years sawmills already had been at work preparing the ground.

So they built the Bancroft House, an acre of it, four stories high, with a gaudy cupola, and back of it a gasworks to light its cut-glass chandeliers. They put a neat box stove and a brass cuspidor in every room and every room had a bellpull of red plush. There was a rococo ladies parlor, a billiard room, a "shaving saloon," a mahogany bar, and a lobby that would have delighted Jim Fisk. The chef was imported from Paris. . . . Saginaw's sidewalks were still of white-pine plank, but by God, sir, when a boss lumberman took his ease, it should be elegant ease.

The Bancroft was opened with a grand banquet and ball on September 7, 1859, and the *Saginaw Cou-*

[1] Saginaw and East Saginaw were built on opposite sides of the river and bickered each other for years before they consolidated. They are here treated as one town, just as are Bay City and West Bay City.

rier next day took columns to report the doings. What the *Courier* did not report was a gorgeous incident that tells more about the time and place than half a dozen histories of the Saginaw Valley.

The incident concerned Curt Emerson, one of Saginaw's pioneer boss loggers and sawmill operators. Old Curt, by his own tell, had kept comfortably drunk for more than thirty years, his sawmill meanwhile cutting enough boards, so he calculated aloud, to build a solid privy, six feet high and six wide, from Saginaw Bay clean through to Albany, New York, at the other end of the Erie Canal. Curt was a bachelor, quick of temper, and for reasons that were never very clear, had a large sign painted across the outside of his sawmill office. "The Halls of Montezuma," it read in bold letters.

Although Curt Emerson was a big lumberman and had a Saginaw street named for him, he was not invited to the gala opening festivities at the Bancroft. Possibly his colleagues didn't like "Caesar," Curt's little dog. Wherever Curt went, the dog went too, and it was Curt's custom, when angered at anyone, to address his dog. "Piss on him, Caesar," he would say. "Piss all *over* him!"

Anyway, when the magnificent Bancroft opened its doors that night in September of 1859, with bands and an orchestra playing, Curt Emerson was not bid to the feast. Thereupon, it would appear in light of later events, Curt went to his Halls of Montezuma, took an extra stiff jolt from the jug he always kept under his desk, and proceeded to the banquet room of the Bancroft.

Gas lights glowed and spluttered from among the ton or more of cut-glass hanging in the chandeliers. The orchestra played chastely. The table, so the *Courier* man reported, fairly groaned under food and drink, including champagne in silver buckets. All the lumber aristocracy of Saginaw and near-by Bay City was pres-

ent, men and women. Unnoticed, Curt eyed the guests
as they sat down to table. Then he acted.

Springing lightly, in spite of his sixty-odd years, old
Curt landed fair on both feet at the head and on top
of the long table; and he strode and kicked his way
to the foot, doing damage later estimated at two thousand dollars, cutting a score of guests with the flying
glass, forks, and knives, and ruining untold yards of
taffeta and bombazine. It broke up the banquet. Next
day, when he had sobered slightly, Curt willingly paid
the damages. He said he was sorry that anyone was
injured, but the hell with the hotel.

Into that incident and its setting is packed the very
essence of Saginaw City—champagne and plank sidewalks; a Parisian chef to do the cooking, a wild and
wealthy sawdust-savage to kick the cooking up into the
cut-glass chandeliers.

Banger and the Penobscot had been quiet and seem-
ly alongside Saginaw City and the Saginaw River. Bangor had a theological seminary to exert a pious influence on its loggers and lumbermen. It bloomed also
under the strong cultural sun that radiated from Boston and Concord. And the Maine Temperance Society had put the fear of God into the hearts of Bangor's rum sellers.

There was none of these things in Saginaw. Saginaw City of the fifties and long after was a town of the
new frontier. Life was more expansive, the tempo faster. They had *steam* sawmills here, of a size and speed
never dreamed of in Maine. Logging was done on a
titanic scale to feed the mills. Ten miles above Saginaw City the Flint, Shiawassee, Cass, and Tittabawassee rivers united to form the Saginaw; and along the
banks of them all, and miles deep on both sides, was
bigger and, men said, better white pine than was ever
seen in the East. Here, sure enough, was more timber
than could be cut in a thousand years. Men talked that

way, in camp and in the elegant lobby of the Bancroft House.

The loggers walked into it, ax in hand, and they filled the four rivers full of logs, spring after spring. Meantime, more loggers were piling logs into the Au Sable River, and into the Bad, the Rifle, the Au Gres, the Kawkawlin—all of them for mills along the dominant Saginaw.

Down the river, twelve miles below Saginaw City, the sawmill town of Bay City was growing, with stacks sticking up from every water-front acre. And every little way between the two cities still more mills arose. One could almost but not quite walk the dozen miles on the tops of piles of lumber.

Saginaw grew to have seventy-four sawmills. Bay City had a mere thirty-six, and Bay City's suburb of Bangor[3] had two more. That made one hundred and twelve mills along the Saginaw. In a "good" year this stupendous concentration of machinery could cut a billion feet of lumber in a short season. In 1882 Saginaw River mills turned out 1,012,000,000 feet of lumber, and for good measure sawed three hundred millions of shingles—enough lumber and roofing to build fifty thousand medium-sized homes.

The Genesee Street drawbridge in Saginaw used to open fifteen hundred times a month, to pass freighters coming and going with lumber for Albany and the world. The Third Avenue bridge in Bay City opened even oftener, for it was nearer the Bay. The famous tug *Witch,* and a hundred lesser boats snorted night and day at moving booms of logs; and the river steamer *Belle Seymour* would load forty tons of pork and beans and other supplies and head for the camps upriver. At one time, when Saginaw had not more than thirty thousand population, it required twelve daily newspapers to report all these doings and, incidentally, to tell the

[3] Hopefully but futilely named for the Penobscot city.

voters exactly why this or that boss lumberman was
fitted to sit in Congress, goal of so many of them.

Everything here along the Saginaw was on the grand
scale. The timber was bigger and thicker than anywhere else. Whores were prettier and more numerous.
The police less bothersome. And while Saginaw's sawmills worked day and night to cut logs into lumber,
Saginaw's businessmen and women labored long and
diligently to entertain the boys who cut the logs and
made the boards.

Making lumber, in fact, was only part, and the pro-
saic part, of Saginaw's life. Educating the vast army
of loggers, fresh from the creeks and loaded not for
bear but for dinosaur, was the town's liveliest industry.
The boys came here from as far West as Green Bay
in Wisconsin to blow their stakes in Saginaw, for Saginaw, as related, had gas lights at an early date and gas
lights brightened the eyes of Water Street gals and put
glint into the forty-rod dispensed along that great
thoroughfare.

The lure of Saginaw was very strong and insistent to
the men back in the tall, straight timber. It was common to see a train pull into the Père Marquette depot
with not one pane of glass whole in the entire string of
ten coaches, while the mating howls of loggers scared
little children and virtuous women all along Potter
Street, which faced the depot.

From this and other depots, both rail and water,
five hundred and sometimes five thousand loggers
would converge on Saginaw's business district. It was
the Red Sash Brigade, out in force—possibly the greatest mob of bottlemen and door-kickers-in that ever
walked. Most of them wore bright mackinaws or shirts,
and the Canadians among them wore a fringed sash
of red wool. All wore calked boots. These gave a dis-
tinctive counterpoint to the tramping—a click, click,
click, as the steel calks punctured the pine sidewalks and pulled out again.

They were headed not for the elegant Bancroft, but
for places like John Scanlon's hotel, and the Valley
House, the Besner House, the Gibbs House, the Tus-
cola, Price's, Kinney's, Jeffers', and half a hundred
other lumberjack hangouts including the justly notorious Perry House, on the site of the present Grand
Trunk station.

By the time they had been shaved and started down
Genesee Street to buy a drink at every saloon along
the way, an eight-piece band would be playing in front
of Little Jake's Clothing Store. Little Jake Seligman was
the Barnum of merchants,[3] and his technique fitted
Saginaw like a pair of spring-bottom pants.

With the square well filled with a thousand or more
milling loggers, attracted by the band, Little Jake himself would go to the second floor of his store and there
throw vests out of the window, one at a time. The logger who got and carried a vest into the store was given
a coat and pair of pants to match, free.

The fighting over the vests was something to see, and
so was a vest itself when a triumphant logger carried
the tattered remains into Jake's store. He got the free
pants and coat, all right, but a new vest to match cost
ten or twelve dollars. Jake lost little in the transac-
tions.

In fact, Little Jake did so well by the loggers that
there is a statue of him in Saginaw today. On top of
what is perhaps the weirdest town clock and tower ever
designed by man is a bronze male. He looks little like
a merchant, in his rather wide hat and long cloak, but
more like a combination of Webster Addressing the
Senate and Grant at Shiloh. Jake presented the statue
and clock to Saginaw, but that ungrateful city would
not accept it until Jake set aside a sum of money to
care for the timepiece for a hundred years to come.

[3]Little Jake Seligman also operated his own bank and a horse-
car street railway, the cars of which were painted canary yellow
and light blue.

Like Little Jake, the city fathers of Saginaw were in keeping with the times. They advised their police to humor the Red Sash Brigade; so long as a logger did not leap through a store's show window or actually commit murder in the first degree, they were to be left alone.

Loggers were never known to molest children and "decent" women, so there was no problem there. They carried no weapons, save their calks. Few of them would steal anything other than hard liquor. Saginaw nights might be made hideous by the howls of men released a few days from the savage forest, and of course there would be mayhem on Water and Potter streets; but it was all just good clean fun, and citizens might go to bed in security if not in quiet.

Theaters, variety halls, and free-and-easys of all kinds flourished in Saginaw, and native talent budded among the piles of sawdust. In a few years little Charlie Harris, bellhop at the Bancroft, would have his name as author on the title page of a very popular song, "After the Ball"; and chubby Lelia Koeber, who attended the Hoyt grade school, would become Marie Dressler and a great actress. George Lavigne, who worked in a sawmill yard and boxed on Saturday nights, was on the way up to having his picture on the front cover of the *Police Gazette* as The Saginaw Kid, lightweight champion of the world (1893-1899). The Kid found plenty to practice on in Saginaw of the eighties.

Of the frail sisterhood who did noble work in entertaining the Red Sash Brigade, doubtless Belle Stevens was the most beautiful and surely the most elegant. Belle never rapped on the windows of her Water Street dive, nor would she allow her girls to be so vulgar. Belle had class. In a two-dollar day and cheaper, it cost three and ofttimes five dollars for a brief stay with Venus at Belle's. But Belle never hurried anyone, say very ancient males of present-day Saginaw whose faces glow at mention of her name. No unseemly rush at Belle's. And long before a movie's line became legend Belle had cards printed on which in demure script was the invitation "Come Down and See Belle When in Town."

They went down to Belle's, no mistake about that; for when the drive was in, you had to be a favored man at Belle's or you took your turn in a waiting list a yard long. When the list was very long or the urge very great, the boys went along to see Emma Keys or one of her girls; or to Carrie Lee's, Long Minn's, or Sue Groves'. And there was always a good, solid backlog in Ma Smith's place.

Ma Smith was very durable and outlasted the lot of them. She kept a stable of from twelve to twenty girls, and when business was real brisk Ma could "bake a batch of rolls, herself," as she quaintly put it. Ma was an able businesswoman, too. She was on the best of terms with the city council, and often that august group would adjourn and go in a body to the Smith place on Water Street.

On the one and only occasion when the forces of Civic Virtue got the upper hand of Water Street, temporarily, Ma Smith had a house hurriedly erected on Crowe Island, in the middle of the Saginaw River about a mile from town, and there she moved her retinue. Henceforth, and until Ma moved back into town, it took some of the towboats an ungodly long time to cover the twelve miles between Bay City and Saginaw. Ma reported that she upped her take by ten per cent when she and her girls lived on the island, but the boat whistles—most of the blasts no doubt greetings from kindly skippers—disturbed the morning beauty sleep of her girls. Hard-working women such as Ma had around the place had to sleep sometime.

In near-by Bay City entertainment conditions were comparable and excellent. Cassie Hawkins, a real beauty of the Lillian Russell type, ran the select five-dollar house; and there were eighty-odd other joints whose rates ran from fifty cents to two dollars.

A dive known only as The Catacombs operated in the center of town, near the Third Street bridge. This was undoubtedly the toughest place anywhere along the Saginaw, given to robbing the customers and reputedly dropping the bodies down a trapdoor into the river.

Bay City wasn't so large as Saginaw, but it was far more literary. Here was published the *Bay City Growler,* a scandal rag that kept one posted on the "sporting life" of town and often printed items revealing the notable sex life of some of Bay City's lusty timber barons. Another lively paper was the *Lumbermen's Gazette,* which printed less about lumber than it did about hell-raising.

Bay City's underworld fairly overflowed with enterprise. One winter a madame and her gentleman friend moved thirty girls to a rangy old barn at Meredith, just west of Bay City, where a very large crew of loggers were in camp, the idea being to get the boys' dough before they went to the big towns in the spring. The attempt was only partly successful, due to conditions. The only furniture was a bar made of planks set on two barrels, and mattresses on the floor. The wind blew in so wildly from Saginaw Bay that it tore the tar paper off the sides of the barn and, as one who was there recalls, "let in too much cold." One grants that it probably did.

Uplift was periodically tried on the loggers when they came to town. Well-meaning but frightfully naïve folk said that loggers acted the way they did because there was nothing offered them but saloons and brothels. They opened coffeehouses and reading rooms and temperance hotels, but the Red Sash Brigade would have none of them. For five months or longer they had gone to bed at twilight and were lulled to sleep by the howling of timber wolves. They were rooted out of

bunks while it was yet dark and herded out into the
snow to chop down the forest. Their light in the long
evenings and early mornings was Borealis herself, who
sent flickering streaks of fire across the northern sky,
and about the only music they had was the chill wail
of ironshod runners over ice roads, with an obbligato
of clanking chain.

Hell, man, when the snow melted and the logs were
driven down, no man wanted coffee, even with cream
in it; and no man wanted to read the temperance
tracts of General Neal Dow who already had brought
prohibition to Maine, thus causing those poor Bangor
Tigers to drink Peruna and horse liniment, and to howl
louder than ever. No, indeed. What a man wanted
came in bottles and corsets.

The end of Saginaw's great lumber days was tragi-
cally sudden. Even the boss loggers themselves seem
not to have known how near was the end of the timber line in their valley. In 1882 their fine sawmills at
Bay City and Saginaw cut more than one thousand
million feet of lumber. A decade later most of the mills
were silent and rusting;[4] while the operators of the
few mills running were frantically bringing logs from
'way up on Georgian Bay in Canada, in a last attempt
to make sawdust. It was no go. The forest was too far
from the saws. . . . Saginaw's clock had struck thirteen, and there was daylight everywhere in the swamp.

However, the towns of Bay City and Saginaw did
not die. There were a few pretty lean years, then new
manufactures came. In her prime as lumber maker to
the world, Saginaw had not more than thirty thousand
permanent residents, Bay City less than fifteen thousand, the two including ninety-eight reputed million-
aires.

[4]The Tittabawassee Boom Company, the mutual concern that
handled all of Saginaw's logs, was dissolved in 1893.

Today, in 1938, the two old sawmill towns can muster a total population of one hundred and twenty thousand. They make slick gadgets to go on super-super sixes, and many other things. Let them be content. Rome came to fall in time, crumbling around the bones of Christian fanatics. It was the host of loggers, on whom the Saginaw fattened and waxed great, that laid the old Saginaw low and buried her in and on top of forty feet of white-pine sawdust.

8

The Hell-Roaring Era

SAGINAW AND BAY CITY were only one scene in the red-eyed drama that was being played in the pineries of the Lake States. True, it was one of the great scenes, but only one, and meanwhile or soon, other scenes were leaping to life all over Michigan, Wisconsin, and Minnesota.

It was a vast stage, nigh two hundred thousand square miles of it, mostly, except for a slice of western Minnesota, in white pine. It was well watered with rivers and lesser streams that could float the roundstuff; and when the water wasn't deep or near enough, the boys would turn to and lay their own logging railroads. Steam was coming in. "My track ain't so long as the Great Northern's," remarked Uncle Al Powers, the old Minnesota boss logger, "but she's just as wide."

The cast of the drama was large. The Census Bureau, which has no imagination at all, allowed that in 1889 a few less than one hundred and twelve thousand men were at work cutting the Lake States' timber and making it into boards. To this should be added some two thousand lobbyists, most of the state legislators, the Congressional delegations, and the many honest bartenders and kindly prostitutes; all of these were as much a part of the show as the man with an ax in his hands. And just as necessary.

The scenery, as intimated, was cheap enough until it was all but gone. No matter how remote the timber, you couldn't lose much money on pine bought at a dollar and a quarter an acre. Then, there were the countless timberland grants to "projected" canals and railroads and "improvement" companies, usually arranged by forward-looking lumbermen. The railroads and canals didn't always get beyond the projected stage, nor were the "improvements" above question, but you may be sure the timber was cut. Sometimes these affairs made a mild stench, such as the notorious "Oconto Grant" in Wisconsin, and got into the papers, but they were soon forgotten; vastly greater and more magnificent skullduggery was being perpetrated in other lines of industry and "development."

That any lumberman in the Lake States stole any timber would appear to be a gross libel. They didn't have to. If they couldn't get all they wanted at a dollar and a quarter an acre, they might get a "Round Forty" and cut it. This Round Forty business was the classic joke of the era and was founded on sober fact.

Say that a boss logger was desirous of getting a hunk of state or federal timber. He might buy forty acres, which was the smallest unit in which timber ordinarily changed hands. He'd send the boys in to cut it, telling his foreman to "log around [approximately] forty acres." So, the boys would cut—ha, ha! it was sidesplitting—a round forty. First, the forty acres to the north, then to the east, the south, the west. It was thought a neat play on words and it tickled everybody, except the harassed timber agents of the state and federal governments.

If this cutting one hundred and sixty acres, in place of forty, were detected, the law read that the trespasser should pay "its estimated value, in any case not less than $1.25 an acre."

The state legislatures, of course, were "packed" as much as possible with yes men of the timber barons; and the capitols fairly crawled with lobbyists, well heeled with rum, cash, and acquiescent ladies who boldly used rice powder and smelled of Jockey Club.

When Horace Greeley went to Madison, Wisconsin, on a speaking tour in 1869, he said he had never seen "such a pack of drunken rogues and ruffians" as were currently engaged there in making the laws.

But the boys out in the timber knew little of how the timber was being acquired, and cared less. There is no record, even, that they thought of themselves as pioneers, although the boss lumbermen did. "Farms are multiplying," wrote Isaac Stephenson, with satisfaction, "and the friendly soil cleared of one harvest is yielding bountifully another."

Popular superstition laid disease to this clearing of the soil.[1] In western Michigan and eastern Wisconsin, first in 1846, with recurrences until 1869, a strange epidemic covered whole districts like a blanket. The people of Green Bay, Manistee, Muskegon, Grand Haven, and other places suffered from a sort of ague-and-chill fever, similar to malaria. It was occasionally deadly, always unpleasant, and it put entire townships to bed. Even the loggers were affected. Axmen shook so they could scarce strike twice in the same place. Settlers were afraid of quinine, yet they came to take it in large quantities. As for the loggers, doubtless they resorted to the one sovereign remedy they knew. What the disease was seems not to be known.

These epidemics had no appreciable effect on logging the Lake States, but the Panic of '57 did. It caused the quick slaughtering of "more oxen than Swift and Armour ever seen," as one oldster recalled afterward. Oxen had been the chief motive power of the loggers. With no money to buy hay, oxen instead of trees went under the ax. In the Lake States the ox never regained the place he had held. Horses took it.

Another thing the Panic of '57 did was to increase the movement into the Lake States of Easterners, some

[1] A similar disease was suffered by early settlers on the Willamette and Columbia rivers in Oregon.

settlers, many loggers. Many of them were Potato-
Famine Irish who had come to the United States
earlier in the decade; now they emigrated again, to
marry French Canadian girls and settle "Corktown"
at Detroit. And all through the fifties a steady stream
of immigrants flowed into Michigan, Wisconsin, and
Minnesota from Germany. Hundreds of them went to
work in the logging woods. The Germans were rated
not so "good on the water," either in calked shoes or
bateaux; but they were hard workers and stable; they
liked to "put in a long route."[2]

The late and honorable Ignatius Donnelly, member
of Congress and author of *The Great Cryptogram,
Caesar's Column,* and other highly original works—
best sellers of the day—played no small part in bringing in the Germans. He founded the town of Nininger
—now a part of South St. Paul, Minnesota—and published the *Emigrant Journal,* in both English and German. The *Journal,* like all of Donnelly's works, was
pretty imaginative. It was shipped into Germany by the
ton and described the ease and suddenness with which
immigrants—and particularly immigrants from Germany—might become wealthy through buying real estate and settling in the coming metropolis of Nininger
and nowhere else.

The crash of '57 gutted Nininger before it was well
under way, but Donnelly's efforts aided in bringing in a
lot of robust men who, for lack of anything else, became loggers.

For a brief period it looked as though the Mormons
might play a considerable part in logging the Lake
States. A group of them leased the sawmill built at
Black River Falls, Wisconsin, by Jacob Spaulding and
company, and cut timbers and boards for the big Mor-
mon holy of holies at Nauvoo. But when Joe Smith

[2]A *long route,* in logger talk, means to remain at work in one
camp for a long period.

was murdered in 1844, the Black River mill was returned to Spaulding.

Roving French Canadians had trapped and hunted the Lake States in the eighteenth century, and now in the 1870s they returned to cut the timber. There was an ebb and flow of them across the Line until the pine was all gone. They liked to return to "Canadaw" every so often, to visit the old folks and scenes, but many of them remained in this country, especially in the northern parts of the three states and along the Saginaw.[3]

The French Canucks were born loggers. A bit too filled with temperament to handle oxen and horses, they could do wonders with an ax. No better men walked in calked boots, or steered bateaux. They were dressy as all get-out, setting the red sash style that lasted as long as the Lake States pine. And they added something to life in the camps with their singing of "Alouette" and "En Roulant Ma Boule," in chorus, meanwhile tramping the camp floor with their *bottes-sauvages*, which were homemade shoepacks.

Along with the Frenchmen came a smaller but still large number of Scotch- and English-Canadians, mostly from Ontario but many of the same breed from Nova Scotia, New Brunswick, and Prince Edward Island. From these ranks a host of great woods bosses were drawn, names like McLean, Macdonald, Chisholm, Cameron, Stewart; and often one of them rose to be an authentic timber baron of the first rank, such as Robert Dollar. Dollar came from Ontario to Michigan to work in the woods as a common lumberjack. By hard work, and aided possibly by some talents not described in the books of Horatio Alger, Dollar acquired and cut millions of feet of timber on Michigan's upper peninsula, naming a town "Dollarville." Then he jumped to

[3] The Saginaw-Bay City 1937 directories call the roll: Boutin, Bourbonnais, Bouchette, Dupuis, Duquette, Fournier, etc. All are old names in these cities.

the West Coast, where his mills continue to make sawdust and a ship line takes his name around the world.
The upper peninsula, in fact, was pretty much peopled
by folks from Ontario and the Maritime Provinces,
with a generous leaven of Germans direct from the
Old Country.

But there weren't enough natives and Canadians and
Germans and Irish to log all that Lake States' timber.
In the eighties began a deluge of Swedes, Danes, and
Norwegians. Encouraged by truly startling literature to
come to God's country, and ofttimes actually imported
in droves for the sole purpose of cutting logs, the
Olsons, Hansens, and Swansons flocked into Detroit,
Grand Rapids, Chicago, and St. Paul, and were presently sent into the woods with an ax in one hand, a box
of snuff, known as Scandihoovian Dynamite, in the
other.

Who among the boss loggers started this mass im-
portation from the Scandinavian countries is hard to
say, but there is no question about the biggest entre-
preneur of the lot. He was Louie Sands, Scandinavian
himself and one of the big operators on the Manistee
district in Michigan. Louie had them coming into
western Michigan by boatloads and trainloads. If there
was a Swede in Michigan who hadn't worked for Louie
Sands before 1900, he was never sighted.[4] Old-time
lumberjacks tell that the classic and standard excuse of
a Swede logger who was quitting the job at any camp
in Michigan or Wisconsin was "Ay tank Ay yump dis
yob an' go vork for Louie Sands."

The Scandies were excellent men in woods or sawmill. Big, strong, and able, and docile as long as they
had plenty of good fresh snuff, they'd step into a forty
of tall pine and whale all hell out of it in no time at all.
They ate like oxen. It took more to feed them than it
did the French Canadians, but they were worth it.

[4]Hansen's camps on the Au Sable River came to be known as
"Little Denmark" because of the many Danish loggers.

They would work anywhere, in any weather, but they preferred Scandinavian foremen and a crew well seasoned with Vikings. By the time Michigan timber was petering out, Scandinavians were as numerous as Canucks. A little later, when Wisconsin and Minnesota were at the peak of lumber production, the Scandies were the dominating nationality, as far as numbers were concerned, in both woods and sawmills.

Aside from racial differences, there were men of numerous talents and dispositions in the crews of logging camps. One veteran recalls a crew near Traverse City, Michigan, in the eighties. The scaler had been a noted embezzler. The barn boss was an escaped patient from the hospital for the insane at Traverse. The night watchman was a youth who had run away from West Point. And one of the cookees had been a sweet singer with Emerson's Minstrels.

With the stage and scenery provided by Nature and the huge cast of actors ready, the Lake States drama went into its rousing third act, which lasted from about 1880 to around 1905. It was a quarter century of throbbing life for the lads in the woods and mills, and likewise for folks who lived in the lumber towns. It was a hard life, sometimes cruelly so. But it was amusing. Nothing stodgy about it. It was gaudy on all levels. Fortunes were made and sometimes lost, all within a decade or less. Poor boys of today, tomorrow had a plug hat, a butler, a mistress, a cellar of champagne, and a seat in Congress—or, at the least, a lake boat named for them.[5]

Even the lesser barons, who did only middling well, had men to drive them around behind a span of white horses. Some of them wore white beaver hats. Others carried gold-headed canes in place of the peavey which

[5] In the summer of 1937, near the Third Street bridge in Bay City, Michigan, was the rotting hulk of a vessel. Dim on the name boards was "Samuel Stephenson," once a very great name indeed.

aesthetically would have fitted them better. But it was
all in keeping. They built monstrous houses that
stagger the imagination of architects. One of the last of
an old lumber line inclosed his grounds with a solid
wall built of mortar and bottles, mostly of champagne
empties. The house has gone but you'll see the wall
there today, near the village of Watters in Michigan.
The bottles are beautifully arranged, as to color and
symmetry, and the number of them tells of lusty
doings. . . . Mark it well, tourist, for it spells an era.

Or, if the poor logger remained poor, as most did, he
at least lived a wild and unshackled life. God, how they
roved and ranged! From Saginaw west to Muskegon,
north to Manistee, Roscommon, and Cheboygan; still
north of Marquette and Escanaba; south to Green Bay,
Wausau, and Oshkosh; west to Chippewa Falls; and
north to Stillwater, Cloquet, Bemidji—and all way
points. Stewart Edward White put some of it into fiction, just as Holman Day had in Maine. A few poets
called it the Golden Age of the Lumberjack. The jacks
themselves didn't know *what* it was, but they told each
other it would last forever.

While there was timber, there was always a job.
When the Saginaw timber gave out, they moved over
to Muskegon to help finish what was left there. The
general movement of the main horde of loggers was
thus: first they cut lower Michigan, moved to Michigan's Upper Peninsula, then into Wisconsin, and last
of all they cut northern Minnesota.

The rafting of lumber from La Crosse and other
upriver points to St. Louis became an industry within
an industry and required a small army of rough men.
They were known as "roosters"—probably from
"roustabouts"—and bleary-eyed pullets at both ends of
the voyage preened their feathers when they heard the
crowing. Many of the roosters were drawn from the
ranks of loggers, attracted by the greater alcoholic possi-
bilities presented. It took only fourteen to sixteen days

to pilot a raft from Wisconsin to St. Louis. Here the boys liquored up for a day or two, then rode a steamboat back to the point of production, to liquor up again while waiting for a new raft. It is probable that roosters did not live so long as loggers.

Making lumber in Maine had been slow compared to what was going on in the Lake States. The speed-up, as usual, came from the sawmill end of the industry.

A bandsaw had been invented in England three quarters of a century before. An "improved bandsaw" was exhibited at the Philadelphia Centennial in 1876. And now, in the eighties, this new rig appeared in the Lake States in the form of a headsaw.[6] It was a long, curling ribbon of glittering and hungry steel that could eat-um-up-fast and whine for more. A Mr. Rodgers of Muskegon invented the friction nigger, a device for automatically handling logs on the headrig carriage, and a Mr. Hill of Kalamazoo improved the nigger by adding direct steam. Somebody around Muskegon also contributed the bull chain, for moving logs in an endless procession from log pond into the sawmill. And all along the line, from headsaw to mill yard, new inventions were coming in to speed the process of reducing logs to boards.

Log-storage and mill ponds, in the Lake States as in Maine, froze solid in winter. This wouldn't do. Some unnamed genius ran a steam pipe from his sawmill boiler into the pond, and lo, the pond was as free from ice in January as in July. This was the celebrated hot-pond; with it mills could cut all winter.

All this and much more tended to hurry things in the woods, for it was up to the loggers to keep the ponds filled with round-stuff. Logging camps grew in size and number as Swedes flocked in to help the natives and the foreigners who had come earlier. Logging inventors got

[6]First saw that logs meet in the mill.

busy. One of them devised a set of two wheels, five feet
from hub to rim and therefore ten feet high, that looked
like something out of Jules Verne, who indeed may
have inspired it. This rig was known simply as the Big
Wheels, and big wheels would roll and rumble through
Michigan, Wisconsin, and Minnesota, and on into
Idaho, Oregon, and California, just as sure as the
covered wagons had rolled.

The big wheels didn't require roads, for their axles
were high enough to clear stumps; and they made
summer logging not only possible but feasible. . . . And
men swore, by the bandy-legged Old Mackinaw, that if
the sawmills would work all winter, then by the hump-
backed ringtailed Old So-and-so, loggers would work
all summer. And they did.

Horace Butters, Maine logger who had settled at
Ludington, Michigan, after the First Migration, had
been having some Jules Verne ideas himself, and in
1886 he came forth with Horace Butters' Patent
Skidding & Loading Machine. This was a complicated
and truly gigantic rig, for the time. It consisted of two
tall spar trees, guyed with ropes, a trolley strung between the spars. Over this trolley a carriage was pulled
by a line from a steam donkey engine. It lifted logs out
of the brush and yanked them quickly to one of the
spars where another donkey and tackle loaded them
onto railroad cars.

Butters' skidder met with scant favor in the Lake
States (there was little time left after 1886, anyway)
but it went South to log the bayous, and it would go
West, also, to log Douglas fir and redwood on the
Pacific Coast, and to have a dozen "inventors" claim
it.

Another item that speeded log production was a
simple change in cutting methods in the woods; some
bold spirit took a crosscut saw and felled a tree with
it. Why this hadn't happened long before is one of the

great mysteries; crosscuts had been used for several years to cut the felled trees into lengths to fit the sleighs. Felling by saw proved an immediate success. Henceforth an ax would be used only for notching the undercut— to direct the tree's fall—and for limbing.

Living conditions in logging camps of the Lake States were never anything to brag about. Yet they improved steadily throughout the eighties and nineties. Boss loggers discovered that good food and a good cook were just as important as a good foreman.

Camp cooks presently became fabulous fellows, white-aproned personages who faced a battery of the biggest and most modern type of ranges and bossed a crew of cookhouse varlets known as "cookees." Canned milk came into use. So did canned fruit and vegetables. Coffee, or at least something approaching that brew, was added to the bill of fare. Fresh meats supplemented but did not displace the pork and beans. Some attempt was made to keep the cookhouse clean.

Properly enough, the tin dinner horns grew in size until some of them were eight feet long. It was a gesture of the expansive time. Cooks vied with one another with true professional pride to see who could set the best table and blow the sweetest call on the horn; and on at least one occasion a logging-camp cook blew himself straight into logging history. He was Fred Maynard.

In the spring of 1898 Cook Maynard left Bay City for West Branch, Michigan, where he was to cook for a summer crew of Scandinavian loggers. With him he took the mouthpiece of a regulation Army bugle, on which he had been practicing, and just before six o'clock on his first evening in camp, he fitted the bugle mouthpiece into the end of the long tin horn. Then he stepped outside the cookhouse door and blew a sweet and stirring blast.

Not before in those woods had such a noble military noise been sounded—something between "Boots & Saddles" and "Mess Call." But not for two hours did any man show up for supper. On hearing it, terrified Danes and Swedes had thrown down their axes and hit deeper into the swamp. It turned out that some of them believed the Spanish fleet had landed on the Huron shore, and others thought it Uncle Sam himself calling them to the colors to help defend the United States against Butcher Weyler.

In Maine the camp store, or *wangan box,* had never amounted to much. Now in the Lake States the store took on size and variety. Here it was called The Van and its stock covered all the needs of a man in the timber, including Hinckley's Bone Liniment for Man & Beast, Dr. Perry Davis' Painkiller, and other remedies of great thaumaturgic power that were good for hangovers as well. In earlier days, but not in the eighties and nineties, many concerns peddled liquor to their crews right in camp.[7]

Logging railroads had been increasing their mileage ever since Wright & Ketchum laid pioneer rails to their woods road out of Averill (née Red Keg), Michigan, in the seventies. Mail and newspapers reached the loggers. The railroads, of course, did not displace the rivers, nor the horse-drawn sleighs. In Maine, sleighs had a six-foot bunk, that is, the loads could not be more than six feet wide. Here in the Lake States it was natural that they should start with eight-foot bunks and rise quickly to twelve-, fourteen-, and even sixteen-foot affairs.

A sleigh sixteen feet across the bunks was hardly a toy. A load of six thousand feet, or some sixty thousand pounds, was the usual thing for two horses on a good iced road. There never was any uphill and the downhills were cared for by snubbers. And when the loggers wanted to show off at the Columbian Exposi-

[7]Said a pious but unidentified boss lumberman of the 1870s in an interview with the *Saginaw Courier:* "No sutler, sir, is allowed on *my* premises."

tion of 1893, they loaded what old-timers still refer to as The World's Fair Load.

This tour de force was accomplished by lumberjacks of the Nestor Estate Logging Company, on the Ontonagon River in northern Michigan. The logs were each eighteen feet long. The load was thirty-three feet three inches high, and scaled 36,055 feet. Although it required nine railroad flatcars to move the logs and sleigh to Chicago, a team of two horses hauled it with ease from the woods to the shipping point. . . . That, mister, was loading and hauling.[8]

Loggers of the Great Days were as willing to work as horses. They took pride in the quality of their work and even more in the quantity. Canny foremen kept this spirit keen by pitting crews against each other and by offering small bonuses. The best foremen often were those who could fell a tree or break a jam faster than anybody else—and of course lick any man in the crew.

A union was unheard of, likewise unthought of. It apparently never occurred to loggers—no more than it had in Maine—that things could or should be otherwise than they were—booze, bawds, battle, and plenty of timber.

Yet the general speed-up was paving the way for a mild revolt. In the fall of 1881 employees of the Muskegon Booming Association at Muskegon, Michigan, went on strike for a ten-hour day. A thousand men paraded the streets with banners announcing "Ten Hours or No Sawdust."

The operators appealed for troops, which were sent, and martial law declared. The strike fizzled out—until spring, when it broke out bigger and better than ever. Mill owners imported men from Ontario. These were met at the Muskegon depot by strikers, "treated polite-

[8]Ed O'Brien, now of Toledo, Oregon, who was a member of the loading crew, recalls that the work was done on a Sunday in February, 1898.

ly, taken to the strikers' hall where facts were explained to them, and they left town next day."

Next, the operators brought in Pinkerton detectives. There was considerable clubbing and fighting around Muskegon Lake. In June, 1882, the strike was called off and men returned to work a ten-hour day.

Four years later a similar and larger strike occurred in Saginaw and Bay City, with Pinkertons and all the trimmings. After a bit of fighting all the boss lumbermen except A. W. Wright & Company acceded to the ten-hour demands. Wright never again operated in Saginaw. When he found miniature coffins tied to the doorknob of his office, it is said, he pulled up stakes and left the valley for good.

The ten-hour day was generally accepted after 1886, except on the drive, where the matter of working-hours was never questioned; when there was a good driving-pitch, you drove logs as long as you could see them.

On the whole, however, the loggers of the Lake States seem to have cared little about how many hours made a day's work in the woods. Their main purpose, by and large, was the same that had driven Maine loggers of a century before. So, of far greater importance than working conditions was the quality of entertainment to be found when the logs were cut and the drive was in.

Crude but lively board cities, lathering with Sin, had arisen around the big sawmills. And around hot, red-bellied barrel stoves, in a thousand logging camps, these cities and their facilities for entertainment, and not Karl Marx, were discussed by stakey[9] loggers as they figured what they had coming in wages, on the log headboards of their bunks.

---

[9] A *stakey* logger is one who has enough wages due him to make him restless to get to town.

Sin in the Pineries

THE FORTY-EIGHT big sawmills that snorted and whined around the shores of Lake Muskegon didn't make quite so many boards as those along the Saginaw River, but in the field of entertainment the city of Muskegon probably had no peer. One can tell something of a city's reputation for hospitality by the way bards have treated its name, and lumberjack bards appear to have been partial to Muskegon. That city is mentioned in more logger ballads than any other along The Big Clearing from Maine to the Pacific Coast. Jack Haggerty's farewell, in the celebrated "The Flat River Girl," alone should cinch Muskegon's place as lumberjack Mecca of the great white pine days. Sang Mister Haggerty:

> Then adieu to Flat River. For me there's no rest;
> I'll shoulder my peavey and I'll go out West.
> I'll go to Muskegon some pleasures to find,
> And I'll leave my own Flat River darling behind.

Why no yearning logger ever sang of Grand Rapids or Detroit or Milwaukee or St. Paul[1] isn't clear, for those towns must surely have provided excellent entertainment and possibly more ways of blowing money

[1] Loggers had a song about a big Swede who went to Minne-a-p'olis to take in "the big state fair."

than did Muskegon. Yet there were a number of good reasons for the latter's great popularity.

For one thing there was geography. Muskegon was close by the "down" end of the Muskegon River, and when a man had finished his work on the drive, well— there was Muskegon. Keen-nosed loggers claimed they could smell Muskegon booze as far upriver as Big Rapids, fifty miles away, and said they detected the first erotic whiffs of Sawdust Flats perfume at Newago, half as far.

Muskegon's Sawdust Flats was a part of the city made by a "fill" and on it were six solid blocks—long blocks—of what a local divine termed "unspeakable whoredom." In Muskegon loggers didn't say they were "going down the Line." They said they were going down "On the Sawdust," and a girl who worked there was said to be "on the Dust." Standard rate on the Dust was one dollar.

The number of girls on the Dust ran sometimes to as many as three hundred, so old rounders recall. Outstanding was one Spanish Lou, who died of old age January 9, 1908, almost the last of her era. Lou was said to have been a highly educated and wholly depraved woman; and she was distinguished less for her beauty than for her extraordinary ability to curse roundly in eight languages. Logging-camp teamsters who went to Lou's got more than their dollar's worth. They learned a lot of new words to try on their horses.

On a slightly higher level than the Dust was the place operated many years by Big Delia, usually known as The Big Deal. Delia weighed two hundred and twenty-five pounds on the hoof, was six feet two inches tall, and she once hit a logger[2] hard enough to break his jaw and Delia's powerful right hand. In her latter

---

[2]It is well authenticated. The logger had refused to take off his calked boots before entering. Delia, unlike the girls on the Dust, did not allow calked shoes in her place.

days Delia took to chewing tobacco—for toothache, she always said—and every day she consumed a full package of Daniel Scotten's Hiawatha, a favorite fine-cut of the time. Old men vow that when Delia spat it seemed like a cosmic disturbance.

Prostitutes of Muskegon were usually on the best of terms with the city fathers, and it is to Muskegon's glory that the gals were allowed to take part in the city's big Fourth of July celebration of 1887.

There had been a huge drive on the river that year. The town was filled with loggers. Demand for lumber was good. Around the lake two score sawmills were working night and day. Money was plentiful. Muskegon decided to shoot the works and stage big doings on the Fourth—parades, bands, "free attractions," sports for prizes, fireworks, and all.

As plans went forward a delegation of the Sawdust sisterhood called on the town officials. Might they, they wanted to know, erect a dance pavilion and entertain their many logger friends? They were told that they might, so long as they kept to the Dust Flats.

Now the girls showed what they could do in the way of civic consciousness. They hired carpenters to build an open pavilion, eighty-four by one hundred and twenty feet, down on the Flats. They sent their pimps to the nearby woods for boughs of pine and cedar; the girls themselves took turns laying a roof of boughs over the rafters, and decorating the interior with bunting. Some patriot among them nailed a good-sized American flag across one end of the hall. It was all very pretty.

While all this was going on, a boss pimp was dispatched to Milwaukee to hire a band for the occasion.

The day dawned warm and sunny, as all Fourths should. Not one but two bands arrived on the ferry from across Lake Michigan. This was due to some sort of mix-up, but Sawdust Flat girls were real music lovers, and they hired both bands. "Fill 'em up with beer and let 'em snort handsome," ordered Big Delia, prominent in committee work.

Putting it mildly, it was a day long to be remembered on the Dust. Downtown, orators did their stuff; bands played, there was a parade, and kids set off firecrackers. But down on the Dust the day was given over entirely to "Terpsichore and Bacchus," as the educated Spanish Lou remarked.

Two small boys, who remember it with awe, sneaked away from the doings downtown and hid themselves back of the lattice work under the bandstand that faced the arboreal pavilion on the Dust.

Soon as bleary-eyed loggers got their morning snifters that day, they headed straight for the Sawdust Flats. By noon, it is estimated, a full thousand of them were present. Those who wore calked boots were gallant; they kicked them off into two great piles that grew until a man couldn't have jumped over them, and danced in their woolen-stockinged feet.

There was no shortage of dancing partners for the loggers. From Chicago and Milwaukee—at invitation of the local chapter—came perhaps eighty or ninety members of the sisterhood, and there was a bright-hued delegation from near-by Grand Rapids. The bands played nobly, or at least one of them did. Important players of the other group fell by the wayside shortly after noon, having overestimated their ability to consume the potent and free Muskegon beer that was hossed-up in kegs on every side of the pavilion.

Only one incident marred the day, if mar it was, when Black Jap, a vixen from the Flats, tied into a sister known locally as John L. Apparently named for the Boston Strong Boy who had licked Paddy Ryan five years before, the female John L. was a hellcat. As Black Jap was waltzing around with a good-looking young logger, John L. cut in with a hefty wallop to the Jap's jaw. The Jap countered and led with her right. The logger stepped free of the fracas.

For possibly half an hour the two women struck and tore at each other, ripping off clothing, tearing out hair rats, and cursing most horribly. Dancing ceased. So did the partly sober band. The two small boys who saw the battle say it was the most magnificent they ever witnessed. And for the first time they saw what women wore under their dresses.

The fight over, dancing resumed and continued to a late hour and was heartily enjoyed by all the merry throng.

Although this convention of the "Western Michigan Whores Benevolent Association," as some low fellows called it, was a great success, it created a local scandal and was never repeated. But business continued as usual for many years on the Sawdust Flats, and in a house of sin famous as The Canterbury.

This establishment was doubtless the most notorious hellhole in all the three Lake States. John Williams, who also owned the Red Light Saloon at the corner of Ottawa and Giddings streets, was proprietor of The Canterbury. It was a combination saloon, hotel, restaurant, dance hall, and out-and-out chippy house. Cockmains were fought there; prize fights, too, and often dog fights.

The Canterbury's management believed in supporting the lumber industry, from which it drew so many of its customers. The place was finished all over inside with matched white-pine paneling. The interior doorways were curved archways of the same material. Even the bar rails were of pine at first, but they were changed to brass because of loggers who enjoyed kicking long chunks out of the wooden ones.

The motto of The Canterbury was "Everything Goes." Upstairs, in one of the rooms, "circuses" often were staged and were reported to cover all forms of perversion. Loggers who ranged the Lake States said you hadn't cut your eyeteeth until you had been to The Canterbury at Muskegon.

It is not to be supposed, however, that Muskegon had nothing but a sporting life. Its other chief glory was a timber baron, one of the biggest the industry produced. He was Charles H. Hackley who arrived at Muskegon on a steamer just before noon on April 2, 1856, with no money, no friends, no letters of credit. He went to work in a sawmill that afternoon. A short twenty years after he was a baron, and by the time he died in 1905 he was one of the Timber Kings.

During his life, which is said to have been a lusty one indeed, Hackley gave $1,389,525 to the city that had treated him so well, and in his will he raised the ante to some $6,000,000. More remarkable even than the large amount of his public bequests were the uses to which he stipulated they should be put. Most timber barons who left anything to the public, left it to churches, foreign missions and such things, thus causing lumberjacks who had worked in their camps—and at their idea of wages—to remark that the old so-and-so "didn't have no more chanct of gettin' into Heaven than a shingle-weaver."

Hackley's money created parks, a very fine library, hospitals, and schools. And he left a good round sum for the purchase of oil paintings to be hung where the public could see them . . . Only those well acquainted with the usual gifts of rich lumbermen can appreciate the beautiful heterodoxy of Muskegon's prime baron. It is almost beyond belief.

Old-time jacks, sitting around a box stove, might differ over the attractions of Muskegon as compared with those of Bay City, Saginaw, or even of Grand Rapids, Ludington, and Roscommon. None would disagree about the well-earned reputation of Seney.

Muskegon was pleasant. Seney was merely tough. It grew quickly—like an ugly and poisonous toadstool, as a man of God recalls—around the terminus and junction of a logging railroad in Schoolcraft County of

Michigan's upper peninsula. It consisted chiefly of a number of saloons and two monstrous fancy-houses on the edge of town. For seven years after its establishment in 1881, there was absolutely no pretense of law, and little enough thereafter. Seney's bid for fame was strangely enough the breaking up of Seney's first house of sin. The town had suddenly swarmed with more than a thousand loggers and railroad construction workers. Buildings and shacks were going up fast but not fast enough to keep up with demand. Men slept on the ground, and saloons set up in the open, doing business over a hewed-timber bar laid across two stumps.

Such was the primitive condition that faced four fancy-men and approximately thirty girls who arrived ready for business. It looked bad. But a big warehouse had been completed at the railroad depot, and into this moved the P. I.'s and their women. Peaceful efforts on the part of the depot clerk didn't get anywhere; the pimps were big ugly fellows, and armed. And business was so good as to call for twenty-four-hour operation.

In Seney at the time were a number of men who enjoyed trouble fully as much as they did liquor, among them such hellions as Con Davis, Jack Wayman, and the lovely Pig-Foot Macdonald. They needed little urging, and when they were offered one hundred dollars to clean out the warehouse, they promptly attacked with vigor and joy. They slugged the pimps and hurled them bodily out the door. When the screaming hussies started to claw and kick the raiders, the raiders slapped them down and towed them around by their long hair.

Pig-Foot and his gang then destroyed all the whorish fixtures, tore the doors off their hinges, took what loose money they could find, and departed with sacks filled with bottles of drinking liquor. They accepted the hundred dollars, although Pig-Foot remarked that it seemed like stealing to be paid for an afternoon of pure fun.

That's how Seney first came into the limelight, a position it held for some twenty years. Dan Dunne came shortly after the raid and installed a stable of twenty-four girls in a big house across the railroad tracks; Tom Harcourt and brothers opened another place. By 1890 twenty-one recognized saloons, the two big bawdy houses, and one church were doing business. Dr. Frank P. Bohn,[3] fresh from medical college, arrived in Seney late in 1890 to be the town's first doctor. They needed a doctor in Seney.

"On my first Christmas day there," Dr. Bohn recalls, "I worked all day and all night treating the fighters who could find their way to my office by following the red trail on the snow that reddened and broadened as the day wore on.

"I doubt there was anywhere another town like Seney as it was in the nineties. I have seen the streets and the broad sidewalks of the town literally swamped with fighting loggers. . . . The Marquis of Queensberry would have been shocked. When a man was down his opponent jumped upon him with both feet, kicking and tearing at him with the cruel calks in his shoes. Yet no man interfered. There was no use. Until a man realized he had been beaten, it was best to let them continue."

The ill fame of Seney's saloons and crude houses of prostitution grew in time to attract the notice of the *Police Gazette,* then in its heyday. The lively journal sent a man to Seney to look things over, and the correspondent did so nice a job that even today the legend of the "Seney Stockades" will not down, but appeared only recently in one of Hollywood's many "epics of the timber."

The *Gazette*'s man wrote, and the *Gazette*'s wondrous artists illustrated, a story to the effect that in Seney were two vast houses of sin; that dozens of heretofore pure girls had been enticed therein; and that

[3]Dr. Bohn served as Congressman, Eleventh Michigan District, 1927–1933 and now lives in Newberry, Michigan.

they were kept there, virtually prisoners and against their will, by big, high, peaked stockades, such as were used to protect forts in Indian days.

The story was sheer invention in the best *Gazette* tradition. "I was in Seney many years," says Dr. Bohn, "and nothing like stockades ever came under my observation—and my profession often took me into the fancy-houses there." But the story had that something about it that cannot be downed. Folks all over Michigan today will tell you about the terrible "Seney Stockades."

Seney was bad enough without stockades. Ears were chewed off there regularly. "Loggers' smallpox" was prevalent, and diseases not mentioned in the public prints of the day abounded. As competition in venery increased the boss sports took to shooting at each other. One night Dr. Bohn was called to attend Dan Dunne, wounded and bleeding from a gunshot, in his own saloon; and at almost the same time he was called to patch up Steve Harcourt, one of the "opposition." Dunne lived—that time. Harcourt died. Dunne swore out a warrant for arrest of the two remaining Harcourts. In custody of an officer on the way to jail at Manistique, they encountered Dunne at Trout Lake. As Dunne came out a door, one of the Harcourts pulled a gun and fired. Dunne fell dead. Seney's great days were passing.

If there were any stockades in the Lake States they would appear to have been at the small, sinful town of Hurley, Wisconsin, a quite noted logging headquarters. Men of undoubted veracity and tolerably good memories say that on the outskirts of Hurley was a true stockade which inclosed women of one-dollar virtue; but details are lacking. It is a fit subject for a thesis by some sociology student at the university in Madison.

For a few brief years Ashland, Wisconsin, was noted for the entertainment supplied at Price Wade's big joint, some three miles out of town. And both

Wausau and Rhinelander in the same state were rated
high as suitable spots for hell-raising; so were smaller
Hayward and Barron.

La Crosse, Eau Claire, and Chippewa Falls were
bedeviled with recurrent and regrettable upheavals of
civic virtue, yet they managed a good open quality of
rough entertainment much of the time. Marinette, Green
Bay, and Oshkosh attracted loggers in eastern Wisconsin
and also tempted many from Michigan's upper peninsula.

Minnesota's earliest and biggest logging center, and
therefore its earliest whoopee-town, was Stillwater. As
early as 1871 two thousand men and five hundred
horses and oxen were working out of Stillwater, and in
1890 a full four hundred and fifty million feet of logs
went through its St. Croix boom. It took a lot of rum
and no few women to get that amount of timber ready
for the saws. Stillwater provided both, but not in sufficient quantity to keep its Red Sash Brigade from helling
into St. Paul and Minneapolis, twenty miles away.

They came in hordes from Stillwater to St. Paul's
Hill Street[4]—to pound on the doors at Mother Mary
Robinson's, a busy and prosperous woman for three
decades; and to visit Lottie Leighton's and Nina
Clifford's and the place of she-who-became the "girl"
of a famous detective, later married a St. Paul city
official, and died in the odor of sanctity.

They came from Stillwater, most of all, to make a
call on Swede Annie, at her place on Fifth Street in
Minneapolis. Swede Annie was a straw-topped Viking,
prettier than any chorus girl a logger could see on the
stage of the Dewey Theater, and so competent and
charming that loggers in the woods along the St. Croix
didn't remark that they were going to Minneapolis.
They said they were "going down to see Swede Annie."

Duluth got a share of loggers from the near-by

<hr>

[4]St. Paul's old red-light district was called "Under the Hill."

Cloquet timber, as they cut their way steadily north-ward through Minnesota. And close to the end of the white-pine era the towns of Brainerd, Bemidji, Hibbing, and International Falls flared with sudden life. The boys were now whacking away at the last of the Lake States' woods.[5]

Hibbing, perhaps, was a fair sample of the latter-day logging towns of Wisconsin and Minnesota. Located in the iron-timber region of northeastern Minnesota, in 1901 it was only eight years old, yet it had, and was proud of, sixty saloons and more than two hundred full-time harlots. It had a race track, a professional baseball team, and some rather important prize fights. Only once in its timber life[6] was Hibbing troubled by re-formers. In the summer of 1901 a local divine shamed the law into prohibiting a prize fight, which was an illegal exhibition in the county, anyway. This lack of realism was met promptly by Uncle Al Powers, big-time logging operator, who ordered a train of ninety of his logging cars made up. Better than half the town jumped aboard and were hauled into Itasca County, where the fight was held.

It was one of the last typical gestures, as far as the Lake States were concerned, of the race of men whose work in Minnesota and Wisconsin was nearly done. Michigan was already in the past. They'd have to move on. Already thousands of them had gone South, and more of them West, far West.

[5]Neither Wisconsin nor Minnesota has put up a statue in memory of the loggers. Michigan did. Through the efforts of William B. Mershon a group of statuary has been erected on the Huron National Forest.

[6]Hibbing survives as an iron-mining center.

10

Fighters, Birlers, and Such

IN THE LUMBERJACKS' trinity of entertainment, Battle undoubtedly ranked a close third to Booze and Bawds. Their fighting was crude stuff and often cruel, but there was little animosity in it. Loggers fought for the sheer delight of it and to see who was "best man." Gun play in these affairs was extremely rare; so was knifing. The gouging of eyes was rather common and ear-chewing was highly thought of. It was a man's right, when he had an opponent down, to jump upon him with both feet and puncture his hide with calked boots. This was called "putting the boots to him" and it usually left the boot-ee in bad shape.

Every river and every sawmill town in the Lake States had its local "best" fighting man, but only one such bruiser grew into an authentic legend. He was John Driscoll, the one and only Silver Jack, known everywhere in the timber from Saginaw Bay to Duluth. Born in Ontario about 1845, he was a moose of a man who was equally "able" with ax or peavey, but apparently he gave more time to brawling than logging. His nickname came from his prematurely white hair.

When he wasn't in the penitentiary at Jackson, Michigan, Silver Jack did enough fighting to make his name a byword among lumberjacks for half a century after his death. Bunkhouse historians agree on almost nothing about him except the fight he had with Joe Fournier in the Red Keg Saloon at Averill, Michigan.

The date is not known, but the time was spring. Both Silver Jack and Fournier—a gigantic French Canadian

—had spent the winter working on the long rollways of logs for which Averill was then famous. Each had fought and whipped a sizable number of men that winter, and there was much talk about what would happen when the two bullies met.

They met, as related, in Averill's Red Keg. Legend has inserted a woman—a beauteous floozy—into the story, but a woman is superfluous. When two such men as these met head-on, room to fight was all that was necessary. The mountainous Fournier opened up by leaping at Jack and seizing him by the throat. The rough plank floor of the Red Keg was said to have shook like an earthquake as the two big men went down in a heap. Fournier held his grip and soon the happy bystanders saw Jack's eyes beginning to bulge in an unnatural manner. No one, of course, thought of interfering.

Some say it was forty minutes, some an hour, that Fournier retained his hold on Jack's throat. It was all Jack could do to loosen the hold now and again and thus keep from being strangled. And every little while the Frenchman would butt Jack with his head, a head, by the way, reputed as hard as boiler plate.

Just when Jack's tongue was hanging out in fine shape, Fournier made a mistake. He put one foot on the brass rail in front of the bar. In a flash Jack drove the heel of a boot, with its long steel calks pointed as ice picks, into Fournier's foot. Fournier let out a bellow and also let go of Jack's throat. Both men got to their feet.

Now Fournier started the head-butting tactics for which he was famous. But Jack side-stepped again and again, while the big *canayen* butted into the bar, splitting the heavy oak in several places and probably making the Red Keg's proprietor groan at the expense. Finally, when Fournier was making another charge, Jack drove a solid blow into the pit of his stomach. It was all over. For some reason, Jack didn't put

the boots to his fallen foe; and soon as Jack could
get his breath he ordered drinks for everyone in the
house—with a double brandy for Fournier, according to the legend.

That, as said, is about the only thing in the Silver
Jack saga on which bunkhouse historians agree. Some
of them tell how Jack all but killed a plug-ugly named
Red Lyons, in the Pine Tree Saloon at Muskegon. He
kicked in Red's face and stepped on him so hard that
the marks remained ever after. Others tell how Jack
once felled an ox with his fist; that incident took place
variously at Grayling, at Roscommon, at Escanaba,
and at Kalamazoo. A popular story of Silver Jack has
him breaking up a show in a Saginaw dance hall and
putting on one himself, ruining the polished floor
by dancing over it in his calked boots, with his lovely
pal, Pig-Iron Jack, for partner. And there was no end
of men who saw Jack twist horseshoes with his naked
hands. There is some evidence that he acted as bouncer
at the Klondike Saloon at Hurley, Wisconsin. The tales
about him, even in 1938, are wondrous and apparently
without end. Every once in a while the Sunday feature
sections of Michigan newspapers break out with a rash
of "fact" stories in which Silver Jack is the hero.

The sober record, however, regrettably shows that
Jack could hardly have done all the great deeds attributed to him; he simply didn't have the time. The
records of the State Prison of Southern Michigan, at
Jackson, reveal coldly that John Driscoll spent 1871
in that institution. Again, on February 26, 1873, he
was sent up for five years from Saginaw County on
the unheroic charge of robbery. Discharged on May
5, 1877, he was again in the pen on July 14, 1880,
on like charges from the same county, only this time
he was sentenced to fifteen years. He was granted a
pardon by Governor Luce on October 24, 1889. When
you subtract fourteen years from the prime of a man's
life, it doesn't give him quite time enough to drive *all*

the rivers and lick all the other "able" men in three states.

Of Silver Jack's death there are many versions. One has it that he was shot and killed in the passenger coach of a train on Michigan's upper peninsula. Another, that he was drowned in the Tahquamenon River; still another that he drifted off to an unknown end in the tall firs of either Washington or Oregon.[1] What sounds more reasonable is that he died with his boots off at L'Anse, Michigan, present-day scene of Henry Ford's lumber operations. Kendrick Kimball, Detroit newspaperman, dug up the story in 1937, from T. G. Bellanger, fire chief of L'Anse.

"Silver Jack was one of some sixty loggers who were boarding at my father's hotel in L'Anse in 1895," Mr. Bellanger recalls. "His years of prison life and dissipation had begun to tell on him. In March he took sick with a cold and we called a doctor for him. He joked a lot about being ill, especially with Oliver Durocher, a simple-minded fellow who worked around the hotel. On March 31 Jack asked my mother to shout downstairs, next morning, that he, Silver Jack, was dead. Jack figured that the simple Oliver would come running to the room at the news. Then Jack would rise up and shout 'April Fool!'

"But next morning mother found Jack dead in bed and already cold. Beside the bed was a bottle of cough medicine. Beneath the rug we found a bowie knife, eighty-five dollars in bills and a note that said the money would be enough to bury him."

Somewhere in the desolate and unkempt paupers' graveyard of St. Joseph's parish, Bay City, Michigan, are at least part of the remains of Fabian Fournier. He was the same gigantic "Joe" Fournier who fought Silver Jack in the Red Keg at Averill. There is little doubt

[1] There is no tradition of Silver Jack in Oregon and Washington camps.

about where Joe died, or how. He died most beautifully at the Third Street dock in Bay City when one Blinky Robinson, bigshot underworld character, struck him quite hard over the head with a big steel mallet, driving Joe's feet, so it is told, six inches into the hard-packed sawdust.

On that day, in the summer of 1876, Bay City folk had gone on a picnic to Bay View, at the mouth of the Kawkawlin River. Fournier was along, and drunk. Wanting to show how "able" he was, he butted and tore to pieces the bandstand at the picnic park, and generally made a nuisance of himself. Whether or not these doings had any connection with Joe's death is not clear; but on return of the picnic party to Bay City by steamer, that day, Joe was met coming down the gangplank by Blinky Robinson, another mean customer, who wielded the big mallet to good effect.[2]

Blinky was tried for murder but found not guilty because of self-defense. For reasons not now clear Joe's massive skull was used as evidence at the trial. Old-timers tell that the skull was for many years a prized exhibit in the Bay City courthouse where its double-thick bone and double rows of teeth[3] were the marvel of all who saw it.

Joe Fournier, dead, soon became a legend, chiefly along the Saginaw. E. K. Hardenburg, old-time timber scaler, remembers of hearing that Joe's favorite girl was one Hattie. Hattie often had fits. In one of them she was thought to have died and she was promptly buried. Joe dug up the body and found that she had torn herself and her clothes in an effort to get out of

[2]Mrs. J. Moran of Bay City, ninety-one years old in 1937, told the author she witnessed Fournier's death. She seemed to recall that few in town mourned his passing.

[3]When in his cups, which was often, Joe is said to have liked to bite a hunk out of the top of a bar. "Dat Joe Fournier, hees mark," he would announce.

the coffin. It is a fair sample of the many legends about both Joe and Silver Jack.

As a spectacular fellow, possibly the noted T. C. Cunnion, the Peterborough Man-Eater, topped everything. Cunnion was a short man, powerfully built, estimated to have been three feet across at the shoulders. The Saginaw Valley was his pasture, and it was his joy when well oiled to stand in the center of Water Street at East Saginaw and bellow: "I am T. C. Cunnion, the Man-Eater from Peterborough, Ontario!" That was his cry, no more nor less. It was heard so often that no old-timer today speaks of "Cunnion"; it is always "T. C. Cunnion," with the full man-eating and geographical title added.

T. C. Cunnion was a dressy fellow in town. He retained his calked boots and mackinaw, but he covered his chest with a stiff boiled shirt, or a white "dickey," made of cardboard to resemble a shirt-front. It was his concession to the genteel.

When in town Cunnion liked to go into a butcher shop and get a hunk of cow's liver. Refusing to have it done up in a package, he would go out into the street, chewing at the bloody morsel. In this wise he would parade through East Saginaw, his hands, face and shirt-front smeared with blood, giving his usual cry about being the Man-Eater from Peterborough. Once when he ran smack into a shade tree on Water Street Cunnion became really angry. Shaking the hunk of liver at the tree he gave voice to the classic promise that is still revered by all students of profanity. "By th' dynamitin' ol' Mackinaw Jesus," he roared, "I'm a goin' to let daylight into this swamp!" This oath was likely as terrible a threat as man ever uttered, but it was a woman who laid the Man-Eater low.

Who this remarkable woman was is not known, but legend has it that she parked her baby in its carriage just outside a butcher shop, on Saginaw's Genesee Street. As the lady started into the shop, out popped

T. C. Cunnion, his face already covered with blood from the liver he was munching. "I am T. C. Cunnion," he began, "the Man-Eater from. . . ." The woman screamed and as she screamed she whaled Cunnion a terrific blow with her umbrella—plumb across his satanic face. The carnivore from Peterborough went down in a heap.

After such a graceless fall, Cunnion left Saginaw for good. He appears to have hung out for a time in Bay City, where he got free drinks for fighting bulldogs. He would get down on all fours and a bulldog would be set at him. Cunnion fought the dog with hands and teeth, biting and growling the while. But police put a stop to this form of saloon entertainment and the Man-Eater faded from lumberjack history.

In early days of railroading, crews of logger-passengers gave much trouble to train crews. Archie Abbott, old-time camp foreman of the Saginaw country, recalls that gangs leaving Roscommon for Bay City were especially troublesome; they had opportunity in Roscommon to get well liquored up before they started for the bigger towns. But when steam heat came into use on the trains, the crews had less trouble. They would shut every ventilator in the car, then pump steam into the pipes for all they would hold. In this way the temperature of a car could be brought to between ninety and one hundred degrees, and most of the drunks would go promptly to sleep.

Before the railroads came, loggers traveled on Great Lakes steamboats or windjammers. All camp supplies were moved that way and no little rumrunning was done by water. The leader of one crew of rumrunners was the formidable "High" Roberts who operated a saloon at Elk Rapids, Michigan. According to Herbert Hall of Grand Rapids, who has delved into the somewhat misty records of the old-time rumrunning industry, High Roberts was remarkable for his foghorn voice that could be heard above the greatest storm; and his magnificent handlebar mustaches were marveled at in a day when large mustaches were much thought of. The damned revenooers never got old High. They closed in on him once, in 1865, when he was heading up Lake Michigan with a cargo of rum for his Elk Rapids joint. His boat was so arranged, the story has it, that when hard pressed he could pull a plug from its bottom and sink her. This he did that time in 1865, and swam ashore. He struck out alone through the forest, not emerging until he came to the Saginaw River.

Tales of sunken cargoes of rum still heat the imaginations of Lake States folk. In recent years a number of attempts have been made to locate the schooner *Westmoreland,* a three-hundred-foot wood vessel that is known to have sunk off Point Betsie, on Lake Michigan, with three hundred and fifty barrels of wines and liquors. That was just before the end of navigation in 1854. Sole survivor of the wreck, it was said, was one Pelky, who marked a tree on shore. He planned to return and salvage the cargo, but never did. He was killed by the explosion of a tugboat boiler at Bay City.

About once a year loggers gave some serious attention to the only sport that has come out of the woods —the sport of logrolling, called "birling" by the jacks themselves. It looks simple. Two men get on one log, floating in pond or river, to turn it with their feet to see who can ride it the longer.

But it is far from artless. Log birling has as many fancy twists, turns, reverses, stops, and tricks as scientific boxing. It makes a difference whether the log has been peeled or is in its natural state of rough bark. A pine rolls unlike a spruce or hemlock. Fir is something else again. Cedar rides high in the water and calls for a special technique.

As in the matter of fighting, every river had its

champion log birler. The early contests were spontaneous affairs, cooked up on the spot—often by saloon-keepers—with a gallon of whisky for the winner. About the turn of the century log birling became a more formalized sport, with official, although unpublished rules, and judges and prizes. Contests were announced months in advance and usually took place on Fourth of July or Labor Day. Ashland, Wisconsin, was the scene of many notable matches.

"On Labor Day 1901 I witnessed the best log birling I have seen in fifty years of following the timber," recalls Jack Mahoney, now of Bend, Oregon. "It was claimed to be for the championship of the Lake States and was held in Ashland. Ten or twelve men, I forget which, got past the preliminaries. Then, they rolled until only Jim Oliver, Michigan's best, and Tom Stewart, of Eau Claire, Wisconsin, were left. It was up to Oliver or Stewart.

"They started in right after noon. Stewart was the taller and heavier man. Stronger, too. With his superior weight he had control of the log at all times. But roll it as he would, he never had the lighter man in danger, while a number of times Oliver nearly got Stewart trapped—making him do a back-roll. At about seven o'clock that evening, the judges ordered the men from the log. It would have to go over until next day.

"It was a great night in Ashland. Probably three thousand lumberjacks were in town and the town knew it. Big doings. Next morning at ten Stewart and Oliver went back to the log, both of them sober, for they hadn't joined in the whoopee to any extent. They birled until noon, when time was called for dinner. When the contest was resumed it was easy to see that Stewart's greater strength was going to win. He was wearing Oliver down with terrific bursts of speed that seemed to turn the log as fast as the headrig in a circular mill. At about half-past four Oliver fell exhausted from the log. He wasn't rolled into the water; he simply collapsed and fell in.

"Tom Stewart received one hundred dollars prize money and a gold medal that said he was the best man on logs in the three states."

Eau Claire was long a hangout of noted birlers, among them being Tom Macaroon, Jack Fleming, Tom Murray, and the Thompson brothers, Abe and Thomas. Incidentally, the Tom Stewart who won the long contest at Ashland was later defeated by Bill Delyea, a Cloquet, Minnesota, boy who followed the timber West and won many contests in Idaho, Oregon, and Washington.[4]

The St. Croix River, which is a part of the Wisconsin-Minnesota boundary, produced many birlers of championship rank and some of the best peavey men on earth. The notorious Angle Rock in the St. Croix gave them plenty of chance for practice. One of the biggest log jams ever known occurred at Angle Rock in June of 1886. More than one hundred and fifty million feet of pine logs were piled in a mass that ran back miles from the rock. Thousands of people came out from St. Paul and Minneapolis to see it. Breaking it took seven weeks and required a crew of two hundred men, more than a hundred horses, two donkey engines and two steamboats.

There are legends of bigger jams than that of '86 on the St. Croix, but the authorities are vague, and most bunkhouse historians admit that Angle Rock probably caused as much hard peaveywork as any pile of stone known to the boys on their way from coast to coast.

[4]In 1938 Bill Delyea, still an able man on a log, lived in Coeur d'Alene, Idaho.

11

Ballads of the Woods

WHEN LOGGERS WERE NOT LOGGING or drinking rum and abetting harlotry, they sometimes lifted their voices in song. That the song was seldom sweet was of no matter. What a logger wanted of a song was that it told a story—the sadder the story, the better the song.

Lumberjacks probably did more singing in the Lake States than they did in Maine. More blown-in-the-bottle logger ballads seem to stem from Michigan and Wisconsin than elsewhere. By the time the main army of loggers reached the Far West, they had taken to bellowing so-called popular songs; only a stray old-timer could recall the words to the famous shanty-boy ballads.

Most of the authentic logger songs are dreary stuff. Practically all of them were sung to the same tune[1] and the tune was anything the singer happened to think of—a weaving up-and-down drone, interminable and, for the most part, lifeless. A few called for chorus work. Singers were of two principal schools—wailers and bullroarers. Only two of their songs appear to have been sung, equally bad, in Maine, the Lake States and on the Pacific Coast, thus following the timber line.

Whoever wrote "The Jam on Garry's Rock" is not known, but whoever he was he knew exactly what

[1]Dr. E. C. Beck, of Mount Pleasant, Michigan, who has been collecting logger ballads for many years, taking down words and music direct from the rendition of old-time jacks, has been forced to the same conclusion as the author, i.e., that all the songs were sung to the same basic music, or lack of it.

loggers wanted in the way of a song. "The Jam" is purest lumberjack. It has *everything:* bad rhyming, or none at all; a meter that calls for plenty of grace notes; place names that can be changed to suit the occasion if not the meter; and an ungodly maudlin "story." There are as many versions of it as there are species of trees in the forest. The following version was sung on the Androscoggin and Connecticut rivers some fifty years ago:

Come, all ye brave shanty-boys,
wherever ye may be;
I would have you pay attention and
listen unto me.
For it concerns a shanty-boy so
noble, true and brave,
Who broke the jam on Garry's Rock
and met with a watery grave.

It was on a Sunday morning as
you shall quickly hear,
The logs were piling mountain high,
we could not keep them clear.
Cheer up, cheer up! brave hearted youths,
Relieve your hearts of fear.
We'll break the jam on Garry's Rock
and to Saginaw we will steer.

Now some of them were willing, while
others they were not.
To work a jam on Sunday they did
not think they ought;
'Til six of our Canadian boys did
volunteer to go
And break the jam on Garry's Rock
with their foreman, young Monroe.

They had not picked off many logs
when the boss to them did say:
"I would have you be on your guard,
for the jam will soon give way."
His lips to this short warning scarce
gave vent when the jam did go,
And carried away the six brave Canadian
youths and the foreman, young Monroe.

Now when the boys up at the camp
the news they came to hear,
In search of their dead bodies to the
river they did steer.
And they found to their surprise, their
sorrow, grief and woe,
All bruised and mangled on the beach lay
the corpse of young Monroe.

They picked him up most tenderly, smoothed
down his raven hair.
There was one among the watchers whose cries
did rend the air.
This fair one most distracted was
a girl from Saginaw town,
And her wails and cries did reach the skies
for her true love who was drowned.[2]

The Missus Clark, a widow, lived by
the riverside.
This was her only daughter (and
Jack's intended bride)[3]

[2]Due to the near-rhyme, this was probably the only time that
a logger approximated the correct pronunciation of *drowned*.

[3]In other versions the "girl from Saginaw town" is variously
named as "Clara Vernon," "Clara Burnham," and "Clara
Dennison."

So the wages of her own true love,
the boss to her did pay,
And a liberal subscription was made up,
by the shanty-boys next day.

When she received the money, she thanked
them, every one,
Though it was not her portion to
live for very long;
And it was just six weeks or more,
when she was called to go,
And her last request was to be laid
at rest, by the side of young Monroe.

They buried him most decently ('twas on
the Fourth of May)
Come one and all, ye shanty-boys,
and for a comrade pray.
Engraven on a hemlock tree which
by the beach did grow
Was the name and date of this sad
fate of the foreman, John Monroe.

No one can say where a Garry's Rock first reared
its ugly head to cause log jams and lay handsome
young river bosses low. Kennebec loggers claim there
used to be a rock above Forks, Maine, that bore the
name, and point out that "Augusta" would fit the song
as well as "Saginaw." But this smells of plain heresy.
In *any* logger song "Constantinople" would fit exactly
as well as "Saginaw," and so would "Cleveland" or
even "Troy."

Ontario loggers say there is a Garion's Rock in one
of their rivers. Aging men of Saginaw and Bay City
will take you a piece up the Tittabawassee River and

point out "Garry's Rock," near the city of Midland.
And any day, now that loggers are getting into books
and movies, one may expect a "Garry's Rock" to pop
up in the center of the Columbia River, near the new
sawmill metropolis of Longview, Washington.

There would appear to be less doubt concerning
the geography of the one other logger ballad that is
known from coast to coast. "The Redlight Saloon" is
the song and the setting was undoubtedly inspired by
John Williams' place of that name in Muskegon; and
that city's name is prominent in nearly all versions,
an exception being the introduction of "Miss Hegan's,"
in place of "Muskegon," in a rendering sung in New
England.

None of the several large collections of lumberjack
or shanty-boy songs has paid the least attention to this
fine and realistic old ballad which is at least as old
as "The Jam" and probably older, and has the geniune
McCoy ring to it:

I arrived in Muskegon the Tenth of July
To make my connection with a train I did try;
Got left in Muskegon and this was my doom;
To pay a short visit to The Redlight Saloon.

I boldly walked in, I stepped up to the bar;
And a dashing young beauty says, "Have a cigar."
I took my cigar, I sat down on a chair,
And this beauty came skipping and tripping
    'round there.

She boldly walked up and sat down on my knee,
And says: "You're a pines-man as well I can see."
She says: "You're a logger right well do I know,
For your muscle is hard from your head to your toe."

The libretto now gets into its full stride—too full for quotation here—and continues to its logical ending, with a rousing final verse extolling Muskegon, the saloon itself, and the charmers in the upstairs department.[4]

A consideration of lumberjack doggerel, either as poetry or music, would of course be absurd. But the songs are useful. Their subjects reveal what lumberjacks thought about, and these subjects had often to do with rum, "love," great deeds on the river drive, and death in all its forms.

In early Maine loggers liked to chant, to the old hymn, "O Happy Day," an endless piece of doggerel that began:

> Who gives us pay
> for one big drunk
> When we hit Bangor
> Slam kerplunk?—
> John Ross and Cyrus Hewes.[5]

This goes on and on, fetching up in pure bawdry, each verse closing with the two big bosses' names. Another song in which John Ross figured was referred to in an earlier chapter and told how Ross was a man so hungry for logs that he wouldn't let one of his slaves take time off to consummate his marriage.

What occupied loggers' minds in the 1850s is made clear by the strophes of "Drink Round, Brave Boys." It begins:

[4]Some unknown cynic, doubtless a man of experience, added a verse or two that makes the whole ballad a moral one. The additional verses concern the singer's dilemma, after leaving Muskegon, and his subsequent return to visit a doctor.

[5]Well-known Penobscot lumbermen of the time.

> 'Tis when we do get into the woods,
> Drink round, brave boys;
> Drink round, brave boys

and continues on, telling of the choppers' work, the swampers, the teamsters, and traces the log from stump to sawmill, each verse closing with an invitation to drink more liquor.

Or, consider "The Lumbermen's Life," a pre-Civil War ditty:

> Transported we are, from the pretty maidens fair,
> To the banks of the Black River Stream;
> Where the wolves and the owls, with their terrifying
>   howls,
> Disturb our nightly dreams.

Neither owls nor wolves disturbed a lumberjack's sleep, and it wouldn't require a psychoanalyst to uncover "subconscious desire" in that song.

Then, there was "Jack Haggerty" and "The Flat River Girl." The Flat River of the song rises around Six Lakes, Michigan, and empties into Grand River. The "Greenville" mentioned was once a great logging center. Old loggers there tell that a strapping big logger, by name of McGinnis, wandered into camp one day. He was drunk and maudlin; his boss had just promoted one Hannah Tucker's lover to be foreman. So McGinnis composed a song about his troubles and what he was going to do about them. How "Jack Haggerty," instead of McGinnis, got into the song is just another of the many mysteries of lumberjack history. He may have been a dirty plagiarist. Anyway, this is "Jack Haggerty" singing:

I'm a broken-hearted raftsman, from Greenville I
    came;
I courted a lassie, a girl of great fame.
But cruel-hearted cupid has caused me much grief;
My heart it's asunder, I can ne'er find relief.

My troubles I'll tell you without more delay;
A comely young lassie my heart stole away.
She was a blacksmith's only daughter from Flat
    River side,
And I always intended for to make her my bride.

I brought her rich jewels and the finest of lace,
And the costliest of muslins it was her I'd embrace.
I gave her my wages for her to keep safe;
I begrudged her nothing that I had myself.

My name is Jack Haggerty where the white waters
    flow;
My name it's engraved on the rocks of the shore;
I'm a boy that stands happy on a log in the streams,
My heart was with Hannah, for she haunted my
    dreams.

I went up the river some money to make;
I was steadfast and steady, I ne'er played the rake.
Through Hart and through Shelby I am very well
    known;
They call me Jack Haggerty, the pride of the town.

One day on the river a letter I received,
That it was from her promises herself she'd relieved;

She'd be wed to a young man who a long time delayed,
And the next time I'd see her she would not be a maid.

Then adieu to Flat River; for me there's no rest.
I'll shoulder my peavey and I'll go out West.
I'll go to Muskegon some pleasures to find,
And I'll leave my own Flat River darling behind.

So come all you jolly raftsmen with hearts stout
     and true,
Don't depend on a woman; you're sunk if you do.
And if you chance to meet one with dark chestnut
     curls,
Just think of Jack Haggerty and his Flat River girls.

But perhaps the ultimate in bathos is found in "Peter
Amberly," or "Peter Emily." All over the backwoods
of New England, but not farther West, one will find
ancients who tell of knowing, or of knowing someone
who knew, the Peter Amberly of the song. They will
relate how Pete "received his deathly wound" while
loading a sled with logs, and how—true as gospel,
mister—Pete composed the seventy-two-line song *while*
he was bleeding to death, thus proving that loggers
die hard. The opening verse will give an idea of this
exquisite ballad:

My name is Peter Amberly, as you might understand;
I was born on Prince Edward Island, close by the
     ocean strand.
In Eighteen Hundred Eighty-Two, when the flowers
     were in bloom,
I left my native country, my fortune to presume.

The thing continues, relating how Pete was driven from home by a beastly father; how Pete came to Maine to work in the woods; and how—right *now,* remember—Pete had received his "deathly wound," which of course rhymed with "sound." To one who has had to hear the song only too often, Peter didn't die soon enough, nor early enough in life, and his death should have been much more horrible than it was.

Another long-winded affair one is likely to hear, if not acutely careful, concerns "The Drowning of John Roberts." After some eighteen or twenty verses John gets the works:

> We think he got his fatal blow
> While struggling in the undertow,
> By some large rock beneath the wave
> When he soon found a watery grave.

Watery graves were always popular in lumberjack song and so were forest fires. Possibly the worst of the lot is titled "The Burning of John Robinson's Camp in 1873." Robinson was a Penobscot lumberman who lived in Brewer. The camp that took sixteen long verses in the burning was located on Ripogenus Stream, the outlet of Harrington Lake in Maine.

Of a different stripe was "The Little Brown Bulls." This had some swagger to it and was popular with singers of the bullroarer type:

> Not a thing on the river McClusky did fear
> As he swung his goad-stick o'er the big speckled
>   steers;
> They were long, fat and thick, girt eight foot and
>   three—
> "Ha, ha!" says McClusky, "the laddies for me."

The song concerns a skidding contest between two crews and how the Little Brown Bulls won over the Big Speckled Steers. It is thought to have emerged from the Wisconsin woods sometime in the seventies.

Also of a lively nature was the "Canaday I O song." This told of an employment agent who dressed and acted the part of a kindly parson in order to get a crew of Yankee loggers to ship to a lousy, haywire camp up in Canada. The *I O* was to fill the meter and take care of any rhymes that might come up. The ballad relates the terrible conditions faced by the imported loggers:

> To describe what we have suffered
> Is past the art of man,
> But to give a fair description
> I will do the best I can.
> Our food the dogs would snarl at;
> Our beds were in the snow;
> We suffered worse than murderers—
> Up in Canaday I O.

Veterans who worked in the woods of Ontario and Quebec in the sixties and seventies reported that the song did not in the least exaggerate conditions. Yet, possibly it was not in "Canaday" at all. M. T. (Mike) Dunten, now of Olympia, Washington, one of the most deadly accurate observers of lumberjacks in this country, recalls of being kept awake by a wholly different —geographically—version of the above song:

> Our logs were piled up mountain-high;
> Our cots were on the snow,
> In that God-forsaken country
> Of Michigan I O.

In only one ballad did religion play a part. It was a Michigan song and tells in sixteen verses of characteristic methods applied to a Freethinker by a good Christian logger. The agnostic of the piece was "Robert Waite" and defender of the faith was no less than the notorious Silver Jack Driscoll, who actually spent most of his mature life in the Michigan pen. When "Waite," during the bunkhouse conversation, remarked that in his opinion the Bible was humbug and hell a fake, Silver Jack took a swing at him. The fight, so the song reports, lasted forty minutes, during which Fundamentalist Jack spat out "a tooth or two" and Heretic Bob lost an ear. Then

> Jack he got Bob under
> And he slugged him onct or twict;
> And Bob confessed almighty quick
> The divinity of Christ.
> So the fierce discussion ended
> And they rose up from the ground;
> Someone brought a bottle out
> And kindly passed it round.
> And they drank to Jack's religion
> In a quiet sort of way,
> And the spread of infidelity
> Was checked in camp that day.

This song was known both as "Jack The Evangelist" and "Religion in Camp." One wonders if it were the serious production of a red-hot Christian, or the sly work of an ironic Unbeliever.

The French Canadian loggers brought their own songs with them. They still sing on occasion, yet not so much as formerly. As for the English-speaking logger, his voice was all but stilled when the radio

2

HOLY OLD MACKINAW

came. Today's loggers on the Pacific Coast have forgotten or never knew the real lumberjack ballads. When they sing at all they are likely to croon the latest love-moon song of the radio tenors.

12

Death in Hinckley

HARD WORK, AND RUM, women, and what they called "song" wasn't all that occupied lumberjacks of the Lake States. Sometimes they had forest fire. It struck worst, perhaps, in 1871. On the dim morning of October 8, that year, one John Mulligan, ex-pugilist who was a logging camp foreman for I. Stephenson & Company, rode a singed and bedraggled horse into the small town of Menominee, Michigan. "The whole town of Peshtigo has been wiped out," he said. "Not a soul remains."

Mulligan didn't exaggerate much. The booming young lumber city of Peshtigo, in near-by Wisconsin, *had* been wiped out by forest fire that swept in so quickly from the surrounding timber that eleven hundred persons were cremated.

Relief was rushed from near-by towns for distribution at Menominee, and a scene remained long in the eyes of a lumberjack. He saw smoke so thick over Lake Michigan's Green Bay that two men were posted on the dock at Menominee, lifting and dropping heavy planks to serve as a signal of port to smoke-bound relief steamers.

Rescue crews found little to do, for the fire had been thorough. They did find old John Leach, logger-settler, sitting disconsolately on a warm rock, smoking his pipe. Inside twenty-four hours he had buried eleven children and grandchildren. John Leach was a sample survivor.

As a relief party moved over the hot and smoking

ground, Isaac Stephenson marveled to see to what small compass the bodies of big lumberjacks could be brought by the heat of a million pine trees burning. "Nothing remained," he recalled, "other than a mere streak of ashes that would scarce fill a thimble."

Yet the Peshtigo holocaust received little attention. The great city of Chicago, down at the other end of the lake, was being consumed by fire at almost the same time. Americans like their disasters to be big, and the magnitude of Chicago's fire shadowed the horror in the Wisconsin backwoods. Reporters flocked to Chicago to make Mrs. O'Leary's cow famous and they missed a true reporters' incident near Peshtigo when, six days after the flames had burned themselves out, a body crashed heavily to the ground from high in a tree. It was that of a young camp foreman, much sought since the fire, who had either forgotten his woods lore or preferred death on a pyre to death on the ground. The body was the last of the Peshtigo victims.

Today, in 1938, not a hundredth part of Wisconsin's citizenry ever heard of the Peshtigo fire. Old lumberjacks know of it, however, for bunkhouse historians have passed it down to classes around barrel stoves. They tell that the Peshtigo fire bred a thousand moose birds overnight.[1]

It was a bit different, later at Hinckley. No Chicago fire got in the way.

There was little of dawn about the morning of September 1, 1894, in the woods of Eastern Minnesota. The clock in the sawmill and logging office of the Brennan Lumber Company at Hinckley indicated the time

[1]Ancient logging myth, dating from early days in Maine, had it that dead lumberjacks are promptly reincarnated as moose birds, also called "camp robbers." This species is of the Jay family, both Canada and Rocky Mountain.

to be eight o'clock. But nothing else did; it was all sort of graylike, neither day nor night.

It had been that way around Hinckley for a week. If the sun came out at all, it was a mere circle of sullen red, to be hidden long before noon as a smoky slate-colored haze slowly settled over everything. Occasionally, when the wind had been from the south, stray flecks of burned-out embers floated into town. When picked up and pinched between the fingers they were like black and white powder—ashes.

Those few Hinckley folk who had been through the great Peshtigo fire of twenty-three years before were nervous. They knew the signs. The grizzled old log scaler at the Brennan mill allowed the sky was as dirty a sky as he ever seen in forty year. But Hinckley seemed too big a town to be worried about. It had a population of twelve hundred, an Oddfellows hall, a fire department, three churches, five hotels and saloons, eight stores, a restaurant, two railroad stations, and a roundhouse, besides the big sawmill that cut two hundred thousand feet of lumber every day. Both railroads ran north to Duluth, and southwest to St. Paul or Minneapolis.

On the morning of September 1, things took a new turn. The pall of gray seemed to lift for a few moments, and everything appeared as though in a ghastly light of pale yellow that seemed not to be any doing of the sun. Human beings and objects looked unreal. The strange light passed and again the gray sifted down, deeper and darker this time. When the mill-office clock pointed to noon, the bookkeeper had a light burning to see his figures; falling ash dried his ink.

Even the kids in town were uneasy, for the bushes around the swimming hole sounded that uneven and ominous rustle that bushes give out before a thunderstorm; they didn't seem to move, just rustled. Town dogs ceased to bark. Not a crow, not a bird was seen or heard that morning.

Shortly after noon a stiff wind blew up from the south, and on the wind were riding coals that burned and smoldered where they fell in a street that was more sawdust than dirt. And soon a cloud as big and as dark as night appeared over the timber line, and the Hinckley station agent of the St. Paul & Duluth said he just had word that Pokegama,[2] nine miles south on the line, had been totally destroyed by forest fire and most of its inhabitants burned to death.

Now the volunteer fire department was called to the edge of Hinckley village where half a dozen fires had sprung to life at once. It wasn't long before Father Lawler, the village priest, came running through town shouting for all to flee for their lives.

And then, in a seeming instant, hell itself roared into Hinckley, riding the back of a rising hurricane.

There was no time to save anything. Mothers snatched babies out of sugar-barrel cradles and fled. The volunteer firemen now numbered hundreds but they quickly saw they could do nothing with *this* fire. They fled, too.

Many folks ran to the Eastern Minnesota Railroad siding where stood a passenger and a freight train, preparatory to passing. The trains were hastily joined, with Ed Barry and William Best at the throttles of the two locomotives.

Men, women, and children ran screaming for the train. Best and Barry held it until four hundred and seventy-five persons were packed into the coaches and paint on the car sides was bubbling into big blisters. Then they pulled her open.

As the train steamed out of town Engineer Best watched Hinckley burn for a moment he never forgot. He saw men and horses stagger in the street, then go down to stay. Fire leaped at the sides of houses and

[2]Now Brook Park, Minnesota.

burned them so quickly that Best saw bedroom sets plainly outlined against the flames.

The train ran north to Sandstone, ten miles from Hinckley, and stopped a moment, while passengers shouted to Sandstone folk, warning them that hell was in the rear and traveling fast. Just as the train pulled off the smoking Kettle River bridge at Sandstone, the structure gave way. And fifteen or twenty minutes later fire belched out of the timber and swept the village, burning forty-five persons and everything else. . . . Forest fire does things like that. But the train was out of danger.

Back in blazing Hinckley Death was hunting out the remaining citizens. Ninety of them took refuge in a cleared space along the Eastern Minnesota Railroad, and there they burned to black crisps or gray-white ashes, every last one of them. More than a hundred others were saved when they got into the shallow water of a gravel pit not far from where the ninety were burned. A few others splashed into the water of a creek on the northern edge of Hinckley, where some lived it out and some were swept away to drown.

Heading up the tracks of the St. Paul & Duluth Railroad, fire caught and stopped thirty-three of a party of some two hundred refugees before they met a south-bound passenger train. The train was Number Four, on its way from Duluth to St. Paul. . . . It wouldn't get to St. Paul.

Jim Root, who had run a locomotive for General Sherman in Georgia, was in Number Four's cab. When he saw men and women running up the track toward his train he stopped it and got out of the cab.

White-faced kids were helped aboard by women whose hair smelled of singeing and by men who had blistered hands but no eyebrows at all.

Engineer Root knew from what Hinckley folks told him that he could not run any farther south. He knew that the nearest water was a swamp hole known as

Skunk Lake, six miles north, or back. He climbed into his cab and reversed the lever.

Root looked out the cab window toward Hinckley and saw a cloud of smoke or dust, he couldn't tell which. Just as he opened the throttle there came a terrific explosion, somewhere outside. It shattered a cab window and the flying glass made deep cuts in Root's neck and forehead. He had to keep wiping the blood out of his eyes. By the time the train got under way flames were racing along both sides of the tracks; the ties were blazing and so were parts of the moving coaches. Root could see that the far end of his train was afire.

About a mile and a half out of Hinckley, at the top of a grade, Root heard shouting. Three men were running toward the train, fire at their heels and fire ahead of them. Root shut off the power and started to apply the air brakes. But he thought better of it; a stop would be fatal. He cut her open again. Two of the men caught onto the pilot, one to ride a few yards and fall into the flames that now walled in the train on both sides.

Ahead in the train John Blair, colored porter in the chair car, was performing like a hero. A young woman, Mrs. Frank Spriggs,[3] remembers it well.

"Our car was afire from end to end," she recalls. "Paint was running down the walls, inside. The lamps were lighted when we left Hinckley, but they were smashed and blown out by several loud explosions which also broke almost every window of the coach. The bits of glass scattered. Many of us were cut and bleeding. The Negro porter was the steadiest man of the lot. He stood calmly by the water cooler, passing out cups of water until it was all gone. He talked to children and adults in a soothing manner; even joked. He acted as if it was all a summer excursion train. Indeed, he was a hero."

[3]Living in St. Paul, Minnesota, in 1937.

Back in the cab James Root wasn't doing so well. The heat was something men don't often live through. Root fainted with his hand on the throttle. When he came to, he saw he had only ninety-five pounds of steam, and the train was moving very slowly. He thought he had instinctively started to shut the throttle when he fainted; it was half closed.

The day was darker than any night Root had ever seen, but a different kind of dark, streaked with fire that gave you no light to see by. Root couldn't tell just where he was, but he didn't think he was at Skunk Lake yet. He pulled her wide open.

The fireman had taken refuge in the engine's water tank. He came out and threw water on Root, which made Root feel better. The engineer's hands were all puffed up. They felt odd, but he didn't dare to rub them for fear the skin would come off. The fireman was in no better shape.

The very coal in the locomotive's tender was burning when Number Four clanked slowly across Skunk Lake bridge. Root shut off the steam. This was the "lake," what there was of it; they could see the muddy water, red enough in the glare.

Grabbing a pail in the cab the fireman got down. He threw water on the flaming coach doors and steps so the passengers could get out. Engineer Root was down and out, on his cab floor.

The entire train broke into fire almost the moment it stopped, and passengers dismounted and looked for a spot where they could live. Mrs. Frank Spriggs had her six-weeks-old baby in her arms. "Throw that kid away," a "big grain man of Duluth" shouted at her. "You can't save it and yourself."

Many tumbled into the water mud of Skunk Lake. Mrs. Spriggs with her child and some other people—she thinks about five or six—made for a large potato patch near the lake. Fire seemed to be everywhere. As Mrs. Spriggs stumbled over the hot ground she saw a tall man running. He was carrying a woman in his arms, and her long hair streamed out behind in a mass of flame. . . . Mrs. Spriggs has often wondered who they were and if the woman with the flaming hair survived.

Engineer Root lived. So did some three hundred others who came to Skunk Lake. But the fire had taken a terrible toll. It had caught loggers in camp and burned them to death, ax in hand, in one savage moment. And it had destroyed the towns of Hinckley, Sandstone, Mission Creek, Pokegama, and Partridge.

When relief trains came next day, the workers heaped the dead in long windrows and buried them. A list of the dead wasn't completed until October 17, more than six weeks after the fire. On that day the body of Fred Molander was found deep in a well on his farm. It was number four hundred and thirteen.[4]

One more big fire bedeviled the last of the Minnesota forests and lumberjacks. On October 12, 1918, it swept into the sawmill city of Cloquet, took seven lives, and destroyed the homes, business houses, and sawmills of twelve thousand people. At the same time scattered fires in the last timbered country around Cloquet took a death toll of between three and four hundred lives. The entire affair made scarcely an item in the national press. Doings on the Western Front in Europe were filling the columns and running over.

There were plenty of heroes in Peshtigo, in Hinckley, and in Cloquet, but only Jim Root at the blistering hot throttle of Number Four stands out in the loggers' folklore of those fires. And Root will do. He drove his train out of the woods into a part of the Big Clearing.

[4] A monument to the victims has been erected two miles east of Hinckley.

13

The Big Jump; Second Migration

BY THE TURN OF THE CENTURY a good deal of daylight had been let into the swamp of the Lake States, and it wasn't until then that the mass of loggers began to realize they were indeed cutting the Big Clearing —possibly from coast to coast. Before that, 'way back in the thirties, Maine loggers said the Penobscot timber would last until hell froze one foot thick; they never thought they would be leaving Maine.

Half a century later, as they moved on again, this time from Michigan into Wisconsin and Minnesota, they figured it would take a hundred years to clean up the last of the Lake States. And then—quite suddenly, it seemed—in 1905, they got a shock. Dull but accurate statistics of the federal government reported that the remote State of Washington had crashed overnight into lumber supremacy with a production of four billion feet, or almost as much as Wisconsin and Minnesota put together.

If that didn't tell the boys in the Lake States that their great days there were over, they had only to look to the South. Down there along the bayous, so the government reported, Louisiana sawmills were cutting almost as much as those in Wisconsin. A year later they topped Wisconsin's cut.

Yes, sir, and by the Holy Old Mackinaw, the boys woulda hafto be moving on. Peering out from behind a billion stumps their startled eyes saw smoke coming from stacks that didn't burn slab or sawdust. Bad sign, that. And St. Anthony's Falls at Minneapolis

145

were grinding more wheat and cutting fewer boards. Wealthy summer visitors were invading the lumberjacks' old haunts and building cottages—folks who fished with silly poles bought in stores and when they went hunting were as likely to shoot a logger as a deer. The descendants of squaws that early loggers had married in order to get a crack at reservation timber were getting lighter every year, some of them showing up with blue eyes and curly red hair.

Even the whisky seemed to be getting weaker, and when a logger did get a skinful of it, the new type of city slickers took to locking him up in jail. Lots of places put up signs saying "Calked Boots Not Allowed Here." And the first faint sickening whiffs of gasoline mingled with and degraded the pure scent of the pineries; utter confusion lay just ahead. . . . The more restless and untamed of the loggers packed up their turkeys again and moved on.

In time, perhaps a quarter of the migrating lumberjacks moved to the Southern States, where they found a kind of pine new to them. The main army moved West.

To a logger "West" meant mostly the great forests of the Pacific Northwest and Coast which he knew about rather vaguely. Maybe he had heard a stray, wide-ranging lumberjack tell of something called Douglas fir that grew to be twelve feet through at the butt and ran three hundred and more feet straight up into the clouds; or of Western pines bigger and taller than ever grew in Maine or Michigan; or of monstrous trunks of redwood whose size passed all belief.

But if he heard of these things at all, the Lake States logger put them aside as the usual tall story that seemed to ooze out of any traveler whose eyes had viewed the Pacific. When he *saw* a single tree that would scale three hundred thousand feet, log rule, he'd believe it.

The vanguards of the Second Migration from the Lake States rolled over the plains and the Rockies in Mr. Pullman's elegant Palace Cars pulled by big-stacked locomotives that burned wood. They were the Timber Barons and their land-lookers or cruisers. Some of the barons were close friends to the Railroad Kings, and the kings had large empires of timber to dispose of. That was in the eighties and nineties.

The barons took one brief look at the huge timber stand shown in the reports of their cruisers and bought timberland, great, large, wide, long hunks of it, all the way from San Francisco Bay to the Canadian Line and as far inland as it grew into Montana. They had to pay more for it than they had in Michigan, but then, an acre here held more timber; and six dollars an acre wasn't too much to pay. Douglas fir grew so thick and so tall that they didn't think they could lose much money on stuff at that price. They couldn't.

The nineties saw the Second Migration getting well under way. By 1900 the movement West was as marked as the Covered Wagon era had been.

In their wake the boys left camps and sawmills where they stood. They deserted entire villages, not even bothering to pull down the blinds or take down the stovepipes. Officials of formerly well-timbered and well-taxed counties were aghast to find nothing left to eat in the public trough.

Most of all, the loggers left stumps in their wake. And why not? That had been their job—to make stumps out of forests so that John Farmer, as lumberjacks somewhat disdainfully termed husbandmen, could get on with his work. No one had objected to stumps; both state and federal governments had done everything they could to get the timber cut as quickly as possible.

Now and again some crazy fanatic had raised his voice about a need for "conservation," or something like that; but the voice was weak and it wasn't a chorus until well into the twentieth century. Loggers were still useful pioneers, the very spearhead of Empire and Manifest Destiny.

So, the pack of them left the Saginaw, the Wisconsin, and the Mississippi behind and started in full cry for the Pacific shore. It is easy to trace the general pattern of their migration.[1] The Walkers of the Minnesota pines went to the sugar pines of California. The Fordneys, who had logged in Maine before they came to Saginaw, bought timber on Grays Harbor in Washington and moved their lumberjacks there. The Merrills had logged Maine, Michigan, and Wisconsin, and now, with the Rings, they left for Puget Sound. The Hollands and Wentworths of Saginaw and Bay City appeared on the Columbia River at Portland.

The Whitneys of Detroit and the Blodgetts of Grand Rapids bought heavily all over California, Oregon, and Washington. Fred Herrick of Michigan, a one-man migration by himself, struck out for Idaho. The Wheelers of Michigan, out of Pennsylvania, picked western Oregon and Washington. The Collins and Du Bois families of Penn's Woods settled again in timber, this time near the Columbia.

The eminent team of C. A. Smith and Uncle Al Powers, famous throughout Minnesota, moved to Oregon's Coos Bay—axes, peavies, a ton of Scandinavian snuff, and an able crew of men, including the noted André Gagnon, a true genius of sawmill mechanics.

The Ayres of the Penobscot moved to Oregon, and so did the Clarks and Wilsons from Michigan's upper peninsula. The Stouts of Wisconsin went to southern Oregon. Knapps of Saginaw moved to Portland. And late in the movement the Brooks-Scanlon and Shevlin-

---

[1]A few names only, of boss lumbermen, are chosen here to indicate the pattern of the migration. A list of former Lake States firms, now in practice in California and the Pacific Northwest, would be imposing.

Hixon moguls of Minnesota migrated to the pines of central Oregon, taking two thousand lumberjacks with them and building in Bend a lumber city that, except for Sin, compares favorably with Saginaw in its prime.

Early but not earliest among the migrants was Frederick Weyerhaeuser of St. Paul, and by the time the migration had been completed his barony was the mightiest of them all. It deserves a passing mention, as does Weyerhaeuser himself.

Frederick Weyerhaeuser was born in Germany in 1834 and died in St. Paul in 1914. He came from the Old Country to Rock Island, Illinois, in 1856 and went to work in a sawmill. He started a small contract business, building houses, district schools, anything that needed doing, taking in pay corn, potatoes, and other produce that he could barter. He went up the Mississippi, then up the Chippewa River of Wisconsin, where he did some logging. But no booze, bawds, and battle for young Weyerhaeuser. He was shy and quiet, both in personal and in business dealings, but he was always acting—and thinking.

The Chippewa River of the sixties was a battleground. The lumbermen there, as elsewhere and at all times, were ripsnorting individualists. They fought each other for timber; they fought each other to see who should have first call on the river for driving purposes. Actual violence in which gun play had a part was a common and sometimes a bloody occurrence.

The young German thought this wasteful and wholly foolish. He was soon a prime spirit in forming the Chippewa Booming Company, chartered in 1870, to collect logs coming down the river and distribute them to the proper mills. This worked well, and in a few years Weyerhaeuser was active in forming the Chippewa Logging Company, another mutual concern, which took charge of *all* logging operations along the river, from stump to sawmill.

Of the first Weyerhaeuser it was said that he would buy timber anywhere, but would sell none. It was true. Yet he was no lone wolf, for he liked to have partners; and he and they bought timber throughout Wisconsin and Minnesota and they made it into boards. And then, with the end of the Lake States timber in sight—for those who could see well—Weyerhaeuser came West with his friend James J. Hill, the railroad king.

The Western timber looked fair enough to Weyerhaeuser. He immediately bought nine hundred thousand acres of it, which was a sizable hunk in itself. But hardly enough. He continued to buy until the total timber holdings of his company reached two million acres, in Oregon, Washington, and Idaho alone.

Migration of the Weyerhaeuser lumberjacks did not begin with the purchase of timber. They started West around 1900 and continued for three decades in a steady stream, as sawmills were erected all over Idaho, Oregon, and Washington to handle the Weyerhaeuser round-stuff.

Not all Timber Barons followed the classic pattern in their migrations. The Popes and Talbots of East Machias, Maine, did not stop in the Lake States. Before the Civil War they built their own rugged vessels in East Machias, loaded them down with men, axes, and saws, and sailed around the Horn to the West Coast.

Also notable was A. B. Hammond. Originally from Quebec, Hammond stopped in Montana long enough to make railroad ties and considerable money, then went on to California and Oregon to buy heavily in timber, build railroads, and create a Hammond barony of lumber and shipping.

Another Quebec timber baron, of only slightly lesser magnitude than Hammond, was Sol Simpson, who settled on Puget Sound and became the admitted king of Washington loggers. Right on his heels were the Polson brothers, Alex and Robert, of Nova Scotia, to lay the

famous "Polson Line" of rails and logging camps in
western Washington.

But in the main, the men who logged, and with their
sons are still logging, the Idaho and West Coast timber
came from the Lake States, just as the fathers of many
of them had moved from Maine to the Lakes.

Along with them they brought some of the cherished
old town names that had spelled sawdust for generations. To California and Washington they brought "Bangors," and a "Saginaw" and a "Portland" to Oregon.
An early sawmill town of Washington was "Machias,"
named for the one in Maine. And transplanted loggers
could always find a "Saginaw Rooms" or a "Bangor
House" in most of the new Western lumber cities.

With them the lumberjacks brought their peaveys
and continued to call them that. They brought "Bangor
Snubbers" to use on the Idaho hills. They brought the
term *wangan* to use on the drive. Their songs were
largely left behind, for they had learned about A Straw-
berry Blond and A Hot Time and The Shade of an
Old Apple Tree from Mr. Edison's talking and singing
phonograph. The earlier migrants brought Peerless and
Spearhead to chew upon, the later their damp snuff in
round boxes. It was said you could trail the loggers
from the Penobscot to the Mississippi by the tobacco
tags they threw away; and from the Mississippi to the
West shore by the empty snuffboxes.

Not only was the peavey tool in the Second Migration; a member of that famous Maine family went
along to follow the timber line into the sunset. He was
Gary B. Peavey, born on the Penobscot and as staunch
and rugged as any steel cant dog. He cut pine in Maine,
stopped a bit in Pennsylvania, then went on to Minnesota where he cut many logs and took the first drive
out of Mille Lacs and down the Rum River to Anoka.
During the Indian troubles the redskins once killed all
his oxen and drove his loggers out of camp. Peavey led
his crew back into the timber, this time armed with

axes *and* muskets, and finished the job. By 1888 he could see daylight in the swamp. He pulled up stakes and went to Puget Sound where he ended his days a-logging. He had ranged three thousand miles in the Big Clearing.

The Patent Log Skidder, invented by Horace Butters of Michigan in 1886, came along West, too, to be known as the "high lead" and to log fir and redwood; and the men who were to log the Western pines brought their Big Wheels with them.

All of the migrating barons brought able foremen and walking-bosses to take charge of their new camps and sawmills. Some of them brought whole trainloads, special trains, of lumberjacks who howled back at the coyotes on the plains. They broke windows of passenger coaches and kicked car doors off their hinges, meanwhile bellowing to such effect that track walkers wondered if a menagerie were passing. Railroad train crews, who had known only Indians, plainsmen, the James Boys, and such sissies, were astounded at the doings. It was the Erie Canal days all over again.

It is pleasant, too, to know that at least some of the fancy-women of the old sawmill towns came West. The girls weren't much given to scanning lumber-production figures and probably didn't know that Oregon and Washington were shortly to take the place of Michigan and Wisconsin. But when they woke up one dismal afternoon and failed to hear the usual knocking at the door, the up-and-coming ones among them went out and bought a new pair of pink brocade corsets and a ticket for Seattle or Portland.

Alert sea captains were ready, for they always read the papers. They filled their holds with barrels of good strong whisky—or at least strong whisky—and stood out of Chesapeake Bay for a trip around the Horn.

14

Bullwhacking the West Shore

WHEN THE FIRST LOGGERS saw the fir that grew along the banks of the Columbia and around Puget Sound they said there couldn't be timber that big and tall. It took, so they told each other, two men and a boy to look to the top of one of these giants.

And thick? Holy Old Mackinaw, the great trunks stood so close that the boys wondered how a tree could be felled at all! And between the trunks grew a jungle of lush growth that no Maine or Michigan logger had ever imagined. You actually had to swamp out a path to a tree and to clear a space around it before there was room to swing an ax. . . . It would take some doing, mister, to let any daylight into *this* swamp.

The first loggers couldn't know it, but it becomes increasingly apparent, in 1938, that they never will be able to let daylight into all of the Western timber. The boys didn't know what manner of forest they were facing—or, forests, rather, for there were two of them.

The forest that hugs the Pacific shore is the outstanding timber zone of the United States or the world, then or now. It is rather narrow, running from thirty to one hundred and fifty miles wide, but it ranges north and south for a thousand miles. It grows very fast. And one acre of it contains more timber than did five acres of the biggest, thickest stuff Maine or Michigan could offer. In the southern part of this forest grows the redwood. North of the redwood the dominant species is the Douglas fir, named for David Douglas, young Scotch botanist who took some of it back to London when

153

his stay with the Hudson's Bay Company at Vancouver, in the Oregon country, was done.

The eastern borders of this forest are the Cascades and the Sierra Nevadas, high and long enough to mark distinctly the firs and redwoods from the pine forest, which grows east of the mountains. This pine forest has a wider range. It extends north and south for a thousand miles. Its width is hard to define because the timber is scattered; but you get an idea of it when you know that big Western pine sawmills are cutting in Washington, Oregon, Idaho, Montana, California, Nevada, Utah, Arizona, Colorado, and New Mexico—with one large plant in South Dakota. It's plenty of pine for a man to range around in.

The pines[1] were inland; they would have to wait a bit. It was to the coast forest that the early loggers gave their attention. Who felled the first big fir tree for a commercial logging venture is not known, but perhaps the earliest picture of an authentic blown-in-the-bottle logger at work concerns one Clement Adams Bradbury. Even the place, the date, and the time of day where this pioneer logger performed are known.

Shortly after noon on the fifteenth of January, 1847, Logger Bradbury, fresh from York County, Maine, stepped up to a mighty old fir that grew by the Columbia River some twenty miles east of Astoria, Oregon, and hard by the new sawmill of W. H. H. Hunt. He observed the tree's butt, which was eight feet in diameter, and he looked upward with something of awe to a top that seemed near the clouds. There had been no such stuff on the Saco, Down East.

But Bradbury was a logger. He spat on his hands, took in the lay of the land, and notched his undercut. When he had cut about sixteen inches into the tree, he was surprised, then alarmed by a "copious flow of pitch that would nigh fill a hogshead barrel." So great

[1]There are three Western pines—Idaho White, Ponderosa, and Sugar.

was the run of pitch that the amazed Bradbury quit
the tree. He returned to it next day, however, when the
pitch flow had ceased, and finished the job. According
to John Minto, a noted observer of the time, Bradbury
soon became "one of the best axmen and loggers along
the river." He learned to cut his stumps high.[2]

The early loggers saw at once there could be no
quick yanking and twitching around, with a team of
horses, such big stuff as grew in the coast fir country.
What was needed was a lot of power and a strong,
steady pull. So the boys reverted to the loggers' ancient
beast of burden, the ox. Only here, they called oxen
"the bulls," and for half a century bulls did most of
the logging west of the Cascade Range.

Sleighs wouldn't do to handle these big logs, and
there was seldom much snow, anyway. The ground was
too rough and too soft to think of using the Big Wheels
of Michigan. And only here and there was a stream
deep and powerful enough to do much river driving.
Faced with such new conditions the boys quickly
adapted themselves. They built skidroads.

The skidroad was the Western loggers' first and
greatest contribution to the science of moving timber.
They first cleared a path in the forest. At suitable
intervals they felled trees across this path, cut them free
of limbs, then buried them half-deep in the soft ground.
These were the skids that made a skidroad, a sort of
track that would keep moving logs from hanging up on
rocks or miring in mud. The completed job looked not
unlike ties laid for a gargantuan railroad.

It was crude, but it worked beautifully. They hitched
the bulls to the logs—five, six, even ten yokes of them,
in charge of the bullwhacker, the teamster, undoubtedly
the master of all profane men, and they pulled long

[2] Visitors to western Oregon and Washington often wonder at
the tall stumps, some of them fifteen feet high. Chief reason is
to escape "nigh a hogs head of pitch."

turns of the big sticks, held together by hooks, over the skids.

It was something to see, this skidroad logging on the West Shore. First, you heard the loud, clear call of the bullwhacker's voice echoing down the forest road that was more like a deep green canyon, so tall and thick stood the fir; and the clank of chains and the wailing of oxbows as the heavy animals got into the pull and "leaned on her." And then the powerful line of red and black and spotted white would swing by with measured tread, the teamster, sacred goadstick over his shoulder, walking beside the team, petting and cursing them to high heaven by turns, the huge logs coming along behind with a dignified roll. Back of the oxen, but ahead of the logs, walked the skid greaser, daubing thick oil on the skid poles that smoked from friction.

Gray old men, sitting around bunkhouse stoves, still cackle in their high voices that it was the noblest sight they ever saw; and they curse the steam that relegated the bull teams to the murals of Western hotels and barrooms.

Skidroads always had one end in deep timber. The other end might be a sawmill, or it might be the waters of Puget Sound or the Columbia or one of its tributaries. If the sawmill wasn't handy, the logs went into booms for towing by steamboats.

By all odds the most important man of a woods crew in the bull-team era was the bullwhacker. He was paid three times as much as an axman, and his opinions on all subjects from oxshoes to the cosmos were considered weighty. He ruled the skidroad, man and beast, with a firm and practiced hand, and his badge of authority was his goadstick, a slim piece of wood some five feet long with a steel brad in one end.

The bullwhacker's profanity long ago became legendary in the Western woods. When he raised his voice in blasphemous obscenity, the very bark of the smaller fir trees was said to have smoked a moment, then curled up and fallen to the ground. No sailor, no truck driver, nor logger who hadn't driven bulls, could hope to touch its heights of purple fluidity. And when both goadstick and profanity failed to rouse the plodding oxen to their best, the bullwhacker might leap upon an animal's back and walk the entire length of the team, stepping heavy with his calked boots and yelling like all the devils in hell.

Small boys of the Oregon country wanted to be bull-whackers when they grew up, and more than one Western timber baron got his start a-whacking bulls down a skidroad.

Earliest record of logging in the West was that that went on to feed the small water-driven mill of the Hudson's Bay Company near its trading post at Vancouver, Washington, on the Columbia River. This mill was built about 1820 under the direction of Dr. John McLoughlin, the post factor, who put two white men and twenty-five Sandwich Islanders to work getting out logs and making boards, mostly for use around the post.

Commercial logging and sawmilling didn't really get under way until 1848, at Oregon City, chief settlement of the early Oregon country. Sawmills had been erected here as early as 1841, but they cut only for the local trade. An event in California brought them a wider market and set them to running night and day, and Sundays.

It was a sawmill man who touched off the event. On a dark rainy evening in January of 1848, John Marshall, millwright who formerly worked at his trade in Oregon City, hurried excitedly into the office of General John A. Sutter, pioneer settler and businessman of the American River district in California. He wanted to see the General alone, he said pointedly. His eyes were set and staring and his speech and demeanor were quietly hysterical. Not until the office door had been locked

would Marshall speak, and his actions counted more
than what he said. From his pocket he hauled forth a
cloth bag which he undid and dumped its contents upon
General Sutter's desk. It was a small pile of yellow
stuff, possibly gold and probably two ounces of it, and
it gleamed a reddish yellow under the oil lamp.

Such, as General Sutter afterward recounted, was the
beginning of the greatest gold strike the world has ever
known. It was to bring men pell-mell from every State
and from every country on the globe. To the incipient
lumber industry of the Oregon country it brought sudden and prolonged prosperity. With the same ship that
brought news of the big strike to Oregon City came a
demand for lumber at any old price. The poorest lumber
brought sixty dollars a thousand feet, ship's side at
Oregon City, and for good clear stuff the astounded
sawmill owners were offered ninety dollars. This sort of
market didn't last forever but it lasted long enough to
give the lumber industry a flying start.

The marvel of steam as applied to saws came in
1850, when the Messrs. Reed, Abrams, and Coffin of
New England put up a boiler and sawmill at Portland,
on the west bank of the Willamette River. Portland was
an upstart, compared to Astoria, Vancouver, and Oregon City, and it was a proud day there when the new
mill was ready to start.

Just south of the sawmill was a camping ground
used by various tribes of wandering Indians, and they,
hearing that the palefaces had built a machine that
could make lumber without the use of water, arrived at
the spot to see what made it go.

The squaws, says a contemporary account, put on
their best beads; the braves were dolled up, too. They
saw smoke coming from the stack and they must have
heard the noise of sizzling steam, but they were wholly
unprepared for the lumberman's traditional way of
starting a day's work in a steam sawmill. There was the
screech of the whistle, and some two hundred red men

and women, their eyes wide with terror, ran for dear life into the nearby woods. It was days before an Indian dared approach the monster that screeched before it began whining.

With a "big" steam sawmill running, Portland soon took the lead in the West Coast industry.[3] As elsewhere, steam came to the mills long before it came to the woods.

Meanwhile, far-ranging lumbermen were peering into the deep forests that grew down to the shores everywhere on Puget Sound. One of them was Henry L. Yesler. He built a sawmill that began cutting in 1853. Seattle grew up around it.

Yesler was a stout pioneer who believed in pioneer ways. He built a huge cookhouse for his sawmill crew that was as generous as it was big. It was open at all hours and for years it was the town's nearest approach to a tavern. Neither man nor beast was turned away from Yesler's camp and barn, money or no, even though Henry didn't have enough ready cash to buy a whistle. Outside the cookhouse hung a circular saw which served as gut-hammer for dinner and as "whistle" for starting and stopping the mill.

Seattle prospered around the sawmill on the sandpit, and so did Yesler. But Yesler was no money grubber who aspired to a plug hat and a span of horses. Most of all he wanted Seattle to grow until it outstripped New York and Chicago. He thought good roads would help the growing, and in 1876 he made a gesture that was characteristic of the man and time.

The Territorial Legislature had voted provision for a "Grand Lottery" for the purpose of raising money to build a wagon road from Puget Sound to eastern Washington, beyond the Cascades. Prizes were to be parcels of timberland. Yesler came forward to donate his saw-

[3]The Jones Lumber Company, Portland, logged with bulls down skidroads that became Portland streets. After seventy-eight years of cutting it is still in business at the old stand.

mill—valued at one hundred thousand dollars on the
tax rolls—as a rather grand first prize in the lottery.
There were no strings to the offer, no ulterior motives,
other than Yesler's great desire to see Seattle grow.

Sixty thousand tickets were printed and sold at five
dollars each, and the affair was "all legal and above-
board" with each lottery ticket stamped "Legalized by
an Act of the Legislature, approved November 12th,
1875, by E. P. Ferry, Governor of the Territory." But
the odd "morals" of the pious had not been reckoned
with. Churchy folk objected and took the matter into
the courts where the lottery was pronounced unconsti-
tutional.

The money was refunded, and it was many years before one could ride through the mountains except on
horseback. It is amusing to think that when the Puritans
of Washington Territory were stopping the "First Grand
Lottery," Seattle's main street was lined with open gambling houses which were dealing cold decks to citizens
who possibly had more need of decent roads. The
gambling houses continued to operate; Henry Yesler
kept his sawmill and the government of the territory
was kept from Sin.

While Yesler was whacking up his first mill at Seattle,
a party of Pope & Talbot's young men, out of East
Machias, Maine, landed at Port Gamble on Puget Sound
and found it a pretty place for a sawmill. And, as Maine
men usually did in such a case, they promptly built
one. The site proved good.[4]

The Popes and Talbots had logged and built ships
in Maine since Revolutionary times. Now they began
building a lumber and shipping empire on the Pacific
Coast. They bought or built other huge sawmills at
Cosmopolis and Port Ludlow, both in Washington, and
they left Cyrus Walker in charge of Northwest operations.

[4]Eighty-four years later much lumber is being made at Port
Gamble.

Cyrus Walker grew into one of the legendary characters of the West Shore. He built at Port Ludlow a New England mansion which had no peer in Washington, Territory and State. It sat on a slight hill overlooking the mill and harbor. It was finished with boards of the biggest and best fir that grew, and there was a lot of it. The main doors didn't swing; they slid—opening like ship's doors. A big American flag topped the cupola. The yard had a white picket fence, and the broad lawn was shaded by maples and elms brought around the Horn as young saplings. On the lawn was a bronze cannon, a relic of the War of 1812, fetched from Boston. It was fired at sunrise on the Fourth of July, but presented no salute to ships except when the slim *Forest Queen* entered and left the harbor.[5] She was Walker's favorite lumber carrier.

The mansion at Port Ludlow was not only Cyrus Walker's home; it also served as an advertisement for the firm of Pope & Talbot. The company's fleet of eighty-nine vessels was carrying Puget Sound lumber all over the world, and to Cyrus Walker's mansion in the deep woods came lumber buyers and brokers, politicians, shipping officials, timber barons, and railroad kings. The food was sumptuous. The cellar was sauve, stocked with everything from Medford rum for old sea captains to marque champagne for the delicate but often thirsty ladies of lumber buyers. The service was cared for by a long line of Chinese—father, son, and grandson—who cooked dishes that would have amazed the folks in Cyrus Walker's native Skowhegan.

Port Ludlow was a colorful place in its heyday, with ships flying the flags of a dozen nations docked at the

[5] Gunner for quarter of a century was Ed Bergren, of Port Ludlow. On the payroll as a head machinist, it was up to Bergren to know when the *Queen* was due. On that day he loaded the ordnance and stood by, ready to fire, until the ship nosed into the harbor.

sawmill. Officers put on their gaudiest uniforms to mingle with the black frock coats of the landlubbers and the hardly less sober gray and brown of bustled ladies. They drank toddys on the broad veranda, or played at croquet on the lawn, while they talked of the new and dirty steam vessels that were soon to drive the winged ships from the sea.

Port Ludlow became known as the mansion in the woods. Other timber barons sought to imitate Cyrus Walker, but none of them quite reached the true baronial character of Ludlow. Yet Walker was no social climber. He didn't care to go to Congress, and it was told of him that he used every day or two to visit the mills where he would pick up with his own hand any stray nails or spikes dropped by careless workmen. These he would show to his employees, telling them that waste was a sin. And Walker in person saw to it that Pope & Talbot's two hundred bulls were kept round and fit to haul long turns of logs down the skidroads.

There was no pay day for the serfs at any of Pope & Talbot's camps and mills. You got your pay in cash, every night if you wanted it, at the company's big general stores; or you could "leave it lay" until you wanted to quit, or got fired. Three generations of Indian and white loggers and sawmill men and three generations of Chinese cooks worked at Ports Ludlow and Gamble. When, finally, the company adopted monthly payment by check, many of the old-timers objected, and one of them insisted that if he must draw what wages he had coming, then it should be in good hard money. This was done, and it is told how the old fellow loaded some eight thousand dollars in silver into a small wheelbarrow and took a boat to Seattle, where he put the cash in a bank.

Although the Columbia River never had such a barony as that of Pope and Talbot, some of the Northwest's biggest tyee[6] loggers were at work along its timbered shores. An early one was John West, who founded the notable sawmill town of Westport. He ran stupendous skidroads back into the hills, spanning ravines with ungodly big bridges of logs that contained enough lumber to keep a sawmill running a month, and raising bulls which, in spite of early castration, were reputed very mean and to bellow louder than anything ever heard in Bashan of old. His crew of loggers roared louder than the bulls, but they were good men in rough country. When, in building a skidroad along Hungry Hollow, back of Westport, they struck a hill that jutted up and in the way, they paused not a moment but dug clean through it, making perhaps the first and only tunnel in the history of bull-team logging.[7]

Another master of bull logging was John Yeon, who came from Quebec and brought no money with him. He bought some timber on tick, borrowed enough money to buy bulls, and dug into the woods back of Cathlamet. For a time Yeon was foreman, bullwhacker, timekeeper, and sometimes cook; and often he took an ax and felled a two-hundred-foot fir, just for exercise. Always liked to keep in trim, Johnnie Yeon said. He kept in trim. In less than twenty years Yeon was one of Portland's wealthy and leading citizens, and built one of that city's first "skyscrapers."

From Norway by way of the Wisconsin woods came Simon Benson—née Bergerson—to become king tyee of all the Columbia's loggers. Like Yeon and many another budding tycoon, Benson drove his own bulls in the early days. He got up at four and it might be near midnight when he tumbled into his bunk. He set the pace. He knew how to pick good timber and good log-

---

[6]*Tyee*, from the Chinook jargon, meaning "chief," hence a big shot.

[7]Still to be seen, and well worth the seeing, near the Columbia River highway, just east of Westport, Oregon.

gers. Best of all, perhaps, he managed to keep his
camps running during the time of the Fourth of July
drunk.

Many of Benson's loggers were Scandinavians, just
over. They soon learned, though, that July Fourth was
a period when all loggers went to town for a snorting
bender, second only to that at Christmas. Keeping a
Columbia River camp running throughout July was unheard of, and sawmills were usually forced to close for
at least three weeks, right when demand for lumber
was at its height.

Legend has it that in the Benson camps, along about
the middle of every June, a barrel of free whisky arrived. The head would be knocked in promptly and a
hundred Scandinavians would belly around, tin dippers
in hand. Following this, naturally, no logging was done
for a day or two. But they remained in camp; and when
the Fourth rolled around, some weeks later, no Swede
nor Norwegian at Benson's camps ever knew it. They
figured they had had a summer drunk, hence the Fourth
was past. They stayed on the job, happy and working
hard, oblivious to what any calendar said. And Benson's camps kept at least one sawmill running throughout July.

This story is legend and is offered only as such. But
it is no legend that Simon Benson was made wealthy
because he was the Columbia River's biggest, and many
said best, logger. Before he retired and moved to California, Benson endowed a polytechnic school and presented to the City of Portland a number of street-
corner drinking fountains, with the avowed hope that
loggers in town would quench their thirst with water
rather than in Burnside Street saloons. As far as it is
known, they are the only fountains ever dedicated to
the race of loggers. Humorously enough, the fountains
were installed but a few years before the veritable
species of lumberjack became all but extinct.

John Yeon and Simon Benson, centering at Portland, were typical of the highly successful bull-logging operators. All the lesser lumber towns of Oregon and Washington had at least one tyee logger who "came up from the skidroad."

Meanwhile, there were doings in the redwoods.

Not long after the boys and the bulls began whacking away at the Puget Sound and Columbia River forests, a party of settlers crossed the bar to Humboldt Bay on the North California Coast. Needing material for homes at once, they did not wait to build a conventional sawmill. They beached the sidewheel steamer *Santa Clara* and with long belts hitched up the ship's main shaft to four saws set up on shore. This was Ryan & Duffs sawmill. It worked slick as skidgrease. The crew lived in the *Santa Clara's* cabins, ate in her dining saloon, and managed to turn out some forty thousand feet of rough lumber a day. The towns of Bucksport and Arcata were in the making, and so was the lumber metropolis of Eureka.

Fir and spruce grew nearest the shore of Humboldt Bay, and only a few hundred yards inland were the redwoods,[8] of monstrous girth and height—trees to make a man wonder what manner of giants must have once walked among them. They took a logger's eye. No such timber had been seen, not even by the Men of Gath. The general run was from three to ten feet in diameter, but it was common to find them fifteen and twenty feet thick on almost every acre. The little ones were between four hundred and eight hundred years old, and some of the monsters had been growing there for two thousand years, raising their tops three hundred

[8]There are two species of Sequoia, or redwood. The professors term the commercial redwood *Sequoia sempervirens*. The kind one usually sees on picture postcards, a coach-and-four driving through the stump, is *Sequoia gigantea*, commonly called "big tree" and not good for lumber.

and sixty feet into the air. Two thousand years. . . .
They were trees to give even a timber-hungry logger
pause before he struck ax into them. And when a jack
said these trees were older than Jesus H. Mackinaw, it
meant something more than a logger's pleasantry.

Cutting such timber was a task no logger had conceived. The force of their fall was terrific, an impact
that shook the very ground for half a mile or more. It
might take a man a full day to clear a spot—"making a
layout"—so that a tree should fall fair and not smash
itself to pieces; and the best part of another day to fell
the tree.[9]

A logger isn't likely to forget the first time he saw a
big redwood fall. With the layout made and the undercut done, the fallers go to work with the saw. A host of
wedges is used to keep the saw from binding and to aid
in directing the tree's fall.

When the giant gives its first slight shudder of death,
the faller sounds the loggers' traditional warning cry of
"Tim-berrrrr!", a wail with a rising inflection—often the
last human sound heard by heedless men.

You see the very top tremble a bit, and presently
there is a sound that might be likened to a close and
"slow" thunderbolt, if there were such a thing. It is a
dry tearing sound, as though the clouds were being
ripped apart. Then, there comes a brief moment when
this tearing, ripping, splitting noise has an undertone
of a great swishing, like a hurricane being born. And
then the long, rumbling crash that booms in your ears
and sends a vast noise echoing through the hills. It is
enough to make the hair stand on the neck of the
dullest barbarian. The ground trembles, and in any
camp cookhouse, if under a mile away, flunkies can

[9]Redwood loggers used crosscut saws for felling timber in the
seventies, a decade before they were adopted by the boys engaged in the fir forests.

tell by the rattle of dishes on the shelves that an extra big one has come to earth.[10]

The growth rings of one such tree showed it to be fourteen hundred years of age; that is to say, when this tree began life, Clovis was on the throne of France, St. Benedict had just taken up his abode in a gloomy cavern amid the ruins of Nero's Golden House, the Catholic creed was less than fifty years old, and the Dark Ages were settling down into their long night.

A cross section of this tree showed a scar of fire that burned in 1595 A.D.—when William Shakespeare was a young man. The trunk was then more than a thousand years old, so it could stand a bit of heat. Fires swept this forest again in 1789 and 1806, but did little damage to this particular tree. A fire in 1820, however, must have been severe; it burned off bark, sapwood, and some heartwood. But new growth worked its way over the burned surface, slowly healing the scar, although being interrupted by recurrent forest fires in 1848, 1866, 1883, and lastly in 1895—when Grover Cleveland was President of the United States. When this tree was felled, the loggers were anxious to return to camp in order to learn, by radio, which of two men named Louis and Braddock[11] had knocked out the other.

Falling such trees was easy compared to transporting the logs cut from them. The early loggers built splash dams on the rivers of the redwood country, and drove redwoods as they had the pines in Maine. The butt logs were too heavy to float, so they left them in the woods, to be dug out of the brush seventy-five years later and made into pickets, grape stakes, and such.

They tried carting. The boys would saw off two sec-

[10]Redwoods may be brought down with ax and saw, yet they do not die in the process. Within a year new growth can be seen everywhere on and around the stump. If fire be kept out, a sizable tree will stand here in a century's time.

[11]Two American prize fighters, 1937.

tions of a log, put an axle between them, and thus make
a sort of Big Wheels upon which oxen pulled logs
thicker than any two fat bulls. It was all very crude,
but with the carts, and the skidroads, such as the fir
loggers were using, they managed to supply the sawmills of the rising town of Eureka.

Eureka was never to be quite a Bangor or a Saginaw,
but ever since its founding it has been the center of the
redwood industry. It had its open piles of sawdust along
the water front, with many mills a-whining, and, true
to the classic pattern, it early developed a Bowery, or
"skidroad," as Western loggers call that part of town
where they blow their money.

Eureka's skidroad was First Street and to it flocked
loggers from all around Humboldt Bay. Not only loggers, but miners, prospectors, Indians, and occasionally
a soldier. It was here in Ryan's store-saloon that young
Captain U. S. Grant, from near-by Fort Humboldt,
drank himself out of the army. That was in 1854. Local
tradition has it that on one well-remembered occasion—
when Grant had stopped overlong in Ryan's joint—he
went pounding down First Street, driving three horses
tandem and dragging a string of three buggies behind.

Somewhat later, F. B. Harte, cub reporter on the
weekly *Union,* in Eureka's neighbor town of Arcata,
used to visit First Street, attracted by the colorful horde
of loggers and miners who nightly packed the Oberon,
the Continental, and other gambling hells. Harte lin-
gered a while on Humboldt Bay, then went down to
San Francisco to manage the United States mint, become a magazine editor, and leap overnight into fame
with *The Luck of Roaring Camp.*

The unknown Grant probably amused the loggers by
his notable ability as a bottle- and horse-man, and old-
time redwood lumberjacks recalled him, after Appo-
mattox; but neither Grant nor Bret Harte meant much
in the life of a logger. John Dolbeer meant a heap more.

John Dolbeer and his partner William Carson were

of the true logger species. At Eureka, in the sixties, they formed a lumber concern that still flourishes. And Dolbeer devised a rig that made his name known for a thousand miles through the redwood and fir forests.

John Dolbeer had an inventive mind. During the sixties and seventies he made many new mechanical gadgets to improve the Dolbeer & Carson sawmill, and he gave much thought to the slowness of bull-team logging. He felt sure the big sticks could be moved faster by some sort of machinery. He went to work, puttering in the mill blacksmith shop, and built a new kind of donkey engine. It had a vertical boiler, a single cylinder, and a horizontal engine with a drum. In August of 1881 the new machine was ready. Dolbeer bolted it to a sled made of timbers and moved it into the tall redwood that grew along Salmon Creek, near Eureka.

It is recalled that the arrogant bullwhackers who drove the Dolbeer & Carson oxen snorted in amused contempt to see such a contraption in the woods. They sat on stumps, chewing tobacco and passing lewd remarks, while their bulls chewed their cuds and batted not an ear as John Dolbeer ran a line out from the donkey drum and wrapped one end of it around a rugged redwood log. Then he returned to the engine and opened her wide.

That heavy log came in a-snorting—in less time than it would have taken for a yoke of bulls to turn around. It marked the exact date[12] when began the conversion of logging bulls into steaks and hamburger.

[12]Possibly other efforts to use steam donkeys in West Coast logging were made as early as Dolbeer's; but the record is vague. Dolbeer's machine was patented in 1882.

15

Steam and Highball

WHILE JOHN DOLBEER WAS PUTTERING with the successful logging donkey engine that took his name, other men were experimenting with steam in the fir forests. They appear to have been vague men who left no clear record, but there is no doubt that they devised a steam donkey with an upright capstan. This engine they called a gypsy, or spool, donkey. By the mid-nineties both gypsies and Dolbeers had brought "ground-lead" logging into style; by means of a line pulled by a turning wheel or capstan, the logs were yarded, or *led* along the ground.

The capstan was the "spool" and the man who stood by the spool to keep the winding line in good order was the *spool tender*. A *line horse* was used to haul the line back into the timber, once a log had been landed at the engine. These animals became very knowing, needing scarcely to be guided at all, and it was the custom of teamsters who drove line horses and took great pride in them, to argue over the cunning and ability of their animals.

A man down on the payroll as a *sniper* prepared the felled logs for easier yarding by rounding their sharp edge with an ax. *Chokerman* put *chokers*—wire slip loops—around the logs; these chokers were hooked to the line from the donkey. On a high stump stood the *flagman* or signal boy, well in sight of both the crew in the woods and the man at the throttle of the engine. When the boss man of the yarding crew yelled "Hi!"

170

the flagman dipped his flag, or waved an arm, and the
engineer put on steam.

The boss man of a yarding crew was called the
hooktender, a name that technically meant nothing in
the machine age but was a survival from bullwhacking
days when logs were hooked together for hauling. The
hooker, as he was more generally known, was the marti-
net, the top sergeant, the Legree of the woods, the vital
driving force of steam logging. As an authority next to
the camp foreman, the hooker took the place of the
howling bullwhacker. Loggers of the lower ranks
claimed all hookers were the progeny of the Devil and
a mythical bitch woman by name of "Molly Hogan."

Hookers soon became almost fabulous. Many a logger will tell you that hookers yelled louder and oftener
than any bullwhacker ever did. They were accounted
the toughest men in a crew. Invective and plain profanity rolled in clouds out of a hooker like steam from
a donkey engine. They became masters of picturesque
pleasantry. "When I hollers 'Go ahead,'" pronounced
one "Highball" Anderson of the Grays Harbor country, "the hemlocks bend double and the clams go down
a foot."

Hookers knew more ways to indict Man, the Deity
and His elements for disorderly conduct than any lawyer could have thought up; and when a log got tan-
gled around a stump and words failed the harassed
hooker, he simply threw his hat to the ground, leaped
upon it with his calked boots, and howled like a trapped
wolf. These and other antics got them nicknames like
Jimmy The Bear, Tin-ass Mike, and Flying Thompson.

Ground-lead logging speeded production in the
woods. It was necessary—if the boys were going to
keep up with what was going on in the sawmills. All
through the nineties and well into the century bigger
and better and faster mills were being built in Washington, Oregon, and California by boss lumbermen
from the Lake States. Lumber cities like Bellingham,

Everett, Hoquiam, Aberdeen, and Tacoma had come into being. Seattle had long outgrown the settlement around Henry Yesler's mill and now had half a dozen big plants. Even Olympia, Washington's capital, was making a lot of boards. Portland was still the metropolis of the Northwest and its biggest sawmill town as well. Down in California sizable towns were growing up at Crescent City, Eureka, Scotia, Fort Bragg, Westwood, McCloud, and Weed. By 1900 the rush of Eastern lumbermen to the West Coast was in full swing and would last almost exactly twenty-five years more. If the loggers were going to keep the mill ponds of these fast new plants filled with round-stuff, they'd have to speed things up—to *highball,* they called it.

The *high-lead tree* was the answer. It was nothing more than the idea expounded by Horace Butters in his "Butters' Patent Log Skidding Machine," back in Michigan of the eighties. It had gone South to log the swamps and bayous of their cypress and pine. It emerged in the Pacific Northwest as something "new."

The high lead[1] was simply the old ground lead with an aerial twist to it. A block, or pulley, was hung high in the big tree. Through this ran the line from the donkey engine. Thus a log could be hauled in with one end in the air, riding free of stumps and underbrush.

It proved to be the genuine McCoy, and it brought into being a new job, that of the high climber or high rigger, probably the most spectacular fellow in all American industry. With sharp steel spurs strapped to his legs, a safety belt around his waist, and an ax and saw dangling beneath him, this steeplejack of the woods hitches himself with a rope up a tall fir,[2] limbing it as he goes. Anywhere from one hundred and fifty to two hundred feet from the ground, he straps himself loosely

[1]The high lead is in use in 1938 but is on the way out.
[2]Some camps use steel towers, called "skidders," instead of trees.

to the tree and saws off its top.[3] Hanging there against
the sky, he must work carefully, lest he cut his safety
belt, for death on the stumps and ground far below
yawns at him from all sides.

And when, after highly skilled work in a cramped
position, the great top of the tree starts to lean, then to
fall, the high climber must brace himself well. The
trunk vibrates wickedly in wide arcs, and top and man
for an instant are little more than a blur. Down, down
goes the treetop, crashing its tons of weight on the
forest floor to send echoes up the canyon and over
the hump to the next camp.[4]

The tree is now a spar and it is first guyed all around
with steel cables. At its top by an elaborate process is
hung a pulley block such as you are not likely to see
elsewhere. High-lead blocks weigh up to a ton and a
quarter each, few of them less than eighteen hundred
pounds. Once in a while one of them falls, and none in
its path has ever needed first-aid attention.

From the donkey engine a monstrous steel cable—
the main line—is run up through this block, then out
into the woods. Logs, around which a steel choker has
been wrapped, are attached to the main line and yarded
to the foot of the spar. Horses aren't used to return
the main line to the woods; a second drum on the
donkey carries a haulback line to do this job. The high
lead almost doubled production.

High-lead logging also brought a noticeable increase
in the accident rate; with stuff flying through the air,

[3] Sometimes dynamite is used. The climber straps the powder
sticks around the tree, hangs a long fuse, lights it, and gets out
of there. The resulting explosion is worth seeing, but the topping job isn't so "pretty" as a sawed one.

[4] Some high climbers are good showmen. When they have
topped a tree, they take a r'ar of snuff, or roll a cigarette, and
stand on their head at the top of the spar. Some low-minded
climbers mark the completed job by attempting one of Gar-
gantua's tricks on the loggers watching below.

rather than moving over the ground, there was considerable more opportunity for a man to get hit. Added to this natural hazard was the "yarding bonus" offered by many operators. The boss would set a footage mark, usually rather high, for a crew. If the crew managed to yard more than this figure, every man got a dollar or so added to his wages for that day. But worst of all, perhaps, were the wilder hook tenders who seemed to think that setting a "world's record" for a day's logging would give them everlasting fame as highball loggers.

A high-lead yarding crew has about the same occupational names as did a ground-lead crew, with additions. The *rigging slinger* hooks the chokers to the main line; the *chaser* unhooks them at the spar tree. The flagman of ground-lead days has given way to the *whistle punk,* the lad who, with a jerk line or an electric device, blows the starting, stopping, and backing-up signals for the *donkey puncher* at the engine's levers. It isn't exactly an assembly line, but it's all routine. Over and over again, it is the same process. The chokerman puts a choker around the log, the rigging slinger attaches it to the main line, the hooker yells "Hi!" to the punk, the punk jerks the whistle, and some two thousand feet away, and often out of sight, the whistle on the donkey toots once. The donkey puncher opens up. There is a great singing of taut cables as the powerful machine goes into the pull, while the log, thick as a man is high, churns and groans in an upheaval that could be likened to a whale thrashing about in shallow water. Once in motion, it is a veritable juggernaut's car, crushing all before it, including only too often a man who isn't "in the clear."

Pulled to the foot of the spar tree, the logs are slapped onto railroad cars by a McLean loading boom[5] or other tackle so quickly that one hardly realizes what

[5]The invention of C. C. McLean, one-time white-water man of the Michigan woods, long-time logging superintendent and still at it, in 1938, at Valsetz, Oregon.

is happening. The long train of big sticks—twenty, fifty, even a hundred cars, is made up, and away they go down the mountain, around curves, and over high, dizzy trestles, so rough is the terrain, to the waiting log pond.

Sober men marveled at the ruthless power and great speed of high-lead logging. They said it was and would be the last word. But it wasn't. Somebody topped and rigged *two* spar trees, and the "flying machine" or sky-line system was born. A taut cable runs between the two spars, a hundred and fifty feet above the ground, and over this cable, on a device called a bicycle, the logs come zinging in to the landing, traveling swiftly through the air and never once touching ground, stumps, or snags. Logs are moved thus upmountain, downmountain, and across wide canyons, with a speed that is amazing.

The donkey engines that run these prodigious rigs have out-grown the name. They are great hulks of steam, or diesel, or electric operation, many of them sixty feet long. Imaginative loggers tell of their power, that they could straighten out the Temperate Zone, just as Babe, the Big Blue Ox, did for Paul Bunyan, time of the Winter of the Blue Snow when the temperature went to twenty-four feet below zero.

The whole effect on the eye of a modern logging operation is a somewhat disconcerting maze of large and small cables running through the air in every direction, and the ground covered with stationary engines, pumps, woodbucking power saws, steel rails, switches, locomotives, cars, telephones, humidity gauges, movable power plants, and traveling machine shops. It is, in short, a gigantic factory without a roof.

Such was the speed-up, the *highball*, in the West Coast fir district after the bulls gave their last despairing bellow, in the late nineties. It was different in the Western pine country. The boys came to log the in-

land pines about a decade after the coast loggers got
into their stride of steam. They brought their Big
Wheels with them from the Lake States, they brought
steam jammers to load with, and they brought horses
and logging sleighs. But they didn't overlook the rivers.
They drove the streams of Idaho and eastern Oregon
and Washington much as they had done back East; and
sometimes they built log flumes down which mountain
water hurried the logs to the sawmills. The Western
pine loggers had to highball, too. Down at *their* mills
somebody had filed teeth into *both* sides of a bandsaw
—and *whisssh,* it cut a slab as the log moved forward
on the carriage, and *whisssh,* it cut another slab as it
moved back. With the double-cut bandsaw, these Western sawmills took slices off a log almost as quick as
lightning. Other parts of the mill were speeded to keep
up. The pine loggers couldn't loaf.

The coming of the Western pine men was dramatic.
Almost overnight a collection of a few pioneer huts
and a saloon on a bend of the Deschutes River became
Bend, Oregon, a city of ten thousand, mostly former
Minnesotans, with two of the largest pine sawmills in
the world. Sawmill towns like Kootenai, Sandpoint, Elk
River, Potlatch, St. Joe, Emmett, and Barber sprouted
in Idaho before the natives knew what was going on,
and the old mining camp of Coeur d'Alene bustled
with new activity as sawmills arose there. Spokane took
to entertaining more short loggers[6] than cowboys. Weyerhaeuser built a huge plant at Lewiston, Idaho, which
doubled that city's population in a year; and another at
Klamath Falls, Oregon, which sawmills had already
changed from cow town to sawdust town. Other pine
men from the East and South moved into the virgin
timber of eastern Oregon to change the style of fighting,

---

[6]On the coast any logger from East of the mountains is a
short logger. Fir logs are cut forty feet long; pine logs, twelve,
fourteen, and sixteen feet.

in old cattle towns like Burns, from two-guns to calked boots.

The forest service figures tell how sudden it was. In 1898 the mills of Idaho cut sixty-five million feet of lumber. Ten years later the cut had risen to half a billion feet. And in the same period mills in Washington had more than doubled production to reach an annual cut of four billion. Oregon had almost tripled its cut, reaching two billion feet in 1908. California in the same year reached a billion feet.

On top of this spectacular increase of lumber making in the West came the World War. It brought a lumber demand that for suddenness hasn't been known before or since, and especially a demand for spruce for airplanes. The West Coast country had the spruce—plenty of it, in a strip that grows close to tidewater from Alaska to Mendocino County, California. It is the Sitka spruce. The professors term it *Picea sitchensis*, yet it is an excellent tree, struggling, in spite of its scientific name, as high as three hundred feet and as large as ten feet diameter at the butt.

When the World War got going all the logging camps then operating couldn't have met the demand for lumber, even without strikes, and when in 1917 the I. W. W. staged the biggest strike the lumber industry had ever known, the federal government moved in, formed the Spruce Production Division,[7] and started logging on a scale that was staggering. The soldiers built logging camps, logging railroads, and sawmills, and at Vancouver, Washington, they erected a single cut-up plant in which forty-five hundred men worked at turning out spruce.

Following the World War still a new migration

[7]Indicative of the great lasting qualities of government bureaus is the fact that the U. S. Spruce Production Corporation of the War Department is still in business, in 1938, and probably enjoying life, now that the rush of wartime is twenty years in the past.

started flowing into the Pacific Northwest. These late-comers were from the Southern pine country. Most of them came to Oregon, but the largest single concern came to Washington. In 1923 the vast Long-Bell interests built the city of Longview—schools, churches, hotel, library, parks, hospital, railroad depot—and in it erected what is probably the largest lumber-manufacturing plant in the world, although there is little to choose between it and its neighbor, a gigantic unit of the Weyerhaeuser company. You get an idea of their size when you know that either plant can—but isn't likely to—turn out better than one million feet of finished lumber in *eight hours*. That's a lot of lumber. One million feet will serve to build fifty good-sized houses. The two plants at Longview, working six days a week, could cut more lumber than all the mills in Maine managed to cut in 1869, which was a very busy year in Maine.

The migrating lumberjacks found bigger timber, bigger logging camps, bigger sawmills. They also found seagoing monsters of log rafts that defied imagination and might well have come out of the mystic land of Paul Bunyan. These were the work of an able and inspired crew of Columbia River loggers and the sight of one has popped the eyes of more than one man from the Lake States.

In 1906 Simon Benson, boss logger of the Columbia, built a sawmill in San Diego, California, handy to what he correctly believed would soon be a great lumber market. But he found that costs of shipping his logs in coastwise vessels took away his profits. Rail shipment was out of the question. Any way you looked at it, it was a haul of eleven hundred miles from the mouth of the Columbia to Southern California.

Benson decided to try a raft. Almost everybody said it was foolish and dangerous. A raft of logs that could withstand the pounding of the open seas had been a lumberjack dream, and nothing more, since 1791, when

Dr. James Tupper of Dresden, Maine, made a bold but unsuccessful attempt to take logs to England in that manner. Again, in the eighties, lumbermen of Halifax had constructed log rafts for towing to New England mills. All of them were lashed to pieces and lost.

But Benson and his men went ahead. In the quiet of Wallace Slough on the Lower Columbia River they first built a cradle, filled it with three million feet of logs, hitched on a powerful tug and started. It made the eleven-hundred mile trip without trouble in twenty days, thus astounding all unduly wise men. More than one hundred similar but much larger rafts have made the trip since, and the Benson sawmill at San Diego is probably the only one in North America to cut logs brought from a forest more than a thousand miles away.

The cradle of a Benson raft is made cigar-shape, more of a perfecto than panatella. Plank and timbers go into its construction and the completed job, bare of logs, looks like the ribs of some monster of the days of dinosaurs. With the cradle ready, a floating derrick moves back and forth, meanwhile lifting, pulling, pushing, and dropping logs this way and that—pickin' 'em up and layin' 'em down, the raft boys call it. It is a job for specialists, because although every size and length of log is used, the strength of the entire raft depends on there being a large portion of tree-length material in its make-up. The long logs give the lap and backbone necessary to resist the action of ocean waves and ground swells.

The derrick working looks like a gigantic game of jackstraws, in reverse, for the process is a threading together rather than of disentangling. The big machine, snorting and puffing, picks up the huge sticks as though they were matches, placing them exactly where the foreman wants them.

As the cradle fills with logs it sinks into the water. When half filled the first chains are put on. A great anchor chain is run through the center of the raft. This

is the backbone. Herring-bone chains are shackled to
the center chain and attached to five circle chains at
each end. A completed job contains approximately one
hundred and seventy-five tons of chain.

When all is chained, the cradle is removed and put
aside for the next raft.[8] A deck load is piled on and
lashed. Towing lights that will burn thirty days are
placed at each end. She's ready for the long voyage.

The completed job is the largest thing currently
afloat in the Pacific. In and on it is not a stick less than
five million feet—when sawed, enough lumber to build
a respectable village. It has a thickness of thirty-five
feet and it draws twenty-eight feet of water. It is fifty-
five feet wide in the middle and eight hundred and
thirty-five feet long—exactly one hundred and forty
feet shorter than *S. S. Queen Mary* of the Atlantic.
More than one logger recently arrived from the East
has looked through the Columbia's mists to see what
he thought was Leviathan itself moving majestically
down to the sea.[9]

The migrating sawmill workers were as at home in
the new Northwest as they had been in Minnesota or
Louisiana, but the migrating loggers had to learn lots
of new things. First off, there was how to fall a tree in
fir and redwood country. Because of pitch or of butt
formations, or because of the very large size, it wouldn't
do for a man to try cutting a stump as close to the
ground as he had done in the pine. Here the faller used
a springboard, a piece of wood, nearly flat, some five
or six feet long. One end is shod with an iron lip. The
logger cuts a notch as high as he can in the trunk of
the tree. Into this notch he puts the iron-shod end of

---

[8]Rafts are put together in fresh water. Otherwise marine
borers would eat up the expensive cradle in one season.

[9]Why Hollywood hasn't used the building and voyage of a
Benson raft for one of its epics is beyond understanding.

his springboard; if he isn't high enough yet, he "spring-boards" up again and again. Then, with his partner on a similar board, they go to work with ax and saw. Sometimes they leave stumps sixteen feet high.

And most of the newcomers had to learn to use logging machinery, and a different kind of clothing. In the fir and redwood country, where winters are mostly rain, they had to learn to get around in "tin pants." These and the tin coats are water-repellent clothing. They are stiff to begin with, and old age and much pitch make them more so. When a pair of pants gets to the point where they will stand alone in all their fullness on a bunkhouse floor, the owner is said to be an experienced logger.

The newcomer logger also had to learn no little new language. For instance: that the job of chopping down trees and sawing them into logs is *falling and bucking;* that the man in charge of such work is the *bull bucker;* that *gyppo,* or *by the mile,* or *by the inch,* or *by the bushel,* means piece or contract work; that the *candy side* is one of two or more logging crews, in the same camp, which is best equipped; that a cookee is here a *flunkey;* that old-fashioned camp bunks—where you crawl in over the foot—are *muzzle loaders,* and are lousy in more ways than one; and that blankets are *sougans.*

The newly arrived logger had to learn, too, that a donkey engine might be a *Humboldt,* a *Dolbeer,* a *Tacoma,* a *Seattle,* a *Willamette,* a *Crackerjack,* a *Duplex* or a *Halfbreed;* that to *give her snoose* means to increase power; that to *highball* is to hurry; that a *hoosier* is a greenhorn; that a *homeguard* is a long-time employee of one certain company; that a *jagger* is often met with and is a steel sliver from a wire rope; that a *nosebag show* is one where midday lunch is eaten not in camp but out of dinner buckets; that a *job shark* or *man catcher* is an employment agent, and that his place of business is a *slave market;* that a *punk* is a young man; that a *stiff* is a member of the proletariat, and that a *bindle stiff* is one who lugs his bedding around with him; and a number of other words, not all of them printable.

One of the first things he learned—whether he arrived on the coast in the eighties or forty years later—was that the place where he spent his hard-earned dough when he went to town was the *skidroad*. The skidroad of a city might be known to the solid citizens thereof as Trent Avenue, Yesler Way, Powell Street, Pacific Avenue, Burnside Street, or by some other official name, but to the logger it was simply the Skidroad of Spokane, Seattle, Vancouver, British Columbia, Tacoma, Portland, or of one of a score of lesser towns. Skidroad meant "Bowery," and Bowery might mean anything—here in country that was tougher and wilder than Maine or Michigan men had ever known—from a paternity-lawsuit shakedown to a forty-four-caliber slug between the eyes.

16

Blowing Her In

MIGRATING LUMBERJACKS found the whoopee districts of Western lumber towns a bit different from anything they had known before. Basically, of course, the bowery-like skidroads were composed of the same things as elsewhere. But these Western joints were wilder, tougher, and more openly sinful than ever Haymarket Square in Bangor, Water Street in Saginaw, or even the Sawdust Flats of Muskegon. In spots they were gaudier; everywhere they were "bigger, wider, and more of it"—in keeping with the bigger, taller timber.

Skidroads were where you blew her in. A skidroad might be one, two, or a dozen streets of a lumber city. You didn't have to ask how to find it, for it had a character of its own. It was usually handy to the waterfront, whether of river or ocean, and not far from the railroad depot. Its places of business catered to loggers, miners, cowhands, fishermen, and sailors, and construction workers, but on the West Coast loggers were the most numerous customers.

Saloons, restaurants, and lodginghouses were in greatest number, and many of them had names with a timber flavor. "The High-Lead" was popular for saloons. Restaurants ran the gamut from "The Loggers Waldorf" to "The Cookhouse." There was generally a "Hotel Michigan," a "Saginaw Rooms," and a "Bangor House."

Next in number were the chippy establishments, and cheap-john stores which seem to have always been stocked with Sunday suits of a particularly bilious and

183

offensive purple-blue color. On the Skidroad, too, one would find the slave markets, employment offices, like Hicks' Loggers Agency in Vancouver, British Columbia, and Archie McDougal's in Seattle. Somewhere along the stem would be an open-front "demonstration room" of Dr. Painless Parker, the eminent chain-dentist, with one of Dr. Parker's men ballyhooing the dangers of decayed teeth, while a stooge dressed like a logger sat in a dentist chair, a bib around his neck.

A tattooing parlor might be next to a show window in which were displayed perhaps a basket of China tea, a bottle of American ink, a carton of soap, and some advertising cigarette cards. Any logger could tell by this display of unrelated wares that here was a Chinese lottery.

There might be a combined shooting gallery and penny arcade, and here and there a mission place where you could get free soup if you would sit through a lecture or a sermon. There would surely be, after 1906, an I. W. W. hall, and always a barber shop with lady barbers, and a barber college where bums could get free shaves and haircuts. And there might be a secondhand book store, like Raymer's in Tacoma and Seattle, or a place that defies definition like Tom Burns' Timeshop[1] in Portland.

Until well into the present century open gambling was a feature of Western skidroads. When pioneer realism faded, the gaming joints were driven under cover by civilized hypocrisy where they still flourish. But gambling, like food, clothing, dentistry, and other minor needs, was of secondary importance to loggers. Saloons and fancy-houses got their stakes.

[1] On Portland's skidroad for more than thirty years, Tom Burns repairs loggers' watches, soapboxes on street corners about everything from Socialism to the need of taxing church property, has a stupendous and excellent library in his basement, writes and distributes pamphlets attacking both God and Public Utilities, and has a show window of curiosities that attracts a crowd from morning until late night.

Of the larger cities, loggers might take in San Francisco's Barbary Coast as a special sort of spree—an experiment, almost—but 'Frisco was never a loggers' town. The boys from the redwoods blew her in at Eureka, on Humboldt Bay and close to the timber.

Earliest and for many years the biggest and liveliest skidroad in the lumberjacks' West was Portland's lusty old North End. The North End was almost anything on and north of Burnside Street, and often south of that red-eyed thoroughfare. Socially, the skidroad centered at Erickson's, without any doubt the widest-known meeting place for loggers in all the West.

Erickson's was primarily a drinking establishment. Founded as a simple saloon in the early eighties by August Erickson, a Russian Finn, it grew in size and magnificence until loggers vowed they had rather see Erickson's, with its lights on, than to view the Grand Canyon or a Chicago World's Fair.

All Western states have been given to bragging of places with a "mile-long" bar that usually scaled a modest hundred feet; but it was sober fact that the mahogany in Erickson's ran six hundred and eighty-four lineal feet. The place occupied the best part of a city block and had five entrances, all of them very elegant. Inside were really five different bars, the one on the Second Street side being known as "St. Petersburg" because it was here that Russians and Finns liked to congregate and drink by themselves.

Bars, fixtures, and mirrors were the best money could buy. There was a concert stage. The mezzanine was cut into small booths for eating, drinking, and, to a certain extent that was well understood, for the making of love, although no sirens were connected in any way with the Erickson payroll. A feature was a "$5,000 Grand Pipe Organ." The free lunch was prodigious, one of its many standard items being the half of a roast ox. Soft bread for sandwiches was cut exactly one and one-half inches thick; the Swedish hardtack bread, round and large as grindstones and almost as hard, stood in stacks. The mustard pot held a quart. Round logs of sliced sausages filled huge platters. Pickled herring swam in a large bucket of brine. Beer was five cents, hard liquor two for a quarter.

Art wasn't overlooked. Besides numerous interior decorations, a huge oil painting, "The Slave Market," took up much of one wall. It depicted an auction sale of Roman captives and was highly thought of by the connoisseurs of art who infested Erickson's, many of them weeping into their big schooners at the sad plight of the slaves.

Yet Erickson's was no place for tears. It was too vital with the surge of life. Here was where outdoors men came to meet—the true club of the working stiffs. Loggers mixed with sailors, salmon fishermen, cowhands, miners, riverboat men, and all sorts of itinerants, all of them heading in a dead line for the noted place the moment they arrived in Portland. Not many of them had drunk liquor in such an elegant place or had been treated so well.

City police were seldom needed to restore order. Gus had his own staff. Of these bouncers a delightful person known as Jumbo Reilly became a fixture. He was a huge man, weighing more than three hundred pounds, and though he wasn't much of a fighter, his size and general appearance were so forbidding that he had little trouble holding down his job. Few arguments reached the fighting stage in Erickson's. Jumbo or one of the other bouncers would try to reason with the opponents, and if this failed, out they went. Loggers liked to tell of the time a jack known as Halfpint Halverson was thrown out by Jumbo. Halfpint returned by another door. Jumbo spotted him and tossed him out again. This continued until Halfpint had been thrown out of four different doors. Going around to the Third Street side, Halfpint made another attempt. Just inside the door he came face to face with the mountainous Jumbo. "Holy

Old Mackinaw!" exclaimed Halfpint. "Are you the bouncer in every jeasley saloon in this town?"

Loggers liked places that were as large as that.

Erickson's was but two short blocks from the water front, and when what is still referred to as the Flood of '94 made most of downtown Portland look like Venice, and his own and most other saloons were inundated, Gus promptly chartered a big houseboat, stocked it with supplies—including the famous Erickson free lunch— and moored the craft in the middle of Burnside Street. Rowboats, homemade rafts, catamarans, and single loggers riding big fir logs came a-paddling for succor to Erickson's floating saloon. The boys lined up at the bar singing "White Wings," the current American equivalent of "The Gondolier's Song." Edward C. (Spider) Johnson, long-time bartender for Erickson, recalls that perhaps a score of loggers never once left the floating saloon during the several days the city was flooded.

Not due to any emergency was the floating hellhole operated by the lovely Nancy Boggs. Year in and out Nancy had her notorious whisky scow moored in the river at Portland. It was really a two-storied houseboat, some eighty by forty feet. The lower part was saloon and dance hall, while on the upper floor or deck were living and working quarters for Nancy's stable of some two dozen hostesses. Nancy anchored in midstream, and from time to time would move north or south, depending on the arrival and docking of steamers, the changing currents of the river, and the changing attitudes of the Portland police department.

In those days the city was composed of two towns, Portland on one bank of the Willamette, East Portland on the other. Nancy paid no license to either. Police of the two cities once made simultaneous raids on the scow. One logger who was present recalls that Nancy met the onslaught with gusto. She grabbed a hose and promptly poured live steam over the raiders. Then she upped anchor and floated down river to the Linnton shore, and business continued as usual.

But the whisky-scow business went out of fashion. Lots of customers fell overboard and were drowned. The police bothered more and more. And many potential patrons wouldn't trouble to take a rowboat to get a drink and a dance when there were plenty of drinks and dancers on shore. So Nancy sold her vessel and moved to the dry land of the North End where she continued to prosper for many years.

Long popular with loggers and seafaring men coming to Portland was the Senate Saloon operated by Liverpool Liz, born Elizabeth Smith. Liz was a short, stocky woman who made up in finery what she lacked in looks. She wore the finest gowns and was never seen on duty without her large and famous gold and diamond necklace, said to weigh four pounds. Liz wouldn't stand for anyone being "rolled" in her place, but she had a system that paid dividends. A flush logger would go into Liz's place and find perhaps only two or three men at the bar. In the goodness of his heart the logger would tell the barkeep to set them up for everybody in the place, figuring that drinks for four would total fifty cents.

"Yes, sir," the barkeep would say politely, reaching for glasses. And at that instant anywhere from fifteen to twenty girls would come trouping in from upstairs, shouting, laughing and calling for "two-bit drinks." A round of drinks in Liz's place cost nearer to five dollars than fifty cents. The matter was arranged by the barkeep who pressed a button that rang a discreet buzzer in the upstairs brothel.

Perhaps the toughest rum-and-women combination house of the period was that of the demure and dainty Mary Cook. Her place was "The Ivy Green," and more than one logger complained that the title needed the prefix "poison"—yet they always came back for more at Mary's.

Mary was large, a behemoth of a woman, not only stout but tall and big-boned. She weighed two hundred and eighty-five pounds on the hoof and never hired a bouncer, preferring to do this interesting work in person. And it is reported that she was most capable. She could be as rough as Erickson's huge Jumbo Reilly and her technique was held to be better than Jumbo's. She would either lift a noisy logger bodily from the floor and hurl him through the air to land in a heap, or she would sort of skid him along the plank sidewalk in a manner that made his behind feel like the back of a hedgehog. Yet she was in no way quarrelsome. She was jolly, good-hearted, and never would go into action until she saw that something had to be done; and when she did, they could hear the groans of the wounded 'way down at the police station, six blocks away.

Mary Cook could be dainty, too. She liked to stand in the barroom, near the entrance, and smoke long and very black cigars as she greeted customers. If you held out a finger to her, she would blow neat smoke rings around it, three to a series, for good luck.

What Erickson's drinking establishment was to thirsty loggers, so was the Paris House to those who sought charmers. It was without question the largest house of prostitution ever to cater to the lumberjack trade. It occupied the second and third floors of a rambling blocklong building on Davis Street, between Third and Fourth, in the heart of Portland's North End. In its crib-like rooms when it first opened for business were exactly one hundred[2] girls; white girls on the second floor, girls of varying shades on the third. It was known less for the beauty of its inmates than for their varied depravity, and the monstrous size of it appealed to loggers.

[2]Largest number of girls taken here in one of the so-called police raids was eighty-three.

The Paris House did extremely well for many years, being, as it was, the outstanding Horrible Example of local reformers who gave it free publicity estimated by the late Duke Evans, the joint's manager, to be worth thousands of dollars to him and the girls. It survived half a dozen moral waves and wasn't closed until 1907, when big "houses" were going out of style, anyway.

It was in Portland's bad old North End where many an unwilling and usually unconscious logger went down to the sea in a ship. This sudden change of calling was cared for by a number of slick gentry, among them Larry Sullivan, the Grant brothers, and the colorful Jim Turk, only local crimp[3] ever to wear a silk hat and to carry a goldheaded cane. These men operated sailors' boardinghouses in Portland, and when there was a shortage of sailors they loaded drunk or drugged loggers onto ships and collected from twenty-five dollars to fifty dollars each "blood money" from sea captains for the transaction. It was known to the trade as the "crimping business," to the public as "shanghaiing."

Most notorious of the Portland crimps was the redoubtable Joseph Kelly, never known except on police blotters as anything but Bunco Kelly. "Nothing like some good sea air for a logger," Bunco used to say, and there are old-timers living who can tell of wearing calked boots into Portland on a Saturday night and of waking up, minus the boots, on Monday morning in the forecastle of a ship just crossing the Columbia bar for China or Australia. One such logger afterward told that the voyage of six months "cured me of consumption"; but more loggers cursed than praised Bunco Kelly.

It was told of Bunco that once when his concoctions failed to drug a big logger into sleep, Bunco was so disgusted that he picked up the huge wooden Indian that stood in front of Wildman's cigar store, wrapped it in a tarpaulin, and shouldered it up the gangplank

[3]A crimp's occupation was getting men, legally or otherwise and usually otherwise, to fill vacancies in sailing-ship crews.

of a British four-master. "Here's the man you wanted," said Bunco to the skipper. "He's a big son-of-a-bitch and he's powerful drunk, but he'll make you a good sailor." Bunco put the figure in a bunk, covering it up well, and then collected his blood money from the captain. That was how next day a crew of Finnish salmon fishermen at Astoria were amazed to haul in a wooden Indian in their nets.

Seattle's skidroad, near and on Pioneer Square, wasn't a really important social center for loggers until after the turn of the century. In 1899 one Joe Backer founded its most illustrious lumberjack hangout. He leased the ground floor of what had been John Cort's first theater and installed a truly grand skidroad palace. He named it Our House and it was an immediate success.

"Joe Backer catered to the lumberjack trade," says James Stevens, who before he became a well-known author[4] was a lumberjack and knew the old skidroads well. "But he wanted only the best of the boys as customers, and this tradition was carried on by the Landwehr brothers, who later became proprietors. It was always a genuine social hall for loggers. The bar was fronted with green tile. Giant pillars flanked the mirrors and above them were panels embossed with intricate carvings. The outside walls were adorned with a brilliant painting of a European tavern scene and gigantic counterfeits of barrel heads. On each barrel head appeared Our House's slogan: 'Only Straight Whiskies for Our House Patrons. We Could Buy Them Cheaper but We Wouldn't. We Would Have Bought Them Better but Couldn't.' Calks were not allowed in Our House. In spite of this restriction, the fame of the place was second only to that of Erickson's in Portland."

[4] Paul Bunyan, Brawnyman, Homer in the Sagebrush, Mattock, The Saginaw Paul Bunyan.

On the floor above Our House, but having no connection with it, was a big gambling hall where twenty-five games operated as long as any customers remained.

Possibly Spokane's best-known meeting place for loggers on spree was Jimmy Durkin's, on Main near Trent Avenue. Its success was due less to the quality of liquor and entertainment offered than to Jimmy himself. "Jimmy Durkin is a man of his word," was a saying among loggers that grew into a slogan, and Jimmy did much of the banking business for the men of the Western pine woods.

But perhaps the city of Aberdeen, on Washington's West Coast, presented a more typical sort of Skidroad than either Spokane or Seattle, or even Portland. Aberdeen was and is a pure sawmill town of classic vintage, nearer to the old Saginaw and older Bangor than anything in the West. Only Aberdeen was tougher, much tougher. Built on the wild shore of Grays Harbor, and backed by a wonderful forest, Aberdeen and its sister town of Hoquiam grew suddenly into a lumber giant shortly after 1900 when boss lumbermen and several thousand lumberjacks moved there from the Lake States.

Aberdeen's skidroad centered around F Street and its greatest ornament was the Humboldt Saloon, founded and operated until Prohibition by "Big Fred" Hewitt.

The Humboldt was unique in more ways than one. No woman was allowed in the place, nor were gamblers or any sort of fancy-men. On the walls were no works of art, for Big Fred was not an art lover but a scientist of sorts. He had a curious mind, especially for anything he considered educational.

In the Humboldt was a respectable collection of minerals from all over the world, classified and labeled. Possibly Big Fred didn't know what ethnology was, but in his place were displayed the tribal garb, weapons and "medicine" of Indians from the Blackfeet to the

Pueblo. A galaxy of ordnance included flintlocks and ball-and-cap rifles and pistols that had played parts in Indian skirmishes, murders, and hold-ups. A meerschaum pipe was reputedly one that Cole Younger, the bandit, smoked during his long stay in the Minnesota prison at Stillwater, after the James-Younger raid on Northfield failed. There was an "Oregon boot" said to have been worn by Harry Tracy, Oregon's notorious bad man.

Stuffed moose, snakes, owls, and cougars stared and glared at customers. There were some huge bones, thought to have been those of a mammoth, that a logger had come across on the banks of the Hoquiam River. Big Fred gave two quarts of his best liquor for them. There were the ribs of a whale. There was an alder log which had grown around a scythe hung in the tree by some early settler. Prominent was a stump which had been made with a stone ax before the white logger came. On one wall was a large glass case that sheltered photographs of noted bull teams and noted bullwhackers, early donkey engines, high climbers at work, and Lillian Russell, alive, and Jesse James, very dead.

Big Fred believed in education and he believed in pure liquor. The Humboldt had its own house brand of liquors of "double stamp" strength, and quality, and its own brand of cigars. A pretty colored lithograph of Big Fred himself, with sweeping mustache and roached hair, appeared on every box of cigars. He was a man who stood solidly behind his wares.

Old-time loggers knew the Humboldt as a trusty bank and Big Fred as an honest man. When they flooded into Aberdeen for the Fourth of July and Christmas shutdowns, many of them went direct to Big Fred's to get their checks cashed. They'd take what money they thought they needed, leaving the rest with Fred. It was common for the Humboldt's big safe to contain twenty thousand dollars, all of it the property of loggers who didn't want to be rolled by Aberdeen's horde of harpies and thugs. The boys knew they could get it when they had need.

But Aberdeen didn't have enough Humboldts and Big Freds. The sudden growth and great industry of the town attracted as evil a gang of men and women as could be assembled. King of this backwoods underworld was Billy Gohl, a true monster of a man who was ostensibly the local agent for the Seamen's Union.

Gohl's place of business was over the Pioneer Saloon, close by the Whiskah River that flows through town, and in the fall and winter of 1909, no less than forty-four corpses, mostly of loggers, their heads bashed in or bullet holes in their chests, were found floating in the river. But "The Ghoul of Grays Harbor," as the press was soon to term him, got too bold. He was arrested on rather strong suspicion of murder. After a sensational trial, in which a hunk of tattooed skin from a victim's arm was the chief exhibit for the State, Billy Gohl was put away in Walla Walla prison for life, being transferred to the insane hospital and dying there in October, 1928.

Bunco Kelly of Portland was already dead. So were Liverpool Liz, Nancy Boggs, and dainty Mary Cook. Big Fred's museum had disappeared. The glamour of Our House had long since departed. Prohibition had driven honest saloon keepers like August Erickson off the skidroad.

Mention has been made of religious bands and soapbox orators of the skidroads. The Christian evangelists made little headway among loggers; nor did the rousers for the Knights of Labor, the Populists, nor the Socialists. Loggers might grumble about low wages and poor living conditions in the camps, but they did nothing about them until a smoldering ember of Karl Marx set fire to their tails. It was the Wobblies who blew the spark into flame.

17

The Wobblies Come

THE SHADOW of whiskered old Karl Marx did not fall athwart the lumber industry until late in 1905. On the evening of December 30 that year, snow covered the ground of southern Idaho. The village of Caldwell lay under a blanket of it, marking the steps of Frank Steunenberg, ex-governor of the state, as he made his way homeward the short distance from his law office in the town.

There was a picket fence around the house. Steunenberg opened the gate, passed through, and turned to close it. At that instant a terrific explosion shattered the quiet dark of the night, and the former governor of Idaho lay dead on the reddening snow.

So great had been the explosive charge, whatever it was, that the blast was heard by farmers ten miles outside town and the windows on the front of the Steunenberg home were blown into jagged bits of glass that were found protruding from interior walls.

The blast was to have other reverberations. It brought into the national spotlight a young Idaho attorney, the present Senator William E. Borah. It brought fame to Clarence Darrow. And it produced a new antichrist in the hulking form of William Dudley (Big Bill) Haywood, ebullient genius of the brand-new Industrial Workers of the World—the Wobblies—soon to be much feared and hated and loved in the lumber industry and elsewhere.

Almost a year previous to the Steunenberg murder the I. W. W. had been organized in Chicago, and Hay-

wood elected general secretary. "Fellow workers," Big
Bill had roared at the first meeting of the order, "the
aims and objects of this organization shall be to put the
working class in possession of the economic power, the
means of life, in control of the machinery of production
and distribution, without regard to capitalist masters."
There had been no loggers at this first meeting, but
there would be plenty at others, and the Wobblies were
to raise more hell in the timber than booze, hurricanes,
forest fires, and Acts of Congress.

Where the Wobblies were, there was always turmoil
and alarums, and in Big Bill Haywood they had an
able leader. He was well over six feet tall, every line in
his body proclaiming the strength of an ox. He could
roar louder than any of them, he loved the smell of
frying capitalists, and he was as clever a publicist as
Barnum. Moreover, he was a first-class organizer.

Following close on the murder of Steunenberg, Idaho
police arrested one Harry Orchard on suspicion. In
jail at Caldwell he denied any knowledge of the set
bomb hitched to the Steunenberg gate. Moved to the
Boise jail Orchard had a long interview with James
McParland, the Pinkerton sleuth who had run down the
Molly Maguire terrorists back in Pennsylvania of the
seventies. To McParland Orchard confessed a series of
bombings and shootings that covered several years and
numbered at least thirty victims. In his confession Orchard specifically charged three men with paying him
for the "jobs," including the murder of Steunenberg.
They were Charles Moyer, president of the Western
Federation of Miners; George A. Pettibone, who seems
to have been a sort of unofficial big shot in the union;
and William D. Haywood, general organizer of the
Miners' Union and head of the new Wobblies.

Kidnapped in Colorado and brought to Idaho without authority, Moyer, Pettibone, and Haywood were
charged with the murder of Steunenberg. The reason
implied for the murder was that the miners "had it in"

for Steunenberg because of the manner in which he acted in a miners' strike in the Coeur d'Alenes, years before.

Haywood and Pettibone were tried and found not guilty. The charges against Moyer were dropped. Orchard was sentenced to imprisonment for life in the Idaho penitentiary.[1]

The trial of Haywood became a national *cause célèbre*. Even before the case came to trial it had created wide interest and more bitter feeling than anything since the Haymarket affair in the eighties. There was no sitting on the fence. Either you were for Haywood and the others, or you were against them. The President of the United States, even, wasn't immune to the hysteria. In a letter that was made public Theodore Roosevelt wrote that whether or not the three men were guilty, they were "undesirable citizens."

This letter made a terrible noise. Writing in his paper, *The Appeal to Reason*, Eugene Debs, then a big figure in the land, made a vitriolic attack on Roosevelt. Loggers in Northwest camps went to work wearing buttons on which was printed "I am an Undesirable Citizen." Labor unions staged monster parades in protest. The letters "I. W. W." went into newspaper headlines, and by July 28, 1907, when he was found not guilty, Big Bill Haywood was more of a national character than the brilliant prosecutor, Mr. Borah, or the brilliant and sardonic counsel for defense, Mr. Darrow. The Wobblies were off to a good start.

Even before Big Bill's acquittal, Wobbly halls were opening in Portland, Seattle, Tacoma, and Spokane, and loggers and sawmill workers were the object of a big organization drive. The fir and pine forests fairly swarmed with lads who were "packing the rigging" in the form of Red Cards and other I. W. W. supplies and propaganda booklets. In March of 1907, when

[1] Harry Orchard, long a trusty, is in 1938 in charge of the prison's turkey farm.

Haywood's trial was in full swing, they felt they were strong enough to challenge the timber barons.

They struck first in Portland, where all except one of an even dozen large sawmills were forced to close. It was scandalous, an unheard-of thing in the lumber industry of the Pacific Northwest; and retaliation was prompt. Police arrested scores of Wobs and clapped them into jail on charges ranging from disorderly conduct to attempted arson. The strike was soon broken, but lumbermen were jittery at this first attempt to organize their notoriously unorganized employees.

The Portland strike was a mild enough beginning. Over in Spokane presently occurred the first of a long series of "free-speech" battles staged by the Wobblies. When a police magistrate forbade them to soapbox on street corners, there deluged on unhappy Spokane a thousand or more wild and footloose "Rebels," attracted by black headlines in the Wobbly press proclaiming SPOKANE TOWN CLOWNS STOP WOB SPEAKERS.

Among the converging radicals was a woman. She was Elizabeth Gurley Flynn, young, handsome—with a Western hat turned up in front, and a flaming red tie around her pretty throat—and she was a hellion that breathed reddish flame; fairly sober reporters affirmed that a flash from the girl's blue-gray eyes would serve to light a Sweet Caporal.

The Flynn promptly entered the fight, shouting on a Trent Avenue corner for the workers to rise up, shake off their chains, and do battle for free speech. In what must have been an unreflective moment, the idiotic police arrested the beauteous firebrand and threw her into jail. TOOLS OF TIMBER BARONS JAIL REBEL GIRL howled the Wobbly press in studhorse headlines that even illiterates found inflaming.

Now it seemed—and they still remember it in Spokane—that every hobo West of the Mississippi had come to town to protest against this inhuman treatment of Beauty and Womanhood. They marched the streets, taking over whole blocks, and they sang rude songs. Logging crews of pine camps deserted in a body to go to Spokane where their calked boots pitted the soft asphalt and their nightly howls frightened little children and all capitalists. The city jail was overflowing for weeks. Citizens who were taxpayers began protesting against this feeding of hordes of itinerants out of the public funds.

The ganging-up was too much for Spokane. All prisoners were released, and henceforth, as the Wob press gloated, Spokane was safe for I. W. W. street speakers. Gurley Flynn returned East to start the Lawrence, Massachusetts, "revolution," and to cause employers in Paterson, New Jersey, to lie awake nights.

The Wobs were now on the upswing. For the next decade they kept the lumber industry of the Northwest in a state bordering on insanity. Indeed, even now when violence on the labor front is common, white hairs curl and blood is pumped faster through the hardening arteries of members of conservative clubs in Portland, Seattle, and Spokane, when by chance some younger member asks who was this Bill Haywood, anyway, who wrote a book and died in Russia.

Outstanding characteristic of the I. W. W. was the amazing rapidity with which they got around the country. When iron miners on the Mesaba Range went on strike, Wobbly loggers of Oregon flooded Minnesota. Dirt movers of Montana construction camps appeared as by magic on the picket lines around California hop fields. In 1908 when Wobbly ranks were torn by factions warring over dogma, what was known as the "overall brigade" and was composed chiefly of loggers, jumped freights heading East out of Seattle and Portland, and captured and dominated the I. W. W. convention in Chicago that year. The overall boys voted, and their vote became a part of the organization's policy, that Wobblies should pay no attention to political activity, which was a snare and a delusion; they should concentrate on bringing the Revolution by means of strikes, sabotage, and the eventual taking over of the sources of production by the workers—who, of course, would all be good Wobs.

The results of the 1908 convention were soon apparent. Strikes broke out suddenly in all sawmilling and logging centers. They were sporadic, never lasted long, and were accompanied by riots, sabotage, and other violence.

A celebrated Wobbly affair was the "Everett Massacre." Denied the exercise of free speech in the big sawmill city of Everett, Washington, the Wobblies on the afternoon of Sunday, November 5, 1916, chartered a steamer, packed her with approximately four hundred determined members, and left Seattle harbor. Two hours later, as the ill-fated *S. S. Verona*[2] nosed the Everett dock, shooting began, and when the smoke had cleared seven men were dead and sixty-eight lay wounded. The affair created a lengthy trial, in which nobody was found guilty of anything, and was chronicled in a Wobbly book. At least two Wobbly songs were written about it.[3]

Wobbly leaders used the riot at Everett for organizing purposes, and when, a few months later the World War came to America, they were ready.

In 1917 the I. W. W. staged the greatest strike the lumber industry has known anywhere. Eighty-five per cent of camps and sawmills went out of production. Spikes allegedly appeared in logs at mills that continued operations. Logging trains were derailed. Mysterious fires broke out in timber and mill. Stickers

---

[2] Bad luck dogged the *Verona*. On January 11, 1936, she was destroyed by fire at a Seattle dock.

[3] The *Wobbly Song Book* had run through twenty-six editions by May, 1936. It contains some humdingers.

showing horribly grinning black cats—symbol of sabotage—were found glued to the windows of camp and sawmill offices. Boss loggers and mill operators became vexed, then worried. BIG BOSSES GET WOBBLY HORRORS, said banner headlines in the I. W. W. press.

There were riots on the log drives of Idaho and eastern Washington, where river crews fought against Wob pickets. Tough mill foremen threw Wob organizers into mill log ponds. Even tougher camp foremen beat them up. Genuine Wobblies were gluttons for punishment; it took nerve to be one in 1917.

The United States Army wanted lumber in a hurry to build its cantonments and it wanted spruce for airplanes—but little lumber was being produced. The wheels had all but stopped.

The Wobs shouted back that *they* wanted an eight-hour day, better wages and working conditions, and white sheets on the bunks in logging camps.

Finally, the government intervened. It formed the Spruce Production Division to log and mill timber. It formed the Loyal Legion of Loggers and Lumbermen, the 4L, of civilian and army employees and employers, and forced boss loggers and lumbermen to grant the shorter workday. Upon this, the I. W. W. voted to "return the strike to the job." That is, to return to work but to continue tactics of slowing work, and other sabotage. Wobbly stickers now showed a big clock on whose hands hung a pair of wooden shoes—sabots—and the admonition "Time to Slow Down."

But the government and the 4L prevailed, and the Wobs went into hiding or into jail for the duration of the war. Bill Haywood fled to Russia, not to return, and Leavenworth prison was filled with Wobbly leaders, many of them to remain until pardoned in 1923 by President Harding.

Once the war was over, the I. W. W. again came into the limelight, this time as the motive power behind the Seattle general strike in 1919. The various services of the city ceased to function, while armored cars patrolled the streets. Fighting broke out in the shipyards, along streetcar lines, and around the yards of local sawmills, and finally grew into the somewhat preposterous "Ole Hanson Revolution," so called from the mayor's name. It was broken with no serious bloodshed.

But the Wobblies were to appear once more in a most dramatic scene. On November 11, 1919, in small Centralia, Washington, the American Legion held a parade. When directly in front of the Centralia I. W. W. hall, the local contingent of the marching Legionnaires halted. Whether by design or because of a gap in the marchers and an effort to close ranks, will never be proved. In any case, the Centralia Legion halted in front of the Wobbly hall. What happened in the next split second has been hopelessly in dispute for the past eighteen years.

What is assuredly and horribly known is that shouts and cries and the dry, sinister crackle of gunfire broke out almost simultaneously, and that parade watchers saw three Legionnaires go down in welters of blood. Then, there was a rush on the I. W. W. hall, and Wesley Everest, Wobbly, went out the rear door, firing as he ran. Chased to the brink of a near-by river, the Wob turned and shot his nearest pursuer dead.

Wesley Everest was taken and put in the city jail, and early that grim evening every light in Centralia flicked out without warning. A group of men moved into the jail, took Everest, and departed. The city lights glowed again. Next morning Everest's bullet-riddled body was found hanging from a near-by bridge.

Whether the Legionnaires had planned to raid the I. W. W. hall, as defense attorneys claimed, or whether, as prosecution held, the Wobblies had committed downright murder, has been discussed in print thousands of times and is the "Tom Mooney Case" of the Northwest. Four Legionnaires were dead, anyway, and so was one Wobbly. Eight I. W. W. members were sent to prison

for varying sentences.[4] The affair was the beginning
of the end of the Wobblies as a power, and a terror,
in the timber of the Northwest.

The Wobbly press was as colorful and as noisy as its
membership. Its editors never troubled themselves about
facts, just so long as a news story was loaded in every
paragraph with dynamite against the Ruling Classes.
They were paid four dollars a day, in good times, and
served but six months at a stretch. Most of them took a
leaf from the book of Hearst and kept a rousing good
"menace" on tap at all times. If no Wobbly hall had
been wrecked for a fortnight, or no Wob organizer
beaten up by police, the editor would hitch up his
galluses and come out with a stirring piece scare-headed
TIMBER BARONS HIRE JESUS-BILLY TO QUIET SLAVES,
the "Jesus-Billy" being the late Reverend Billy Sunday,
considered by many operators a good sedative for employees who had begun to grumble about the wages.

A nice thing about working on a Wobbly paper was
that it was no more confined to English than is the
theatrical weekly *Variety* today. The Wobs had a lingo
all their own. To start with, there is the word *Wobbly*
itself. Its origin is somewhat hazy. Many Wob neolo-
gists say it was conceived unconsciously by a China-
man, a member, whose heathen tongue was not equal
to the letter "w." When the Chinese wanted to tell the
boys that he was a good I. W. W. man, the best he
could do was "Me likee Eye Wobbly Wobbly." It
proved enough.

Wobbly spread from man to man, as such things will,
and by mysterious, unseen jungle-news channels, from
camp to camp, until it was picked up by the Wobbly
press and later became a part of everyday speech in all
Western states, Wob and layman alike.

And Wobbly editors were quick to appreciate other

---

[4] Still in Walla Walla penitentiary in 1938 is Ray Becker.
Other defendants are dead or have been paroled.

terms used by the boys out at the "points of production." A worker who was not filled with revolutionary spirit was labeled a *scissorbill*. The Wobs wanted logging concerns to furnish employees with blankets and sheets, so the ancient practice of carrying one's own blankets from camp to camp was made ludicrous by *carrying a balloon*, with appropriate front-page cartoons. A *sab cat*—from *sabotage*—might be merely an organizer or he might be one well versed in the safest methods of wrecking machinery. A *hoosier* was a working stiff who didn't know his job; to *hoosier up* was to slow work purposely. *Pie in the sky* was a cynical reference to the bourgeois heaven. *Gyppo* was any sort of work done by contract and was much frowned upon. A town policeman was a *clown*. The prosecuting attorney was the *cutor*. The Wob press used *hijack*—"Hi, jack!" a command to throw up the arms—long before it came into general usage. A *red card* was evidence of membership. A detective, company guard, or stool pigeon was a *fink*, by all odds the dirtiest word in the Wobbly thesaurus. There were many others, fully as pointed and all of them founded on sound etymological grounds and most of them containing humor.

Reading an I. W. W. newspaper in the heyday of the order was an exciting and an interesting experience. Its star columnist was one T-Bone Slim, who liked to razz a great colleague in the pay of Hearst and referred to his stuff as *brisbanalities*. Slim rode the rods all over western Canada and United States and took time out to write a blistering column every week.

And many of the footloose correspondents were good reporters. Consider this from *The Industrial Worker*, printed in 1923 under the heading of "Job News":

Aberdeen, Wash.—Coates-Fordney Camp—Highlead layout; two sides, rig-up crew and steel gang. Wages: gandy dancers, $3.75; rigging, $4.25 to $6.50. Garbage, $1.45 per day. Mattress furnished, but carry your own balloon. Slaves dissatisfied with conditions, but talk nothing but dehorn and world's series. Two of us Fellow Workers just started to line up a few of the boys when the push hit us on the behind with paychecks. He has the Wobbly horrors bad. Fellow Workers coming this way should lay off the bull-bucker here. He is a fink. Pretends to favor the One Big Union but when you ask him to stamp-up, he turns you in.

That would be good clear reporting on any man's newspaper.

From its membership peak of around one hundred thousand in the 1917 period, the I. W. W. has faded to a mere shadow. There are probably not five hundred of them in the Northwest woods, and probably not five thousand of them in the United States. What caused their decline and fall is something that is occasionally argued around bunkhouse stoves by a few old-timers who don't care for the C. I. O., the A. F. of L., or the Communist Party. It would appear there were several reasons.

First were the big federal raids on Wobbly halls in 1917 and the arrests, convictions, and incarceration of members. These discouraged all but the most stout-hearted. The Centralia affair, referred to, made several Wobbly martyrs but brought a loss rather than gain in membership. Then, in 1924, came a serious split in the very ranks of I. W. W. officials. They first resorted to slugging each other for possession of I. W. W. General Headquarters in Chicago. The strife was finally taken into the courts—capitalist courts—for injunctions and other mumbojumbo of the Ruling Class with which old-time Wobs would have no truck whatsoever. The result of this split was two distinct groups, each claiming to be the original, blown-in-the-bottle I. W. W. Chicago, New York, San Francisco, Portland, Seattle, and Spokane each had two halls carrying the I. W. W. trademark. Two papers appeared with I. W. W. on their mastheads. It was all very demoralizing. They called each other bad names in their schismatic newspapers, and organizers were embarrassed when they approached workers, for the purpose of collecting dues, to find that a delegate of the "other" I. W. W. had been there first. The effect on simple, dues-paying members can readily be imagined.

Moreover, the Communists—"comicals" to the Wobblies—bagged a number of Wobbly editors and speakers. The Communists also continue to promise a lot more to the downtrodden than the Wobs ever did. Although the Wobblies still spend as much or more effort in fighting the Communists, the C. I. O., and the A. F. of L. than they do in reducing capitalism to pulp, their ranks have been greatly thinned by desertions to Browder, Lewis, and Green.

The two Wobbly newspapers that survive in 1938 seem mild, genteel, and even reactionary when compared to the screaming headlines in red and black ink which, as late as ten years ago, called upon the slaves to arise, unite, and shake off their chains in six different languages. There is little in them to pack a Spokane full of bellowing pickets or to cause a Judge Gary to toss fitfully in his sleep.

During the summer of 1936 the Wobblies stirred in the logging camps of North Idaho, but they stirred feebly and to small purpose. Only one man was killed in the rioting, and the principal result of the whole upheaval was to halt work, for a few days, on the filming of a log-driving scene in what Hollywood has since announced is "an Epic of the Big Timber."

18

Log Pirates on the Sound

WHEN BOSS LOGGERS and lumbermen weren't suffering from the Wobbly Horrors, they sometimes had log pirates to bedevil them. That is, those on Grays Harbor and Puget Sound did. Log stealing wasn't a new racket when it was introduced on the West Coast; there had been log thieves on the Great Lakes and before that along the coast and rivers of Maine. But nowhere before had the business been an organized racket and carried out on a huge scale.

The great heyday of log pirates on Puget Sound was roughly from 1917 to 1928. It was swell pickings. Until 1925 there was no adequate legislation to handle the situation, and the log pirates were in clover. Once in a while they would make away with an entire raft, or boom, containing one million feet of logs; but usually they were content to steal a section of a raft, or roughly eighty thousand feet. The little fellows who worked the racket as a part-time job were happy to snitch even one or two logs.

The classic theft of all time took place on the Fraser River in British Columbia in the summer of 1920. Theoretically on watch in a little floating boom house near a big raft of Douglas fir was a good-natured Swede by name of Halstrom. The raft, he knew, was destined for a Seattle sawmill, and he knew that a tug was due the next morning to take it away.

Along about sundown a strange tug put into the cove where Halstrom watched the logs. He noted that it was the *Daisy Ann* and that its home port was

Seattle. The *Daisy Ann* hove to at the boom house. A
pleasant fellow, obviously the captain, hailed Halstrom
to know if the tug were heading right to reach the
logging town of Mission. Halstrom replied yes, that
Mission lay a few miles upriver. One thing led to another and the *Daisy Ann's* captain and crew of three
men joined Halstrom on the deacon seat outside the
boom-house door. The captain finally asked Halstrom
if he would like a snort.

Watching boom is a lonely sort of task, and Halstrom
was really a gregarious soul and a notable drinker. He
thought, he said, that a snort would be pretty good.
The tug skipper produced a bottle and they all drank.
They drank some more. Next morning when Watchman
Halstrom was roused by a towing crew come for the
raft, he looked out on a cove bare of so much as one
stick of timber. More than one million feet of fir had
disappeared.[1] Mr. Halstrom disappeared also, without
waiting for any wages due him.

Such gigantic thefts, of course, were rare, but it
shows what could be done when log pirates were organized and had an understanding with operators of what
came to be known as bootleg sawmills.

Nowhere in timbered North America is there a place
so happily designed for log thieves as Puget Sound. Its
thousands of miles of shore line, its innumerable bays,
sloughs, rivers, and islands lend themselves beautifully
to log piracy. And before the formation of the State
and other log patrols, the racket had grown into a
business that cost legitimate loggers and sawmills at
least one hundred thousand dollars a year and probably
more. Not a large racket as rackets go in Eastern cities,
but considered important money on Puget Sound.

Late in 1925 the Washington State legislature passed
what is now known as Chapter 154—"An act to protect
the title of the owners of floating logs, timber and

[1] No one was convicted, but the stolen raft was made into
lumber at a Seattle sawmill.

lumber." It prescribes in detail the branding of forest products by owners, and the registration of brands with the State. It provides for penalties for dealing in "maverick" or unbranded logs, or in logs branded by another, much as did the cattle-branding laws of an earlier day.

Next, the logging operators and mill owners incorporated log patrols—one on Grays Harbor, three on Puget Sound. Any one of the four patrols has had an interesting life, and the experience of the State Log Patrol, which has headquarters in Tacoma, is typical.

The State Log Patrol went into action on February 1, 1928, with W. E. Craw, a former police captain of Everett, Washington, in charge. Previous to public announcement of the patrol's formation, Captain Craw spent three months investigating the ramifications of log pirates. His findings were positive and startling. Working with operatives posing as boom men and log-pond men, he uncovered a ring of log thieves that included the owner, general manager, superintendent, and head boom man of a respectable sawmill concern of Seattle. These fellows had been doing jobs on a large scale, stealing entire booms or at least entire sections of booms at a time and cutting them in their own mill. Prosecution followed and convictions were secured.

Captain Craw found that the trail led still farther. He discovered the officials of one county on Puget Sound to be in league with the pirates. A sheriff and his deputies were getting a cut on every thousand feet of "hot" logs moved in their "jurisdiction." So Craw had himself commissioned as a deputy sheriff in five counties bordering the Sound. In this manner he could make arrests without tipping his hand to county officials, a large number of whom Craw felt sure were playing the game with the actual thieves.

Craw obtained eight fast tugboats. On each of these he placed a powerful searchlight and two determined

men armed with rifle and revolver and a deputy
sheriff's badge. These men had to be—and apparently
they were—a combination of navigator, mariner, policeman, detective, and sea lawyer. Each boat had its
particular district to patrol, and part of the business was
to check up on sawmills and to observe the appearance
of logs they were cutting. A number of small and
medium-sized mills were notorious for operating with
"hot" logs, for which they paid about a fifth of the
current market price.

Captain Craw, dressed as a hunter or fisherman, usually operated alone in a sixteen-foot speedboat which
carried a thirty-two-horsepower outboard motor and
could make twenty-five knots without trouble. He had
the opinion, which proved to be a good one, that
stealing could best be discouraged by "turning the
heat" on mills he suspected of sawing stolen logs. He
found no less than twelve in his patrol district of the
Sound. When he could, he put operatives to work with
the pirates. When he couldn't, he took to dropping in at
awkward times and catching the mill owners with logs
they couldn't account for.

Then, there were the beachcombers, men who on the
Sound usually refer to themselves as "stump ranchers."
They live in shacks on tidewater and their ways of
living are many. Often they were content to pick up a
stray log now and then which had jumped some raft
being towed by. The more ambitious would sneak up on
a raft tied to shore when the tide was in. They would
take out the boom chains that held the last or outer
section of logs. When the tide turned to ebb, the section tampered with would open and anywhere from ten
thousand to eighty thousand feet of logs would be
carried out where they could be corralled several at a
time and taken to the beachcomber's favorite cove.

Once safely in his snug harbor there were two things
a pirate could do. He could laboriously saw off the
branded end of every log and then brand them with his

own registered and legal mark or with the brand of the bootleg mill with which he did business; or, he could take a homemade branding ax and so mangle the original owner's brand that the devil himself couldn't have said what the mark had been. Then, of course, he would apply his own brand to the log ends.[2]

Thus rebranded, the pirate could not be convicted in court—at least not on any evidence supplied by the logs themselves. But in log piracy, as in most forms of crime, there is always something to tell the tale, and in more than one case on Puget Sound it has been a boom chain.

A boom chain is used to hold two logs together and thus form part of a boom or raft. It is about four feet long, weighs some seventy pounds, and has a ring in one end, a toggle in the other. They are worth around six dollars apiece to the pirate and are consequently valuable secondary loot. Besides, it is difficult to steal and move more than a log or two without using boom chains.

In 1929 Captain Craw was trying to get some evidence against a notorious Sound water-front character known as High-Pockets Peterson. He knew that Peterson was stealing logs, lots of logs, but Peterson had managed to keep out of the hands of the patrolmen. Then, High-Pockets made away with a big batch of boom chains. The captain, after some rather neat detective work, trailed him to Seattle, where Peterson left the chains in a small blacksmith shop on the West Waterway.

The officer went to the King County courthouse to get a warrant for arrest of the blacksmith and Peterson. When it was served on the smithy a day later, it was discovered that not a single chain in the shop carried an identification mark of any kind.

This was curious, because all boom chains around

[2] There is nothing to prohibit a beachcomber from registering his own log brand.

Puget Sound are marked with the owner's brand stamped into the toggle, and the brand is registered with the State just as the log brand is. But look as he would, Captain Craw found the toggles of all chains in the shop to be clean and smooth and free of any mark.

The log-patrol captain knew something about iron. He took one of the chains to a convenient emery wheel and had an assistant hold the smooth toggle against the wheel a moment while the sparks flew. When he looked at the toggle again there appeared as though etched in black on silver the pattern of an eight-spoked steering wheel. This was all he needed to know. Referring to his book of State-registered brands, which he always carried handy in his coat pocket, the patrol captain found that an eight-spoked wheel was Brand Number 102—and No. 102 was registered to the Cavano Logging Company, with headquarters in Seattle.

Whether or not the blacksmith knew it, it is a fact that merely heating a piece of iron and then pounding it smooth with a hammer on the anvil will not remove the brand from the grain of the iron. Invisible to the naked eye, any emery wheel will bring out the hidden mark in an instant—as both the blacksmith and High-Pockets found out in King County court. The mark was sufficient to convict them.

The news of High-Pockets' conviction probably aided in discouraging log thievery, but it didn't stop it; it made the pirates more wary. Captain Craw's patrolmen caught two men operating from Whidby Island who had cleaned up eight thousand dollars by log stealing in the fall and winter of 1929. Another time patrolmen intercepted delivery of two hundred thousand feet of stolen logs, good ones, too—the work of four men and a thirty-foot gas boat.

During the depression years log prices dropped to almost nothing, and so did log stealing. Then, No. 1 fir logs went up to twenty-six dollars and more a thousand feet in 1936. An average log contained about six thousand feet and would be worth, say, around one hundred and fifty dollars at a legitimate mill. A bootleg mill would pay possibly twenty dollars for it. Twenty dollars is considered good pay for a night's work by any beachcomber.

But there isn't likely to be any big revival of log piracy as an organized racket. It's too difficult to beat the log brands. On file at Olympia, the State capital, are ten hundred and ninety-five registered log brands. Their patterns run to letters, numbers, and combinations of the two. Then, there are "Character" brands—squares, circles, diamonds, and triangles.

Some of the Character brands are as gaudy as anything ever conceived by imaginative writers of "western" cattle-range fiction. A logging concern of Montesano has a six-pointed Jewish star. A Tacoma firm brands a bear's-foot mark on its products. Other brands depict an ax, a butterfly, a wine glass, a circular saw, and a Nazi symbol.

Important, too, are the "Catch" brands. These are a secondary line of defense against the log pirates. Catch brands work this way: Say that Brown, a logger, sold a boom of logs to Smith, a sawmill man. The logs, at Brown's camp, were branded with Brown's registered mark—that is, his letter, number, square, or whatnot. Before Smith's towing outfit starts to move logs from Brown's camp to Smith's mill, they stamp Smith's Catch brand onto the log ends. Thus the subsequent ownership is made legally clear. Catch brands differ from all other brands in that the dominant part of the mark is in the shape of a large letter "C."

The open cattle range is almost a thing of the past, even though cattle are still branded. What marked its end were the miles and miles of barbed-wire fence that spread over the grasslands and foothills. Barbed-wire fences can't help Puget Sound, however, and the Sound will always be open range. But the log patrols, backed by a law that has teeth in it as long and as sharp as a picaroon, and aided by the elaborate system of registered brands that is all but unbeatable, have wiped log piracy as an organized racket from the waters of the Sound.

The turning point probably came when the lads learned, from High-Pockets' conviction, that even "un-marked" boom chains will tell tales that a court will listen to.

19

Around the Barrel Stoves

BEFORE HIGHWAYS and automobiles and radio and
women and kids and schools and a hundred other de-
plorable things caught up with the timber line in the
Pacific Northwest, the transplanted but still unchanged
race of loggers lived in a world apart, much as they had
done in Michigan and Maine for three centuries.[1] Ten
months of a year their lives centered in the bunkhouse;
the other two months were spent in lush alcoholic delight on the skidroads of the lumber cities.

The work in Western camps was hard and dangerous
enough to weed out the sissies and weaklings, thus
keeping the breed pure and rugged. But life in camp
wasn't so bad. Living conditions had improved slowly
but steadily. By the time of the World War loggers in
the West were feeding and bedding better than sailors
and construction workers. With the aid of the War and
the Wobblies they got the eight-hour day and other
concessions in 1918. The old-time bunkhouse, built of
logs and housing a hundred men to a room, was a thing
of the past. The new camps had a large and clean
building for cookhouse and dining room. The men
lived in small and rather neat bunkhouses built for six
to eight men each. There were windows. Electric lights

---

[1]M. T. Dunten, ex-logger and a keen observer, now of
Olympia, Washington, recalls that loggers were so well recognized as a distinct species that even the press took cognizance.
In reporting a Puget Sound steamboat accident (*circa* 1912) a
newspaper said that ". . . three men and a logger were
drowned."

215

were becoming common. Spring cots with mattresses, later with company sheets and blankets, were furnished. Far-sighted logging operators vied with each other to set a good table. Some of them put in recreation rooms, with pool tables, a phonograph, and magazines.

But the camp was still remote. You walked into it, or at best you rode a flatcar over a bumpy and crooked logging railroad, or you went by steamboat. Mail might come in once a week. It mattered little, for loggers of those days didn't expect much mail. Wartime and a shortage of men brought girls into camp to wait on table, but otherwise the life of a logger remained aloof and monkish.

Females in camp made many loggers restless. They brought sharply to mind things that heretofore had been relegated to Fourth of July and Christmas holidays. Most of the waitresses were either good or careful girls and usually married a hook tender or a high climber, which didn't help the other loggers any.

So, the boys got restless and took to moving around. It was common enough for a logger to start the season in January at a camp on Grays Harbor in western Washington, move to Hama Hama on Hood's Canal by April, to Skycomish in northern Washington by June, to the Tillamook Line in Oregon by August, and wind up at remote Coos Bay on the South Oregon coast in time for Christmas. Instead of two enormous sprees every year, he had half a dozen small ones.[2] By 1920, or thereabout, loggers in the coast fir country had the travel habit bad. The old-timers who still figured on two and only two blow-ins a year called them short-stakers, camp inspectors, and drummers and boomers.

True enough, there wasn't a great deal to do in camp when a day was done. There were cards, the old stand-by, and loggers had begun to read a few newspapers

[2] The men of the inland pine districts of the West have never moved around so much as those on the coast.

and pulp magazines. But most of all they entertained
themselves by sitting around the box or barrel stoves of
bunkhouses and talking.

The short-stake travelers reported what was going on
in other camps from Humboldt Bay in California to the
Queen Charlotte Islands, up near Alaska. Thus they
ranged in the fir and redwood from about forty degrees to well North of fifty-three degrees—calked boots
on their feet and a can of snuff in the pockets of their
tin pants. That was goodly pasture to range in, and lots
of them saw many things.

As for the veterans, the oldest men, they had done
their ranging; but they could tell of great men and
doings back in the ground-lead days and the bullwhacking era. Legends grew out of these bunkhouse
discourses—not the made-up tales of Paul Bunyan, but
tales of actual men who did thus and so at such a
place on such a time.

There were no written records of course. All the reporting of present and past events was done by word of
mouth. Although some of the stories were tinged with
the marvelous, all of them were founded on fact and
many of them were sound reporting of events that had
touched the life of loggers. Like their academic colleagues, bunkhouse historians did not always agree on
interpretation, or even on fact. And it was only natural
that in time, no matter how commonplace the subject, it
took on a fabulous quality by the very retelling. Many
characters of bunkhouse biographers were legend even
while they lived.

When widow-making winds howled through the tall
fir trees and winter rain beat gloom into the forest, the
barrelstove historians liked to tell how the celebrated
wild man, John Turnow, had added to the common
dangers of logging in western Washington. That had
been in 1910 and for two years after.

This Turnow was no part of imagination. In 1910 he
was thirty-one years old, six feet five inches tall, and

weighed some two hundred and fifty pounds, all of it coiled-spring muscle—as undertakers one day soon would know. And Turnow himself prepared six customers for this final profession. Bunkhouse historians came in time to tell that wherever John Turnow walked in the woods, Death walked close by; they said he lived in treetops, swinging from limb to limb like a gorilla. But these were decorations. The bare facts of Turnow's life were strange enough.

Born in Grays Harbor County, Washington, of a respected pioneer family, John Turnow had been "queer" since early boyhood. He liked to be alone. By the time he was ten he often ran away, always into the deep woods, where he lived for a week at a time, living on what he could kill. He was a dead shot who could bore a grouse through the eye at fifty yards. He made fire Indian-fashion, and shoes out of bark and deerskin. He could call any bird or animal to him.

In 1909 this "Thoreau without brains" was committed to an institution at Salem, Oregon, from which he escaped. About a year later, John and Will Bauer, young men of Grays Harbor County, did not return from a bear hunt. Searching parties found their bodies, each drilled through the head, tucked neatly under a pile of brush.

Turnow was suspected. A man hunt got under way with posses numbering two hundred able woodsmen beating the forest. Not one of them caught sight of the outlaw. When snow came, efforts were redoubled, but Turnow left no tracks and the hunters were forced to the conclusion that Turnow had denned up like a bear, as he probably had.

Then, in March of 1912, word came from a trapper that the wanted man was camped not far from a spot on the Satsop River known as Oxbow. It was thirty-five miles in deepest timber. Colin McKenzie, Grays Harbor sheriff, and A. V. Elmer, ex-logger turned deputy game warden, started for Oxbow. They did not return.

Thirteen days later a searching party found the two missing men. Each had been drilled once through the head, and an effort had been made to bury the bodies in a shallow trench. Most of the dead men's clothing had been removed and their rifles and ammunition had been taken.

Now the hunt for the "Wild Man of the Olympics" began in earnest, with a reward of five thousand dollars on his head. And now, too, began the alarums. Turnow had been seen here, there, everywhere, at the same time and at points two hundred miles apart. A logging camp storehouse of the Simpson Logging Company was entered in the night and a pair of calked boots stolen. Lone log buckers working in the woods sighted a monster vanishing through the timber mists. Other loggers saw some great body disappear into thick tops of fir. The crews of the Simpson company, operating in timber that the wild man was said to have claimed for his own domain, went to work with fear in their hearts.

If you didn't know the Olympic country of Washington you might have thought it strange that more than one thousand hunters, all of them at home in the woods, failed to find the outlaw in a hunt that lasted a year. But it's vast territory that Turnow ranged in, and in 1912 it was pretty much virgin timber, a dense jungle, well watered and through which man could go but slowly—very slowly when looking for such a fellow as Turnow. Somewhere in that forest the wild man laid out the winter of 1912–1913, seen by no one. Spring came and the hunt continued without abating.

On April 16, 1913, Giles Quimby, logger turned deputy, sighted a small rude hut in a natural clearing, perhaps a mile from the scene of the murders of McKenzie and Elmer. With Quimby were Louis Blair and Charles Lathrop, Grays Harbor loggers. After a brief council the three men decided to approach the hut from three directions. They began the advance slowly, cautiously, with rifles cocked.

Deputy Quimby was moving ahead, picking his steps and halting now and then to listen. He heard nothing at all until a sudden burst of gunfire shattered the silence. At the same time he saw Louis Blair tumble headlong, blood spurting horribly from his head.

Quimby's gun was now at his shoulder. For a flash he saw a great head and an ugly bearded face pop out from behind a hemlock. Quimby fired. The head disappeared. Quimby knew the head belonged to John Turnow—but had he hit it with his shot?

He didn't wait long to know. There was another burst of fire and Quimby saw Charles Lathrop throw up his arms and go tumbling to the ground. Again the great ugly head peered quickly from behind the hemlock. Quimby fired and fired again until the magazine of his gun was empty. Then he crouched to reload.

All was silent, except for the worried whining of Quimby's hounds who were sniffing at the two dead loggers. But, had one of Quimby's shots found the bearded giant? Quimby couldn't know. As quietly as possible he made his way through the woods to a safe distance. Then he hurried to Camp 5 of the Simpson logging outfit.

Quimby led a posse of some twenty-five loggers to the sinister clearing where the hut stood. They found John Turnow quite dead. There he was, the wild fellow, sprawled on his back, his big old-fashioned rifle across his chest and clutched in his two hands. He was a sight that loggers who saw him remember vividly. The huge man with matted beard and hair, dressed now in ragged garments made from bark and gunnysacking, laid fold upon fold and filled with fir and hemlock needles. On his feet was the only conventional bit of clothing he possessed, a pair of comparatively new calked boots. In the rude hut near by the posse found six dollars and sixty-five cents in silver, a small knife, and more gunnysacking. Not in the hut or elsewhere could they find any sign of food.

A pack horse was brought in. They strapped the big wild man across a saddle blanket and took him out to Montesano, county seat. And up at Simpson's Camp 5, a kindly cook set out a gallon of lemon extract—approximately twenty-two-proof alcohol—in honor of the occasion.[8] With John Turnow out of the way, loggers could now give both eyes to the business of logging.

Sometimes the bunkhouse discussions turned to more technical subjects, such as who used the first logging locomotive in the West. Old-timers generally agreed it to have been the three Blackman brothers, out of Maine, who came to Snohomish, Washington, in 1872 and proceeded to become big loggers. In a day when bulls were considered the last word in logging motive power, the Blackmans had invented and patented a queer sort of logging locomotive that looked like a big teakettle. They had strips of rock maple shipped to Snohomish from the Atlantic Coast. These they laid like rails and over them the big teakettle puffed and chugged. It worked, too, and made the Blackmans a lot of money while other boss loggers scoffed at the idea.

The town of Snohomish was quite a logging center in those days—'way bigger than Seattle. The Loggers' Saloon there advertised "Champagne & Billiards" in the columns of *The Eye,* one of the town's two newspapers, and rum and girls could be had at a score of places. They didn't like Chinese in Snohomish. When the laundries got too thick, they were all blown into the river—Chinese and all—by a charge of dynamite that was heard twenty miles away and got into the daily papers.

Another subject the veterans talked about was log

[8] In Grays Harbor County courthouse, Montesano, Washington, is a placque in memory of the six men who lost their lives in the Turnow affair.

driving, and of the time a smart-aleck boss lumberman thought he would drive sugar-pine logs down the
Middle Fork of Oregon's Willamette River. He
wouldn't listen to his loggers who told him that sugar-
pine butts wouldn't float; but dumped some five
million feet of them into the Willamette at Pine open-
ings, and there they sunk like so many steel poles. The
old-timers wondered, and still wonder, if the famous
sugar-pine drive will ever be retrieved.

A minor oddity much talked about in the camps of
the Willapa Harbor district of Washington was the Big
Black Cat of Walville. The cat was five feet high, made
of wood and painted and nailed to the white lattice
work of the Walville sawmill. Its whiskers were made of
staunch haywire. The cat's back was arched, its tail
high, and when you got close up you could see that the
animal was snarling, showing wicked teeth made of
clamshells and painted red. The Japanese sawmill
workers thought the cat some kind of good magic, and
on a Sunday you might see a Japanese father lead his
wondering children into the mill yard and point out the
cat to them. Many loggers thought the Big Black Cat
was a survival of Indian "medicine," but it was really
the symbol of the Order of Hoo-Hoo, for many years
a fun-organization of lumbermen. The Walville cat was
put where it was to mystify nonmembers.[4]

The sawmill town of McCormick, Washington, presented another oddity. It was an enormous sun dial
that ran in a wide arc clear across the front of the mill.
Its Roman numerals looked odd in the forest, and many
a logger passing by on his way to camp cynically wondered that any mill owner should want his slaves to
know what time of day it was.

[4]When the Walville mill was torn down in 1936, the Big Black
Cat was presented to the man who made it thirty-five years
before. He is Charles Caverley, old-timer from the Michigan
woods, now living on a farm near Walville.

Arguments as to who was the first high-climber to top a spar tree in the West have been going on for thirty years and the question never will be settled. Many hold it to have been an unnamed Finnish sailor whom Merrill & Ring brought from Seattle to their Snohomish camp to do the job. That was about 1902. The Finn topped the tree, all right, but that night he took aboard too much *aquavit,* proffered by the hospitable loggers, and disappeared, probably returning to Seattle. Now that the tree was topped, somebody had to climb it and hang the block and rigging. Ben (Red) Illige, a young logger, volunteered to do the job. He "dressed" the tree and right then and there was made the camp's official high-climber at the staggering wage of six dollars a day.[5] He may well have been the first of his kind in the Northwest, although there have been a dozen claimants to the honor.

The doings and sayings of noted camp foremen and superintendents—bulls of the woods—have always been a bunkhouse topic, and countless stories, both true and apocryphal, were told of such characters as Bill Chisholm, Gus Wiest, Cyclone Miller, Ronald McDonald, Cutler Lewis, Black Dan McClanahan, Pete Cline, Joe Flora, Red Roberts, Fay Abrams, and the noted Tugboat Wilson. The life of any one of them would make a book, and an interesting book; they— some of them still live—have seen a lot of fancy logging and a lot of wild doings in the woods and elsewhere.

Among minor loggers who became well enough known to be subject for bunkhouse discussion was one Ike Ocean, who ranged through Oregon and Washington and is said never to have worn either shoes or sox on his feet. He carried a dollar watch inside a snuffbox. He hitched his galluses to his tin pants by strands of

[5] In the 1920s high climbers were paid as much as fifteen dollars a day.

haywire. In snow or rain his outfit consisted only of pants and a red woolen undershirt.

In former times each district had a lad who was something of a fighter, but here in the West loggers appear to have done less fighting than in the Lake States, and no eye gouger and ear chewer attained the stature of a legend, such as Michigan's Silver Jack Driscoll.

Down in the redwood camps old-timers told with amusement of a shipload of settlers who arrived on Humboldt Bay bringing knock-down houses of sheet iron with them. These were to "protect them from the Indians." For pig and goose pens the early Humboldt settlers used the hollow stumps of great redwoods, and to this day a native of Humboldt County, California, is said to have been "born in a goose pen."

Mostly, though, the redwood loggers argued about the tallest redwood that ever stood. Some claimed to have seen a sequoia that was more than four hundred feet tall, but the tallest one ever measured still stands on Dyerville Flat, a few miles south of Scotia. It is three hundred and sixty-four feet from ground to tip.

The boys in the Western pine woods talked of the hectic days of the sheep and cattlemen's wars, when a number of loggers who were good shots and liked trouble hired out in the gangs of cattlemen in their bloody and futile effort to keep sheep and barbed wire off the open range. There was considerable shooting and many casualties.

Wherever there was a Wobbly—in pine, fir, or red-wood country—bunkhouse forums were sure to hear of Wobbly Joe Hill (Hillstrom), best known of the I. W. W. martyrs and a writer of "songs of discontent," who was convicted of murder and went down in front of a firing squad of the State of Utah, at Salt Lake City, on November 19, 1915. "Joe Hill's Last Will," reputedly written on the eve of his execution, was famous bunkhouse poetry:

My will is easy to decide,
For there is nothing to divide.
My kin don't need to fuss and moan—
Moss does not cling to rolling stone.
My body? Ah, if I could choose,
I would to ashes it reduce,
And let the merry breezes blow
My dust to where some flowers grow.
Perhaps some fading flower then
Would come to life and bloom again.
This is my last and final will,
Good luck to all of you—Joe Hill.

The Western pine boys never had a Hinckley fire to talk about, but they saw many forests burn. There was that blazing summer of 1910. From mid-July until August 21, an army of three thousand men, mostly loggers and forest rangers, fought timber fires on a one-hundred-and-twenty-mile front in Idaho. Seventy-four of them were burned to death and more than a hundred went to hospital. Out of the welter E. C. Pulaski, forest ranger, emerged a hero.

Caught in a gulch with fire on all sides, Ranger Pulaski led his crew of forty-five men into an old mine tunnel. When the flames swept over it panic seized the men and some started to bolt. Pulaski pulled his gun and vowed he would shoot the first who tried to get out. He wet clothing in the shallow mine water and hung it at the tunnel entrance. Finally he was overcome by gas and heat, and fell, but he survived and so did all his crew. It was one of the classic scenes the Western pine loggers talked about.

They had fabulous bulls-of-the-woods in the pine country. Outstanding was Bill Deary, a boss and timber cruiser so noted that the town of Deary, Idaho, was

named for him; and Moonlight Joe, the wild foreman
for Humbird's. It was told that neither wolves nor owls
were ever seen in timber around the Humbird camps.
It was the howling of Moonlight Joe, hungry for more
logs, that scared them away permanently.

In all camps, everywhere, bunkhouse forums discussed, and often blasted, the emerging *gyppo*, or contract system of woods work. Who invented it, no one
knows, but *gyppo* quickly spread throughout the fir,
the pine, and the redwood camps. How it got its name
nobody knows, but cynical old-timers said it came from
gypsy, and especially the gypsy's well-known habit of
taking everything not nailed down. You get the connection if you know what Wobblies term the "ideology of
the class-conscious worker." That ideology is that the
more you produce for the boss, the worse it is for you.
Hence, when you work hard and hurry, in order to
make big wages at so much a thousand feet of logs, the
boss is gypsying, or gypping you out of just so much
more that should be yours by divine right.

Along the Columbia River, old-timers like to tell
about the time *Blue Jeans* played the Marquam Grand
Theater in Portland. *Blue Jeans* was possibly the only
melodrama that had a scene laid in a sawmill. It was of
the era of flesh and blood drama, when the blood was
very red and often flowed copiously.

In that day sawmills played a major part in life at
Portland, and it was not strange that the advance man
for the *Blue Jeans* show soon had the sawdust-conscious
citizens agog. Lurid posters in every saloon and barber-
shop on the skidroad announced the coming of the
world's greatest dramatic effort, and these posters were
the work of an artist. They depicted the interior of a
huge manufacturing plant, with a gigantic circular saw
eating into a log—a log that was as big as any ever seen
on the Columbia. Wheels, pulleys, and belts cluttered
up this sawmill, until you wondered where there was

room for the workers. It was, in short, the height of
mechanical wizardry. And all on the stage, mind you.
Never had such a sawmill been conceived even in saw-
mill-sophisticated Portland. And there, in the picture,
tied firmly to the log and scarcely a foot from the
whirling saw, was a handsome blond youth.

There was some local discussion as to why there
was no sawyer at the levers in the picture, and it was
obvious that the log carriage had no dogs to it; at least,
they couldn't be seen. But these things were put aside
as of minor importance, due probably to the ignorance
of the artist. Yet the job was done in six bright colors
and it was eye-arresting, when viewed through a number of beers at Erickson's.

Here was the first sawmill drama to appear in Portland. The old Marquam Grand was packed to the
doors.

The action of the show went smoothly forward
through two acts, but there was only mild interest in
the audience. It was apparent why most folk had come
that night, and that was to see the widely advertised
"Great Sawmill Scene—Mechanically Perfect in Every
Detail." And at last when the curtain arose on this
scene the crowd sat up in their seats. They not only
sat up in their seats but they gaped in astonishment.
There were whisperings, too, and mutterings. And no
wonder.

The mastodonic sawmill of *Blue Jeans* was revealed
by the searching glare of the footlights to be nothing
more nor less than a stage whereon rested a very small
sawmill carriage made chiefly, as one customer estimated aloud, of Number 4 common boards; and a
pitifully small circular saw attached to a very wobbly
frame. The saw was turning so moderately that it was
possible to count the teeth as it turned. The log on the
carriage was not "a Giant of the Forest," as advertised
on the posters, but an obvious cull, approximately ten
feet long and some twelve inches thick at the butt—

the kind of thing Columbia River loggers left in the woods to rot.

Old head sawyers in the audience puckered their brows at such an offense against the dignity of their calling. Loggers announced audibly that the stick on the stage might do to make matches from but nothing else. The actors, however, went ahead with the drama. In due time the handsome blond youth got into the clutches of the mean devil with the silk hat and riding crop, and was tied to the rig on the carriage. The log rolled uneasily. The saw continued to turn, even if but slowly, and the log moved slowly in the general direction of the saw. The silk-hatted villain made one more adjustment of some sort of a wheel attached to the log —something new in the sawmill line—and laughed a sneering laugh at his brave but helpless victim. "Die like a dog, you . . ." he began, but was interrupted.

"Set over your blocks, mister," came a clear, bellowing, and only slightly alcoholic voice from the audience. "Set over your blocks or you won't get no clears outa that log."

This technical and brotherly advice brought down the house, and the manager of the *Blue Jeans* company brought down the curtain on the world's greatest sawmill drama. It is a fact that since then no *Blue Jeans* company ever played the city of Portland.

Yes, sir, you could hear no little folklore and real history around the barrel stoves of bunkhouses. And every year from about 1900 on they had more and more to talk about. Things that affected the life of the loggers—the new machines, the Wobblies, the new white sheets, the new white crockery on the table, the new girl waitresses, the electricity, the mail and newspapers that now came daily, and most important of all—although the loggers didn't know it then—the coming of radios, married men and their families, and the highways. Presently these latter things would do away with all bunkhouse discussions. In a decade, or a little more, they would all but do away with the loggers themselves—that is, with the true, ancient, and wild strain that started logging near South Berwick, Maine, A.D. 1631.

20

The Passing of a Race

THE LOGGERS never looked backward—eastward. Had they done so the more reflective among them might have seen what was happening—that as fast as they abandoned their old works a horde of farmers, traders, and city slickers moved in to grub stumps, plat town sites, and make highways out of the grass-grown logging roads. It was the loggers' ancient enemy, Civilization, following hard on their tails, and they wanted none of it.

There was always timber, plenty of timber—just over the next hump. The first hump was Bangor. The boys duffed in and cut so much white pine that Maine's founding fathers put a replica of *pinus strobus* on their state flag. They gave New England a close shave—once over for pine, once for spruce—then swept on into York State and Pennsylvania, pausing a brief moment at Glens Falls and Williamsport to whack hell out of what timber was left. York's and Penn's woods went down before the onslaught like so much wheat in a storm, and the boys piled into Michigan, making sawdust forty feet deep on which to build Saginaw. They went West and North in Michigan, clearing the upper peninsula last of all before they moved into Wisconsin to fill the rivers full of round-stuff and make bedlams out of Ashland, Wausau, and Chippewa Falls.

Michigan and Wisconsin lasted a goodly time, as time was reckoned by loggers, but it had an end. When it came the boys stopped only long enough to file the teeth of their saws, then swarmed into Minnesota like locusts. Like locusts, too, they took everything in their path. They cut the white men's forest. They drove most of the remaining red men from the reservations, often married their squaws, then cut the reservation timber. The Twin Cities reared up from the piles of chips and sawdust they made. But daylight got into the Minnesota swamp powerful sudden, and this time the boys faced a long jump before they could hide in more timber.

Most of them took an extra gallon of drinking liquor, to lighten the ghastly trip across those plains where there weren't even stumps to look at, and struck out for the Pacific Northwest and California; many of them moved direct to British Columbia. The others went to the Deep South, from whence they would have to move again, and move West, too, for the virgin timber beyond the Great Plains would outlast all else.

They came down the Columbia River into Oregon and Washington with a monstrous clanking of peaveys and immediately sailed into bigger and thicker timber than any of them had ever known. And now, although probably not one of them realized it, the loggers were in their last stronghold, their backs to the sea. There was no hump to go over from here. Civilization had caught up with them at last and civilization would lay the true species of logger lower than any stump they ever cut.

Meanwhile, and unknown to the mass of loggers, certain outside forces were at work on the lumber industry. To show what had been and still is going on a certain few statistics are necessary.

In 1909 the sawmills of the country made better than forty-five billion feet of lumber. It was the all-time peak and it will probably never be reached again. But the fall in production since 1909 has not been due to lack of timber. It has been due to lack of demand. Before 1909 the per capita consumption of lumber had started to drop and it has been dropping ever since—

from a top of five hundred and twenty-three feet per American in 1906, to one hundred and thirty-five feet in 1935. Cities were first built of lumber only; today they are built of almost everything else.

Meanwhile, too, the boys had cleared more forest land of timber than was needed for farms; the great hunger for land that played such a part in American development was on the wane. In 1936, so the National Recovery Administration has determined, more than fifty million acres of abandoned farm land were reverting to forest. This shutting daylight *out* of the swamp may well continue for years.

The federal government, once so free with its timber, began holding on to what it had left, then to acquiring forest lands which appear today as the National forests and parks. Public opinion turned quickly against the logger and lumberman. As pioneers the loggers had done their work well, only too well to suit a people that suddenly had gone urban and wanted some forests to play in. These urbanites accused the loggers of leaving nothing but stumps in their wake. The charge was only partly true. The loggers left stumps but they left farms and towns and cities as well.

Boss loggers and lumbermen were surprised one day to find themselves public ogres who fairly sweated destruction from every pore and who ate up everything but the sawdust, which they left in unsightly piles. The Timber Baron became a notable figure in the American demonology—complete with peaveys for horns, and the tail a long, curling ribbon of bandsaw.

During the first decade of the present century the public attack on the Timber Barons was fierce and constant, and the stench of the Oregon Timber Fraud cases was wafted higher than the tallest fir. It was a good thing, one would judge, from the viewpoint both of the public and of the lumber industry. The attack had no effect on the oldline Barons; they simply retired into their mansions, picked their teeth with solid gold toothpicks, and had their pictures and "biographies" put into mugg books which told of the Christian lives they had lived and the amount of money they had given to churches. But the attack had an excellent effect on the younger generation of timber operators.

Long ago the best men of the industry began looking to the future to mend the past. They talked no more about timber that would "last forever." The talk turned to actual conservation measures. Selective logging is a term the public is going to hear more and more about. Practiced for more than a decade already, selective logging means that timber cutting is done in such a manner as to leave seed trees of mature growth on every acre of land logged over. The cheering results can be seen on thousands of acres of logged-*over* but not logged-*off* lands. Small forests of rugged saplings are springing up.

The largest operators have their own private nurseries from which selected tree stock is removed for planting on suitable ground. One such nursery near the Columbia River sets out two million seedlings annually, and there are a score of others in Western states.

But if given a chance Nature herself is the best forester of them all. Fire is the great danger to second-growth forests. So, in all modern logging camps there are fire-prevention measures that would astound an old-time lumberjack whose only idea on the subject was to refrain from knocking live coals out of his pipe in July and August. At every logging camp of any pretension there is a hygrometer, an instrument for measuring the humidity in the air. When the figure drops to thirty, in most districts, logging ceases, either by state law or by agreement of logging operators. And camp fire departments are equipped with miles of hose, water-tank cars, and heavy duty pumps. Government airplanes are used for spotting fires and often for dropping supplies to beleaguered fire fighters.

Such great concerns as the Weyerhaeuser and the Long-Bell interests—and many smaller concerns—have their logging operations planned in a cycle. When the last virgin timber has been cut, the first sections logged over will be ready for reharvesting.

This may sound unduly optimistic to the layman, in view of the past record, but to anyone who has been a close observer it is a condition reasonable to expect. For two hundred years and more the American people, and much of the rest of the world, couldn't seem to get enough lumber. All efforts of the lumber industry were bent toward bigger and faster production. This condition ceased shortly after the World War and it isn't likely to be met with again. Long before 1929 the big camps and sawmills of the Pacific Northwest and coast were running only part time.

In 1935 those big mills in Washington cut a total of three and one-half billion feet, in Oregon three and one-tenth billion feet. California cut one and one-half billion feet, Idaho six hundred million feet.

As for the remaining stand of timber in the United States, the Forest Service figures give it, for 1935, as sixteen hundred and sixty-eight billion feet, more than two-thirds of which is on the Pacific Coast.

Thus the industry has gone into a thoughtful and a quieter period than it has ever known. The marketing of the product of a log is of vastly more importance than the cutting of that log in the forest. It is a more stable industry, and a far less colorful one, for all these regrettable things have left their mark on the logger strain. Contact with civilization over long periods has never failed to kill off a race of pure savages and such a process is now well advanced in the pine and fir and redwood forests of the West.

Horse-logging and bullwhacking were the lumber-jacks' manner of work for two hundred and fifty years. It was a primitive method, and because it exactly suited the race of primitive men who used it, it survived for many years after steam-driven machinery was common everywhere except in the woods.

But steam finally drove the "hay burners"—the horses and oxen—out of the timber and with them went the colorful teamsters and bullwhackers. With it steam brought a bewildering amount and variety of machinery and an industrial routine and discipline that tended to make proletarians out of a race of men who had belonged to no order or class but their own. Steam did away with the cant-dog men. It drove the white-water men from the rivers—to be jammed on Garry's Rocks no more. In 1938 gasoline-driven machinery bids fair to drive the fallers and buckers—the very last of the manual laborers—out of their lair in the swamp.

The old-time log bunkhouses, as related, disappeared and in their place arose barrack-like structures; then the barracks were made into neat bunkhouses where every man has an army cot to himself and a locker in which to put his store clothes. Once started on improvements the boss loggers went wild. They stocked white sheets and pillow slips and added a bedmaker to the payroll. Lamps and lanterns gave way to electricity. Many of the companies threw out the grand old privies—some of them truly monumental jobs—and installed flush closets. A camp without a showerbath became a curiosity many years ago.

At about this time the girl waitresses put in an appearance. They made loggers restless, but they married loggers quickly and this fact gave some canny timber baron a bold and provocative idea: It might be possible to hire loggers who would stay married more than one night. It was tried and it worked beautifully. With the missus right in camp, the logger had no need to visit the fleshpots of the cities. Labor turnover was reduced, production speeded. The logging operators were quick to build houses in camp for married men.

Such doings naturally resulted in children. Today there is no large camp in the West that does not have its school and schoolmarm. That is, except in camps which are not camps at all, such as that of a large redwood operation where there are no camp buildings of any kind; everybody drives his car to and from his home in one of five towns within a radius of thirty miles of "camp."

The highways, in fact, have done as much or more than the women to reduce the logger to proletarian status. When the hard-dirt or paved road got within shouting distance of camp, the first shout loggers heard was that of automobile salesmen. You'll find a garage in almost any camp today, large or small. Unmarried loggers who, in older and more moral days, never saw a gaslight between late December and July Fourth, run to town on Saturday night and sleep it off Sunday afternoon. The highways are doing other things to the camps. Just as steam drove out the bulls, paved highways are driving out the steam locomotives. Trucks are doing the hauling to sawmills these days; gasoline-driven tractors are laying the fires in the donkey engines.

Comforts, marriage, and children, machine logging and highways—from this point onward it is easy to trace the complete disintegration of the tough and hairy species that was formed on the grim wooded shore of Maine three hundred years ago.

The Western loggers began subscribing to daily newspapers and to correspondence courses in everything from Personality to saxophone playing. Instead of spending all their money for booze and other necessities, some of them began carting radios into camp, where they still bleat nightly to the disgust of the few remnants of veritable *Pithecanthropus erectus* who had rather stove log about the time so-and-so loaded too high with the cross haul and came down Seney Hill like yaller hell and busted runners, with the snub line broken and no hay on the road. . . .

Loggers changed their tobacco habits. Thirty years ago a man who came into camp smoking a cigarette was usually eyed coldly, allowed to eat his supper, then sent packing down the trail.[1] "A man who will smoke one of them pimp sticks," old Jigger Jones said soberly, "won't stop at nothin'." Jigger and his contemporaries considered a cigarette smoker to be worthless as a logger, and a degenerate as well. Today's logging-camp stores sell more cigarettes than smoking and chewing tobacco combined.

The camb stores now carry other items. They stock baby diapers these days; and rouge, lipstick, hairnets, and two-way-stretch girdles. A logger couldn't buy a red woolen undershirt even to save him from consumption, but he has his choice of four dainty colors of rayon. And the rustle of a magazine back in the timber is far more likely to be *McCall's* than the *National Police Gazette*.

A casual visit to a modern logging camp will show what has happened to the race that cut a three-thousand-mile swath through the forest, shaved with an ax, and bit mouthfuls of wood out of white pine bars. A number of the new camps have full-sized tennis courts, backstops and all.[2] Many a camp has a nightly movie show, with Saturday matinee for the kids. Radio tenors are heard cooing every evening in formerly remote camps that were quiet except for the soughing of the wind in the firs and pines, or enlivened by the screaming of cougars and, on occasion, the even louder howling of loggers tanked on cookhouse lemon extract.

---

[1] Sam Blakely, logging superintendent at Bend, Oregon, recalls his amazement when, in the winter of 1897, the foreman of the camp in which Blakely was working, allowed a cigarette smoker to stay overnight in camp.

[2] The ultimate, perhaps, has been achieved at the Franklin River camp of Bloedel, Stewart & Welch, Ltd., on Vancouver Island, British Columbia, and it appears in the form of a badminton court. Cricket is undoubtedly just around the corner.

When the logger is now roused of a morning it is not to the melodious notes of the gut-hammer pounded out by a bullcook who has pride in his artistry. Hardly. He is fairly blown from his bed by a blast from an electrically operated siren or foghorn. Nor after breakfast does he hear the cheery bellow of the camp push: "Roll out or roll up!" Instead, his ears are shocked by a locomotive whistle or the braying of the horn on the boss truck of the convoy. The factory has caught up with him.

Should he raise his voice in the wilderness, the song is likely to be a pansy croon. He has forgotten if ever he knew the stirring strophes to "The Little Brown Bulls" and "The Redlight Saloon." The talk of the logger is just about the same as that of his city brother, whom he so long scorned and shunned—the make of car, radio programs, and the World's Series. His argot, instead of the virile cant plugged full of the imagination and color of the pioneer, has largely degenerated into the wisecracks of the city which he has heard over the superfidelity, sixteen-tube cabinet radio in his bunkhouse or home in camp. His profanity, once of noble stature and attaining to an art, consists of a weak and plagiarized "Jeez!" There is nothing here to equal T. C. Cunnion, the Peterborough man eater, and his "By th' dynamitin' Ol' So-and-So, etc." It took men who slept on fir boughs and not in white sheets to get things like that off their chests.

Nor will you, if you ever were in camp of a morning, hear the happy obscene greetings and observations that made of reveille a vaudeville well worth the hearing. No, sir. Today you will hear soprano voices, feminine voices, twittering over back-yard fences about bridge and "permanents," while underneath all is the civilizing drone of the electric washing machine.

It's all pretty doleful for the few old Nestors who survive. The ancient bullcook, his handle-bar mustaches drooping—symbolically, perhaps—makes his daily round of the bunkhouses, pausing now and again to feast his dim but startled eyes on the camp wash lines. Here he contemplates with mixed emotions the filmy underthings of mauve and peach and azure that flutter in the pine-laden breeze—and he curses the flesh that is now much weaker than it was in Saginaw days.

Down the track a piece, a woman comes to the door of the camp schoolhouse and rings a bell—nothing short of a knell to the old-timers—while kids, *loggers'* kids, whoop and yell for a last moment before they go inside to be taught that Democracy makes all men free and equal and that the old Timber Barons and their kind were very bad men.

Nor is this all that the old-time logger has to put up with. When the still strange and dismal day's work is done, he may sit down in his bunkhouse to take a look at the *Morning Oregonian,* the *Seattle Star,* or the *Chronicle* of Spokane. But there is no comfort here, no forgetting. Even his newspaper informs him of still more unbelievable yet true happenings in what was once his realm. Late in 1937 something like the following dispatch may well have caught his eye for a moment:

LOGGERS VIE FOR CUP

ASTORIA, Ore., Sept. 17—Leading the field in open play at the Pacific Logging Congress at Seaside yesterday, George Drake, Simpson Logging Co., Shelton, Wash., went around the Gearhart course in a neat 74. Bruce Morehead, Mt. Emily Lumber Co., and Bob Conklin, Weyerhaeuser's, Longview, were runners-up. The game attracted a large gallery.

If the old-timer read any further, which is doubtful, he would have learned that virtually every logging superintendent and about half of the camp foremen of

Oregon, Washington, Idaho, and California played in that tournament, or watched it.

But the caption alone would have been enough for any old lumberjack. Reading that far, he would sneak away to the darkness of the cookshack to lay hand on a jug of prune juice and drink to the moon, while an owl, frightened by backfire from loggers' pleasure cars, hooted far up the mountainside. . . .

The new breed of loggers live a much easier life than did the shanty boys, the white-water men, the red-sash brigade. They dress and live very much as do their city contemporaries. So do their wives and children. They are good citizens, even to the extent of voting in elections. They are up-to-date in all things. During 1937 they spent much of their time fighting, not at fighting for fun, not even fighting their employers; but fighting among themselves for domination by this or that labor union. Their automobiles are streamlined and, like so many other Americans, the measure of a man is the make of car he drives. Their work day has dropped to seven hours, or forty hours a week.

It's just as well, perhaps, that most of the old-time lumberjacks have already crossed over the Round River from which no man returns. They wouldn't know what to do with so much time on their hands.

21

The New Era: A Postscript

BACK IN THE 1920's, I used to hear gray old bullcooks,
bewhiskered as Moses, sit on the deacon seat of an
evening and curse the "modern" methods, by which
they meant the age of steam in the logging woods; and
weep for the days when bullteams lurched down the
skidroads, bellowing and grunting, and the bullwhacker
cried aloud in protest to a God who had made such
miserable oxen. In *that* great time, it seemed, men had
been men. Hair not only on their chests but on their
faces too. My own generation, according to these
veterans, was a collection of sheared weaklings depen-
dent on machinery, coddled with mattresses, even
sheets, and only too often given to matrimony and
other fatal illusions.

Thus memory gives me pause when I look around
today, in the middle 1950s, to see how little has survived of the so-called modern era which I knew only
yesterday. That era did not come to an end with a
bang. Eras seldom do. They overlap, but the new times
never cease their advance; and before one realizes what
is happening, the logging railroad has virtually disappeared and the geared locomotive is an antique
drowsing in a park—a park past which highway trucks
loaded with logs rumble at speeds to dizzy the long
retired engineers of Heislers, Climaxes, and Shays.

This makes my generation men out of Genesis. We
can remember when Northwestern loggers preferred
snuff to cigarettes, when fallers and buckers used crosscut saws, when steam did the yarding and loading, and

logs came down the mountain behind a Shay that
rocked and rattled and had a voice to frighten a cougar
in the last Forty of the most remote quarter-section on
the claim.

The logging railroads were the first to go. I kept a
record of their heyday, and it tells me that between
1920 and 1937 I rode the locomotives or the cars of
292 privately owned logging railroads in four Western
states and one province of Canada. Had I got around
more, I might have ridden another 200 similar roads
in the same region. How many remain, I do not know;
but a vast majority have gone where the skidroads went.
With them went the steam donkey engines. The internal
combustion engine is doing their work—gas or diesel
donkeys moving the logs from stump to loading works,
and trucks taking them from there direct to the mill or
the log dump. The trucks are as efficient as they are
dull to contemplate. Locomotives were living animals.
They breathed, snorted, sweated, shivered, and belched.
They had voices to warn and demand and protest; or
simply to exult with the pride and joy of being a steam
locomotive, hence a sentient thing.

Though they were not quite in the class of locomotives, the great pounding steam donkeys were something to see and to hear. When the old-time whistle-
punk yanked his signal-wire, the steam donkey
responded with a startled cry of a quality to alert the
most sluggish mind. And when it was running, it
emitted sound and smoke and steam and cinders in
satisfying profusion. The diesel donkey is small,
smooth, quiet—even its whistle an effeminate beep. It
required three, even four men to handle a big wood-
burning donkey. One operator keeps a diesel busy.
Many outfits do not use donkey engines at all, but yard
and load with crawler tractors equipped with one or
another of the elaborate and efficient arches that have
been devised.

There can be no argument about it, save on the

ground of aesthetics; and industry has no place for aesthetics.

In my time, trees were felled by muscular men who stood on springboards notched in their trucks high above the forest floor and pulled the long shining blade of a crosscut; and bucked into suitable lengths with the same sort of tool. Fallers and buckers were mostly of Scandinavian origin—big, blond men with magnificent sweeping moustaches. Then, the power chain-saw was perfected. Labor shortage during World War II brought it to the camps quickly and almost universally. It did away with the Swedish Fiddle. The chain-jobs are infinitely faster, easier to operate, and their use tends to leave less stump. They are, to be sure, charged with starting more forest fires than seem necessary; but the record improves.

Prevention and suppression, or rather control, of forest fires have kept up with logging techniques. Good roads, over which gasoline-powered pumpers and other equipment can be moved swiftly thread both the old-growth timber and the cutover areas. Foam and fog materials complement water but have not supplanted it. The United States Forest Service, which has pioneered in so many things having to do with fire, developed the smoke-jumping battalions, which are delivered by plane and parachute to what otherwise would be inaccessible fires. The bulldozer equipment used in making logging highways is used also to batter and plow lines around fires. Long-time studies of weather, including relative humidity, wind, and other factors, have resulted in something like a scientific measure of fire danger. Long-range forecasting of dry periods has made enormous strides in the past decade. The woods still burn. They burn for the basic reason mentioned earlier in this book; namely, that man never yet has been able to put out a forest fire in big timber, once it had a start under favorable conditions. In such a case, the best that can be done is to confine its spread in some measure. Nothing will put it out except a radical change in the weather.

Almost as new as the truck, the diesel donkey, and the chain-saw is the company forester, the man who turned logged-off land into tree farms. He began to appear in the 1920s, but only on rare occasions. To most logging bosses he was no more welcome than mumps or a union organizer. Not because he harassed the loggers with his ideas. He was not permitted to harass them. But he was an "educated" man—a "professor" as Jigger Jones put it. He knew a whole raft of fancy names for pine, fir, and hemlock. He talked about sites and cycles. He held theories about a "climax forest." He called evergreens "conifers." He aired several downright dangerous ideas, among them the proposition that, given a chance, the forest would renew itself.

The influence of both private and government foresters has been mentioned in earlier pages; but their influence since, say, 1940 has been astonishing. Private or company foresters began to appear in the late 1930s, in increasing numbers; but they were still on tolerance. The production man was the hero, at least to most of the older logging operators; *he* got out the logs, come what might. He didn't like to be told that he ought to leave a few seed trees here and there, or to hear other suggestions foreign to his very nature. Meanwhile, time was taking its toll of the old-style operators, men to whom a standing, living tree was final and revolting evidence that their employees had failed to let all available daylight into the swamp. They died.

The forestry schools meanwhile grew more subtle. Instead of turning out what the late Gus Wiest termed "botanists," they began to turn out graduates who were not only foresters but production men. This was it. One by one, and by dozens, these capable young men have gone to work for logging concerns from Maine to Oregon. (And in the South.) By the early 1950s at least 4,500 of them were on the payrolls of the lumber industry in the United States. Their influence is no less imposing than their number. They are bringing to fruition the hopes of generations of honest conservationists, many of whom would not understand that sound forestry, if ever it came, was to be based less on the emotions than on economics. It is likely, indeed, that the fantastic popularity of Joyce Kilmer's poem "Trees" helped to set back the cause of forestry a good forty years.

Even so, the forester-logger, along with the tree farm and the Keep America Green movements, could never have come into being without the radical adjustments that have taken place in the idiotic and confiscatory tax structure which bedeviled American timberlands.

These young forester-loggers were quick to adopt the new production tools and techniques, and to apply the knowledge of silviculture that has advanced steadily since the advent of the forestry schools half a century ago. Fewer loggers produce more board feet while working thirty-five to forty hours a week than my generation did working forty-eight hours. And with infinitely less muscle exertion.

Of more importance is the fact that logging concerns no longer permit their cutover lands to revert to the state for taxes. They are no longer called "cutover lands." The term is "tree farms." Tree farms are not just any cutover or logged-off land; they are young forests which their owners are pledged to guard against fire, disease, and even public entry; to be thinned where and when necessary to improve growth and quality; to be planted if necessary; and to be harvested in cycles proper to the type of tree wanted, either for pulpwood or for saw timber. Tree farms are registered with American Forest Products Industries, a national organization supported by national and regional associations of lumbermen.

The very name of this tree-farm group is indicative of the times. It represents what is less the lumber industry than the forest products industry. For three centuries this industry was predicated on boards and timbers made from old-growth forests. In less than three decades it has changed to include much else. First came the many fiber products, the countless improved types of paper for many uses; the wallboards and insulating materials. Then came the marvelous new plywoods; the wood plastics; and finally the impreg and compreg woods—tough as mild steel, fire-resistant, decay-resistant. Laminated timbers of any length have been found to be stronger than solid timbers. Sawdust becomes Pres-to-logs. Bark is made into various chemicals. The use of lignin, the substance which with cellulose composes what we call wood, is still in embryo; but it already promises a whole new field of products made from the present waste materials of pulp plants.

The company laboratories in the Northwest of Crown Zellerbach, of Simpson, and of the Weyerhaeuser interests are staffed by men trained in research. They and the staffs of researchers employed by forest products concerns in other sections have complemented the pioneer efforts of the United States Forest Products Laboratory at Madison, Wisconsin. Only the needles of conifers await a commercial use that will result in an almost complete utilization.

Thus a tree is no longer merely timbers and boards and shingles and fuel. A tree, no matter its size, is a storehouse of cellulose and lignin; and such a storehouse is what the forest products industry of the present and the future needs. Volume of wood, not the age of a tree or the number of growth rings to the inch, is what will count. A quick-growing forest will be the goal of most tree farm forester-loggers. Cubic wood volume, not board feet, will be the measure of the forest.

The commercial timber stand in the United States at mid-century, according to Forest Service figures, was approximately 1,644 billion feet, of which 834 billion feet was in virgin, or old-growth trees. This figure includes both hard and soft woods on both privately and publicly owned lands. How much faster timber is cut than it is grown is a matter of almost metaphysical proportions and is best left to the prophets' union, of which there are thousands of members, all eager to (1) name the day when the last tree will fall or (2) declare that the wilderness is about to overrun the clearings again and that the wolf packs are returning. One may hope, even believe, that they will be able to argue the subject until Gabriel blows.

The forest products industry appears to be operating in a more stable manner than was the rule when it was based on lumber alone. The old Timber Barons have gone. So have the Wobblies. Strikes still occur, but they are largely business affairs composed of big talk, threats, and horse trading—the marshaling of evidence of market prices, cost of living, production figures, and the like. The strikes occasionally develop into long closures of camps and mills. But the strikes of the C. I. O. and A. F. of L. unions are not the savage affairs of I. W. W. days, which were also the days of hard-boiled employers. The Red Dawn hasn't been mentioned in years.

The unions and the other factors already mentioned, all have had an influence in stablizing logging crews. The old-time slave markets—as employment offices were known—have largely been supplanted by union hiring halls. Time was when the skidroad districts of all logging towns were lined with employment offices. They have gone. Gone, too, are the Wobbly Halls and the Wobbly soapboxers. The burlesque theaters have faded along with several varieties of honky-tonks. Lodging houses with a sign proclaiming "Calked Boots Not Allowed" have mostly disappeared. There are fewer shops selling loggers' boots and clothing. "For Rent" signs mark many store fronts in the skidroad districts.

Much of this obsolescence has come about because

of the practice, already cited, of holy matrimony by
loggers. They just don't congregate in the big towns any
more. In April of 1950 the once celebrated Skyblue
House of Fan Jones, in Bangor, Maine, was torn down.
In Portland, Oregon, the sinful old Paris House was
demolished in 1938; and the famous bar in what used
to be Aug. Erickson's saloon and ran a full six hundred
and eighty-four lineal feet, has been reduced again and
again to its present modest forty feet. The well-known
Our House in Seattle has gone. Jimmy Durkin's place
in Spokane has disappeared. "Big Fred" Hewitt's Humboldt Saloon in Aberdeen, Washington, is now a machine shop. Much the same thing has been going on in
scores of towns where loggers once congregated to get
their teeth fixed. Speaking of teeth, the offices of Painless
Parker, which once fronted on Portland's skidroad, have
now been moved well uptown.

Even the useful term "skidroad" has been corrupted
in many places and turns up in press and conversation
as "skidrow." Ignorance and carelessness bred the
bastard "skidrow" from a term that originated in
Seattle seventy years ago. (See page 182.) "Skidroad"
is a word of unsullied etymology, derived from the
saloons and fancy houses that grew up along Henry
Yesler's logging road in the Puget Sound metropolis and
is now Yesler Way. (See page 159.) The great Webster
Unabridged will have none of "skidrow," though it
gives both meanings of "skidroad." Use of the corruption is confined to those who wish to be known as men
who get around, men of the world, and who patently
don't know what they are talking about.

As an old settler, a things-aren't-what-they-used-to-
be Tory, my greatest regret in all the changes is the
virtual disappearance of the logging camp. Here was
a bit of civilization of the American frontier. It stood
in Maine as it stood in Oregon, a unique community.
In it fifty, or one hundred, or three hundred men lived
and worked in comparative isolation that was broken

twice a year by trips to town. You went on foot or by tote-team to a camp in Maine. In the Lake States and the Far West you went to camp by a logging railroad.

The population of a camp in the Pacific Northwest was composed of several score single men, and perhaps half a dozen young women who worked in the cookhouse. There was usually a house for the boss, who was married; and row upon row of small bunkhouses with quarters in each for from four to eight men. There was also the cookhouse, or combined kitchen and dining room; a blacksmith shop, an office, and a roundhouse or shed for the locomotives. The camp differed in appearance and flavor from a conventional village, or a mining camp. It was a logging camp. There was nothing like it.

Such camps in the Northwest are now as rare as the geared logging locomotive. I still recall the shock I got on Humboldt Bay, California, in 1937 when I saw a logging outfit that did not have a camp. The work was carried on by men who drove over every day from their own homes, which were complete with wife and children. Although the sight made me uneasy, I did not possess the prophetic sense to recognize this as a vision of things to come, but put it down as an anomaly due to special circumstances.

It was no such thing. The dreadful idea caught on. Now, less than two decades later, a genuine logging camp is something you have to look for—at least in the Douglas fir and redwood regions along the west coast; while in the Western Pine area camps grow fewer by the year. In Maine and the Lake States much of the pulp-logging is carried on by gyppo crews, without benefit of camps.

Nearly all the few camps surviving in the Northwest are less camp than village. Most have garages attached to the family homes of employees. There are schools for the children, community theaters, and small department

stores. Only here and there are camps about which
clings the old-time flavor. To the new generation of the
1950s, and to most of their elders, too, a genuine
logging camp has the derogatory connotations of horse-
and-buggy, though a more accurate comparison would
be rail-and-locomotive.

Occasionally, in the past decade or so, I have come
across a deserted logging camp. There is no scene more
conducive to an irrational but pervasive nostalgia for
times past. There is also no evidence more striking of
the infinite persistence of the forest. Turn your back
a moment on camp and clearing, and the woods begins creeping back. First comes the ground cover of
assorted ferns, grasses, and that strange lovely flower
called fireweed. About the same time sunlight releases
the myraid seeds that have fallen, and they become
small conifers. Alder and willow spring up along the
creeks. A year or two will bury the railroad tracks.
Only a few years more and trees will be peering in the
bunkhouse windows. In a decade the whole camp will
be sunk in an ocean of greenery, jays will be holding
the roundhouse, pack-rats will be disputing the office
with mud-wasps, and the great echoing cookhouse will
be presided over by owls, fit symbols for this ghost of
a frontier settlement.

I recall visiting one camp that had been deserted for
less than four years. It was a place of the deepest
melancholy. The shacks stood beside the plank walk,
all but lost in fireweed six feet high that was shedding
its white down. Moss was climbing the bunkhouse
roofs. Curling like an anaconda through the underbrush
was a long piece of wire rope. The bright red target of
a forgotten railroad switch reared above young firs,
warning train crews that had gone of trains that would
no longer pass. Near the cookhouse door was a half-
hidden pile of rusty fruit and vegetable cans, and
struggling up through choking brush was an apple tree,

once the pride of some cook emulating Johnny Apple-seed.

Inside the cookhouse, the long tables stood naked, still nailed staunchly in place as if waiting until the new forest should be ready, fifty or a hundred years hence, for a new crew to come and cut it. A faucet at the kitchen sink still dripped as doubtless it had dripped since the last cook took off his apron and called it a day, remarking that it was time to go. Daylight had been let into this swamp.

Yet, daylight in the swamp was already fading, for the view from the window by the mixing board was almost wholly obscured by young firs and hemlocks whose leaders showed they had put on a foot or more in height in a single season. Inside, the kitchen was in twilight, ideal for the occupying owls.

Inside and out, all over the camp, the silence was so complete that one subconsciously walked softly and spoke accordingly. A shout would have been as un-seemly as horseplay at a funeral. The clatter of flickers on an old snag merely accentuated the quiet.

The water tank reared up out of the new growth to show its mossy round roof. It still leaked in small rivers as it probably had done when it served the boilers of Shays and Heislers and Climaxes, those geared oxen originally conceived back in the seventies by bearded Ephraim Shay of Cadillac and Harbor Springs, Michi-gan, who meant that logging should no longer be de-pendent on snow for hauling. In the roundhouse near the tank one could still detect the combined aroma of coal, grease, and burned iron—true smell of a locomo-tive's lodging place for the night. It gave me to wonder which of the senses was most effective in reviving mem-ory of a scene far in the past. Was it the smell of the roundhouse? or the sight of a rusty stove in an empty bunkhouse? or the sound of flickers drilling on hard dry wood?

I sat down on an old powder box to muse, and looked along the plank walk of the camp street, splintered and chewed by the calks of hundreds of boots. I reflected that if I had never known a logging camp these ruins would not have caused me to muse. I should have passed them with a glance and perhaps the casual thought that here was a place as deserted as Goldsmith's Auburn, but with little interest and no understanding. But I had known and loved logging camps, and it was natural to reconstruct this one in imagination, to conjure up its life and times, to recognize the significance of the relics and read in them the hieroglyphics of this forgotten bit of civilization. It was a purely sentimental exercise, prompted less by the scientific urge of an archeologist than by what is commonly called nostalgia but is really regret for lost youth.

That was many years ago. Though I have never returned there, I know well enough that the place could now scarcely be found without a compass, and scarcely recognized if found. It will be deep in the shadow of thick and tall trees. The foresters are right. If given half a chance, the dynamic woods soon cover the scars left by the loggers, and even obliterate the symbol of their occupancy of the forest, the camp.

And now that symbol is disappearing. Both the camp and the railroad are on the way to joining the bull-teams and the skidroads. I imagine that few of today's loggers, who are thoroughly and I trust happily domesticated, regret their passing. Here and there, perhaps, one will remember a dawn when the sun came over the mountain to slant through the swirling mists, while the bullcook beat the daylights out of the gong and two hundred young single men came stomping down the camp walk, their calks clicking in the planks, for an incredible breakfast, a box of *Copenhagen,* then a thundering ride behind the rolling Shay to where the spar tree rose high above the big round stuff lying among the stumps. I thought then it was a great and wonderful era in the woods. Thirty years later I know it was.

A Loggers' Dictionary and Compendium

of Useful Knowledge

A FEW OF THE WORDS listed here are already archaic, although they survive in what little bunkhouse conversation is being held in 1938. Many other words, also listed, are fast becoming archaic, for the age of gasoline, highways, loggers' wives and families, and other regrettable items are sweeping the bunkhouses clean of a fine old argot; more and more, the talk of loggers is indistinguishable from that of city slickers.

Some of the words and terms given—such as *bullcook, peavey,* and *corks,* are known and used in the Northern timber from coast to coast, while others are confined to one or more regions.

Barroom. That part of a New England camp where the loggers sleep.

Barroom man. Common name for a bullcook, New England.

Batteau. Type of boat used on Eastern river drives.

Big blue. A large butt log, with much taper.

Bindle. Blanket roll carried by a man.

Bindle stiff. A worker who carries his blankets with him.

Birling. The loggers' game of logrolling.

Boiler. A bum cook.

Boiling-up. Washing one's clothes.

Boomer. A short-staker.

Brains. Man from the head office.

254

Branding ax. A tool for marking ownership on a log.

Bridle chain. Chain wrapped around a sled runner for a brake.

Brow logs. Logs on each side of the track at loading landing.

Buck. To cut a tree into lengths after it has been felled.

Bucker. One who saws trees into logs.

Buckskin. A log from which bark has fallen off.

Bull. By itself, the boss of a camp or logging operation. It is a sort of generic term and, when used as a prefix, except in the case of *bullcook,* denotes the superlative in size, power, or authority.

Bull block. The main pulley-block used in high-lead logging.

Bull bucker. Man in charge of a crew of fallers and buckers.

Bullcook. The chore boy around camp. He cuts fuel, fills wood boxes, sweeps bunkhouses, feeds pigs; is often the butt of camp jokes. But when he rings the gong in the morning, the so-and-so's have to get up.

Bull of the Woods. The camp foreman, logging superintendent, or supreme authority of a crew or crews.

Bulls. Used to mean *oxen.*

Bunkhouse. Where the loggers live.

By the bushel, by the inch, by the mile. Contract work, but usually applied to contract falling and bucking.

Candy side. That crew of a high-lead camp which has the best equipment. The other side is naturally the *haywire* one.

Cant dog. The rivermen's tool. Same as *peavey.* Once described by a greenhorn as a "stick with a hook hanging on it."

Cant hook. Shorter than a cant dog, and lighter. It
has no spike in the end of it. Used for loading
sleighs.

Cat. Any tractor. (From Caterpillar.)

Cat skinner. Driver of a tractor.

Chaser. Man who unhooks logs from choker,
high-lead logging.

Choker. A loop of wire rope, used for yarding
logs.

Chokerman, or *choker-setter.* Man who puts chokers around logs.

Clam gun. A shovel.

Cock shop. Camp office.

Cold deck. A pile of logs left for later loading
and hauling.

Cookee. Any sort of cook's helper in Lake States
and Northeast.

Cookhouse. That part of camp where the cook
performs, plus the dining room.

Corks. Calks; short, sharp spikes set in the soles
of shoes.

Crotch line. Device for loading logs onto railroad
cars.

Crown fire. Forest fire that goes into tops, or
crowns, of trees. When it does that, the boys
say "she's crowning."

Cruiser. Same as *land-looker.* Man who estimates
standing timber.

Crumb boss. Low name for a bullcook.

Deacon seat. The one classic piece of camp furniture. Usually made of one half of a log, flat
side up; and runs from one end of a camp to
the other.

Dehorn. Any sort of booze. Used by old-time
Wobblies to denote anything that takes the
mind of the worker from the class struggle.

Donkey. A stationary engine.

Donkey doctor. Donkey-engine mechanic.

Donkey puncher. Donkey engineer.

Drag day. That day of the month when a man can draw his wages in advance of the day they are due.

Driving pitch. High water suitable for driving logs down a river.

Duplex. A type of donkey engine that both yards and loads logs.

Faller. In the West Coast district a man who cuts down trees.

Fink. A stool pigeon, company guard, private detective. If you don't mean it, you better smile, and smile wide and handsome, when you call a man that.

Flunkey. Same as *cookee.* Cookhouse help.

Fore-and-aft road. A skidroad in steep country for sliding logs into water.

Forty, A. Forty acres of timber. Smallest unit in which timber usually changes ownership.

Gandy dancer. Pick-and-shovel man.

Gin pole. A short spar, used for loading and unloading logs.

"Give her snoose." To increase power. A tribute to the potency of snuff, or *snoose,* used by loggers.

"Got her made." Quitting the job. He's got his stake made.

Ground lead. Type of logging, now rare, where a steam donkey yarded logs along the ground. (Note: *Lead* is always pronounced *leed.*)

Gyppo. Any sort of contract work. See *By the bushel.*

Hair-pounder. A horse teamster.

Halfbreed. A type of donkey engine.

Hardtack outfit. A concern that sets a poor table. It derives from the hard and cheap Swedish bread.

Haulback. The line that returns the chokers to

the woods after a *turn* of logs has been pulled in.

Hayburner. A horse.

Hay hill. A hill on a road on which hay, or dirt, has been sprinkled to act as a brake on sleigh runners.

Haywire. Originally the wire that bound baled hay together. Now means *broken, busted, crazy, foolish, flimsy,* or almost anything you think of that isn't as you'd like it.

Head dam. A storage dam for holding water for driving purposes.

Head tree. In skyline yarding, the spar at the donkey engine.

Highball. To hurry.

High climber, or *high rigger.* The man who tops and prepares a high-lead tree for logging.

High-lead tree. A tree which has been limbed and topped, and from which blocks and tackle are hung for yarding logs.

Homeguard. A long-time employee of one company. The opposite of *boomer* and *short-staker.*

Hooker. Short for *hook-tender.* The boss of one yarding crew in high-lead country.

Hoot-nanny. A small device used to hold a crosscut saw while sawing a log from underneath.

Ink slinger. A logging camp timekeeper.

Iron burner. Camp blacksmith.

Jagger. A sliver of wire rope.

Jammer. A steam engine for loading logs onto cars. Western pine country.

Jerk wire. Wire attached to whistle on yarding donkey, by which the *punk* blows starting and stopping signals.

Job shark. An employment agent. Same as *man catcher.*

Kennebecker. In New England any sort of knapsack.

King snipe. Boss of a track-laying crew.

Landing. Where logs are assembled for loading, or rolling into the river.

Long logger. A logger in the fir and redwood country of the West Coast. So called because logs are cut as long as forty feet.

Macaroni. Sawdust.

"Make her out." What a logger tells the time-keeper when he wants his pay check. "I'm quitting." Sometimes "Mix me a walk" is used instead.

McLean boom. A type of loading boom widely used on the West Coast.

Mulligan car. Railroad car where midday lunch is served.

Muzzle loaders. Old-fashioned bunks into which you crawled over the foot of the bed.

Nosebag. Lunch bucket.

Nosebag show. A camp where midday meal is taken to the woods in lunch buckets. Not highly thought of in these latter days.

Packing a balloon. Carrying one's blankets.

Packing a card. Means he's a union man.

Packing the rigging. Used by Wobblies to denote a man who is carrying I. W. W. organizing supplies—literature, dues books, etc.

Pass line. The line by which a high rigger moves up and down at his work, once the tree is topped.

Peavey. A cant dog.

Pie in the sky. Wobbly reference to the bourgeois heaven.

Pike pole. Long pole with sharp spike in one end, used where logs are floating free in the water.

Pot. A donkey engine.

Powder monkey. Man in charge of blasting operations.

Punk. Any young man, but specifically a *whistle punk.*

Push. Camp foreman.

Rigging slinger. Man of a yarding crew who attaches the chokers to the main yarding line.

River hog. A name for river drivers.

Road monkey. Man who keeps sleigh road in good shape.

Rolled. Robbed while drunk.

Route. Total length of time at any given camp; viz., a *long route* means a long stretch of employment on one job.

Sawdust eater. One of those fellers who works in a sawmill.

Sawyers. The men who fell trees and cut them into logs, Western pine country.

Scaler. The fellow who says how much lumber a log contains. His rule stick is said to be the *cheat stick.*

Schoolmarm. A crotched log, consisting mostly of two trunks.

Scissorbill. A worker who is not filled with spirit for the Revolution.

Short staker. A very migratory worker.

Show. A logging chance. Spoken of as a *good show* or a *poor show.*

Side. One complete yarding and loading crew, with spar tree and donkey engines. A *two-side camp* has two spars and crews.

Side push. A minor foreman.

Sizzler. See *boiler.*

Skidder. A yarding and loading engine which has a steel tower in place of a spar tree.

Skidroad. In the old days a road over which oxen pulled logs. Today it means that part of a city where loggers congregate when in town. As such, its meaning approximates *Bowery.*

Sky hooker. Top man in a sleigh-loading crew.

Sky line. A logging method where a taut line reaches between two spar trees.

Slave market. An employment office.

Sleigh. What a New England *sled* is, once it gets as far West as Michigan.

Snoose. Damp snuff for chewing. Also known as *Scandihoovian dynamite* and *Swedish condition powder.* No one knows what is in it, but all agree it is most powerful chewing tobacco. A pinch of it once floored the late John L. Sullivan.

Snubber. A device for braking sleighs down steep hills.

Sougan. A heavy blanket.

Stamp ax. Same as *branding ax.*

Spar tree. Same as *high-lead tree.*

Springboard. A narrow platform on which fallers stand while falling a tree.

Steel gang. Railroad track-laying crew.

Stiff. Any working man without a white collar.

String of flats. Flatcars; griddle cakes.

Swedish fiddle. Crosscut saw.

Swing donkey. A donkey engine used to supplement a yarder over a long haul.

Tail tree. The No. 2 spar of a skyline hook-up.

"Tim-berrr!" Traditional cry of warning.

Tin pants. Waterproofed clothing used by West Coast loggers.

Tote team. Horses and wagon or sleigh used to take supplies into camp.

Town clown. Small-town policeman.

Turn. A unit of logs being yarded.

Van. The camp store (Lake States).

Walker, The. Superintendent of two or more logging camps.

Wangan. This has a dozen spellings and means two wholly different things: (1) where the camp stores are kept; and the payroll charges for such goods; (2) wherever camp is made by a crew of river drivers.

Whistle punk. The boy who blows signals for a yarding crew.

Widow maker. Tree or branch blown down by wind.

Windfall bucker. A man who is engaged in sawing up trees that have been blown down by wind.

Wobbly. A member of the Industrial Workers of the World.

Wobbly horrors. Said of an employer who fears labor trouble.

Yarding. The assembling of logs.

In the camps of the Pacific Northwest loggers use a number of Chinook words. The Chinook language is also called *Siwash,* for in early days all Indians of the Northwest Coast were called *Siwashes,* a corruption of the French *sauvage,* meaning *savage.* The words most commonly used are given below.

Cayuse. Horse or pony.

Hiyu. Plenty, large, enough, many; viz., *hiyu muckamuck,* plenty to eat.

Klatawa. To go.

Kloochman, or *klooch.* A woman.

Kultus. Bad, worthless.

Memaloose. Dead, or death.

Potlatch. To give; a gift. An Indian party or social gathering where gifts are exchanged. Commercialized in Seattle, as "round-up" is in Pendleton, Oregon.

Skookum. Strong, stout, brave, great.

Tillicum. People, a man, a person, but ordinarily a friend.

Tyee. A chief or big shot. Hence, a tyee logger is head of a large logging operation.

Acknowledgments

ALTHOUGH THE PRINTED RECORD is necessary to any serious work, there is much history, and authentic, too, in the memories of men and women who knew the logging woods and lumber towns in their great and golden heyday. As far back as he can remember, which was around the turn of the century, the author has known and listened to veterans of the woods—some of them patriarchs who dated back to the times of the Aroostook War in Maine. To both dead and living lumberjacks the author owes a great deal.

Because a small part of the history of many lumber cities is considered scandalous, it might be embarrassing to reveal certain sources of information. But those sources are beyond reproach. Everybody from ancient madames to present and former judges, mayors, and businessmen have been consulted. Even the gentlemen of the cloth contributed something.

Wherever possible the author has used the printed record to bolster the witness of old-timers. Especially is he in debt to the competent and charming women of the following institutions. Every last one of them took time and pains to help him: Public Library, Bangor, Me.; Maine Historical Society, Portland, Me.; Public Library, Boston, Mass.; Hackley Public Library, Muskegon, Mich.; Public Library, Grand Rapids, Mich.; Hoyt Public Library, Saginaw, Mich.; Public Library, Bay City, Mich.; Chippewa Valley Historical Society, Eau Claire, Wis.; Public Library, St. Paul, Minn.; Public Library, Spokane, Wash.; Public Library, Seattle, Wash.; Public Library, Everett, Wash.; Public Library, Aberdeen, Wash.; Oregon Historical Society, Portland; Public Library, Portland, Oreg.

Books

Adamic, Louis, *Dynamite*. New York, 1931.

Allen, C. E., *History of Dresden Maine*. Augusta, 1931.

American Lumbermen. Chicago, 1905.

Bagley, C. B., *History of Seattle*. Chicago, 1916.

Brissenden, Paul, *The I. W. W.* New York, 1919.

Butler, Ovid, *American Conservation*. Washington, 1935.

Carey, C. H., *A History of Oregon*. Portland, 1935.

Darrow, Clarence, *The Story of My Life*. New York, 1932.

Defebaugh, J. E., *History of the Lumber Industry in America*. Chicago, 1906.

Disston, H., *The Saw in History*. Philadelphia, 1916.

Dwight, Timothy. *Travels in New-England and New-York*. New Haven, 1821.

Ekstorm, F. H., *The Penobscot Man*. Boston, 1904.

Ekstorm, F. H., and Smith, M. W., *Minstrelsy of Maine*. Cambridge, 1927.

Ford, H. A., *History of Penobscot County*. Saco, Me., 1830.

Forrester, G., *Historical and Bibliographical Album of the Chippewa Valley, Wisconsin*. Chicago, 1891.

Fox, W. F., *A History of the Lumber Industry in the State of New York*. Washington, 1902.

Gaston, Joseph, *Portland, Its History and People*. Portland, Oregon, 1911.

Gudde, E. G., *Sutter's Own Story*. New York, 1936.

Hanzlik, E. J., *Trees and Forests of Western United States*. Portland, Oreg., 1929.

Hempstead, A. G., *The Penobscot Boom*. Orono, Me., 1931.

History of Humboldt County, California.

History of Snohomish County, Washington. Everett, Wash.

Hotchkiss, G. W., *History of the Lumber and Forest Industry of the Northwest*. Chicago, 1898.

Howd, C. R., *Industrial Relations in the West Coast Lumber Industry*. Govt. Printing Office, 1924.

I. W. W. Songs. Chicago, 1936.

Kendall, E. A., *Travels through the Northern Parts of the United States in the Years 1801 and 1808*. New York, 1809.

Kingsbury, H. D., and Deyo, S. L., *Illustrated History of Kennebec County, Maine*. New York, 1892.

Lanman, C., *Adventures in the Wilds of The United States and British American Provinces*. Philadelphia, 1856.

Larson, A. M., *When Logs and Lumber Ruled Stillwater*. Minnesota History, Vol. 18, No. 2. St. Paul, 1937.

Michaux, F. A., *The North American Sylva*. Philadelphia, 1859.

Mills, J. C., *History of Saginaw County, Michigan*. Saginaw, 1918.

Reynolds, R. V., and Pierson, A. H., *Lumber*

Production 1869–1934. United States Forest Service, 1934.

Rickaby, F., *Ballads and Songs of the Shanty-Boy.* Cambridge, 1926.

Springer, J. S., *Forest Life and Forest Trees.* New York, 1851.

Stephenson, Isaac, *Recollections of a Long Life.* Chicago, 1915.

Thoreau, H. D., *The Maine Woods.* Boston, 1868.

West Coast Lumbermens Association, *Forest Facts.* Seattle, 1937.

Wilkins, A. H., *The Forests of Maine.* Augusta, 1932.

Wilkinson, Wm., *Memorials of the Minnesota Fires.* Minneapolis, 1895.

Williamson, W. D., *The History of Maine,* Hallowell, Me., 1832.

Wood, R. G., *A History of Lumbering in Maine.* Orono, Me., 1935.

Magazines and Newspapers

Sprague's Journal of Maine History, Vol. IX, No. 1.

Michigan History Magazine.

Wisconsin Magazine of History.

Oregon Historical Quarterly.

Files of the *Bangor Commercial, Bangor Whig & Courier,* Bangor, Me.; *Lewiston Journal,* Lewiston, Me.; *Saginaw News-Courier,* Saginaw, Mich.; *Bay City Times,* Bay City, Mich.; *Muskegon Chronicle,* Muskegon, Mich.; *St. Paul Pioneer Press,* St. Paul, Minn.; *Oregon Spectator,* Oregon City, Oreg.; *The Morning Oregonian,* Portland; *Daily World,* Aberdeen, Wash.; *Four L Lumber News,* Portland, Oregon.

INDEX

ABOUT THE AUTHOR

Stewart Holbrook, Portland's outstanding informal historian, was born in Newport, Vermont, but moved to the Northwest in his youth. From lumberjacking, he turned to writing, and his account of the lumberjacks, whom he knew first-hand, is lively, hard-hitting, plain-talking narrative, full of color and excitement. His natural ability to write spontaneously, and his concern for facts about the *people* he describes have charted a new path for historical writers in the twentieth century.

During his active life, he was a prodigious worker, writing reviews for the New York HERALD TRIBUNE, and editorials and feature articles for the PORTLAND OREGONIAN—and at the same time writing many bestselling books. Articles by Stewart Holbrook appeared regularly in THE YALE REVIEW, AMERICAN FORESTS, FRONTIER, THE NEW REPUBLIC, and BARRON'S. He was Assistant Professor of English at Portland (Oregon) State College, and also worked as a literary agent, consultant for various public commissions, and Executive Secretary of the Legislative Interim Committee on Natural Resources.

An eminent historian, he was referred to by Lewis Gannett as "the only ex-lumberjack who has lectured at Harvard University on American History." He died in 1962.

Comstock Editions

HAVE THE BEST OF THE WEST AGAIN ON YOUR BOOKSHELF

☐ MOONTRAP, Don Berry	5000	$2.50
☐ TRASK, Don Berry	5001	$2.25
☐ SKID ROAD, Murray Morgan	5030	$2.75
☐ A MAJORITY OF SCOUNDRELS, Don Berry	5028	$2.95
☐ THE LADY OF THE HOUSE, Sally Stanford	5013	$2.25
☐ TALES OUT OF OREGON, Ralph Friedman	5004	$1.95
☐ A TOUCH OF OREGON, Ralph Friedman	5005	$1.95
☐ THE GRIZZLY, Enos Mills	5006	$2.25
☐ TOUGH TRIP THROUGH PARADISE, Andrew Garcia	5008	$2.95
☐ THE SAGA OF THE COMSTOCK LODE George D. Lyman	5012	$2.25
☐ THE MADAMS OF SAN FRANCISCO Curt Gentry	5015	$2.25
☐ THE FLYING NORTH, Jean Potter	5018	$2.25
☐ THE KILLER MOUNTAINS, Curt Gentry	5020	$1.95
☐ THE LAST DAYS OF THE LATE, GREAT STATE OF CALIFORNIA, Curt Gentry	5021	$2.50
☐ THE IRON TRAIL, Rex Beach	5022	$2.25

Available at your local bookstore, or order direct from the publisher.

Comstock Editions, Dept. CS, 3030 Bridgeway, Sausalito, CA 94965

Please send me the books checked above. I enclose $_____
(plus 75¢ per copy for mailing)

Name _____

Address _____

City _____ State/Zip _____